ALSO BY D.V. BERKOM:

Leine Basso Crime Thrillers

A Killing Truth

Serial Date

Bad Traffick

The Body Market

Cargo

Dark Return

Absolution

Dakota Burn

Shadow of the Jaguar

Kate Jones Adventure Thrillers

The Kate Jones Thriller Series, Vol. 1

Cruising for Death

Yucatán Dead

A One Way Ticket to Dead

Vigilante Dead

THE LAST DECEPTION

A Leine Basso Thriller

D.V. BERKOM

Cover by Deranged Doctor Design

ISBN: 0997970863
ISBN-13: 978-0997970869

For Mark...the best partner a girl could have

CHAPTER 1

Tripoli, Libya

The predawn call to prayer resonated through Tripoli's old city as Leine Basso raced along the whitewashed corridor of the medina. She was running out of time. The traffickers had continually changed Munira's location and finding verifiable intel had been sketchy. The latest report put the fifteen-year-old Yazidi girl at a residence in the labyrinthine maze of shops, apartments, and restaurants near the harbor, but even that information was several hours old.

"Leine, what's your position?" Lou Stokes's voice crackled in her earpiece.

"Five minutes out."

"Hamid?"

"The same," Hamid answered.

"Copy that," Lou said.

Minutes later, Leine turned the corner and entered a second corridor leading to the entrance of the trafficker's safe house. Slowing her pace, she raised a suppressed MP-5SD and followed the wall. Hamid emerged from the other direction through the predawn gloom with his gun drawn. They both paused near the arched doorway to listen. Hearing nothing, they entered the enclosure.

A dry fountain in the shape of an eight-pointed star stood at the center of the empty courtyard. Tiled steps to Leine's right led to a second-floor passageway bordered by an ornate metal handrail. Two closed doors could be seen at the top. Hamid continued through the lower level to clear it while Leine quietly ascended to the second floor.

She stopped at the first door to listen, heart thrumming in anticipation.

Nothing. When she tried the handle, the catch disengaged easily. She stepped to the side and pushed the door open.

Empty.

Leine backed away from the room and moved to the second door. This time muffled voices filtered through. She leaned over the railing and gestured to Hamid, who had finished clearing the first floor. He nodded and silently climbed the stairs, continuing along the passageway to check the rest of the structure. She removed a tiny fiber optic camera attached to a cable from the tactical vest she was wearing, and threaded the cable through the gap at the bottom of the door. The two-and-a-half-inch LED monitor flickered to life, showing a partially illuminated room with three occupants.

Two armed men were at a table on the left. The third person, a dark-haired female dressed in lingerie, sat on a mattress on the floor with her knees drawn up to her chin and her hands behind her back. A black plastic zip tie bound her ankles. She matched the photograph Lou had given her.

Munira.

Hamid returned and she showed him the screen before she removed the camera and put it back in her vest. They each took a position away from the direct line of fire and raised their weapons. Leine rocked back and forth three times as Hamid grasped the door handle. On three, he disengaged the lock and she kicked the door open. Leine entered first, with Hamid close behind. The first man shouted to the other one and leaped to his feet, knocking the chair back as he raised his weapon. Leine fired a three-shot burst into him and he dropped to the floor. The other gunman tried to do the same but Hamid shot him twice in the head before he could fire.

While Hamid kept watch at the door, Leine lowered her weapon and turned toward the young woman, now cowering against the wall. Dark bruises covered her face and chest, and several angry red welts marked her arms and legs. *The bastards burned her with cigarettes.* Leine clenched her teeth and tamped down the anger rising in her chest.

Her captors were dead. It was a start.

"Don't be afraid, Munira," Leine said gently in Arabic. "We're here to help you."

Munira shook her head in confusion. "Who are you? What do you want?"

"We're from SHEN, an organization that helps people like you." Leine slid a tactical knife from her vest and bent to cut the tie binding her ankles. "Are you able to turn around so I can cut your hands free? We don't have much time."

Munira nodded and struggled to her knees. Leine reached behind her and slit the hard plastic tie, releasing the young woman's wrists. Leine sheathed the knife as she straightened and held out her hand. The young woman grasped it and pulled herself to her feet. She was tall, though not as tall as Leine, with dark hair that fell to the middle of her back. Leine scanned the room for something to cover the fifteen-year-old.

"What did these men use to dress you?" Leine didn't think the traffickers would risk taking her from place to place dressed in lingerie.

Munira nodded at the sheet covering the mattress. "This." She picked up the pale blue fabric and began to wrap it around herself.

"This is taking too much time," Hamid muttered from the doorway. "We must hurry."

Leine helped her secure the ends of the makeshift abaya and led her toward the door, giving a wide berth to the dead gunmen. Hamid checked the passageway in both directions before giving the all clear and exiting the room. Leine and Munira followed him down the stairs to the first level.

Leine protected the rear as they advanced to the arched doorway leading to the rest of the medina. Hamid scanned the outside corridor and motioned that it was safe to exit the courtyard. She turned, intending to follow them, when a man with an assault rifle slung over his shoulder appeared on the upper floor, headed for the room with the dead gunmen. His eyes met Leine's and alarm swept across his face. He scrambled to raise his weapon.

"Eleven o'clock!" Leine yelled and pushed Munira behind her as she aimed the MP-5 at the trafficker. Hamid was faster and fired a prolonged burst, chewing up the tile near the gunman's feet. The man dove for cover before returning fire.

"Go!" Hamid yelled, ejecting the spent magazine and jacking in another.

Leine grabbed Munira and propelled her through the archway into the maze of the medina. They raced down the corridor through the twists and turns of the old city, retracing the route Leine had memorized on the way in.

"What's happening?" Lou's voice came over the mic. "Leine? Hamid?"

"A third gunman," Leine replied. "Hamid's engaged, but he should be right behind us. I've got her, Lou. We'll be at the square in under five."

"Roger that."

A short time later, the two women emerged from the medina into a small, empty square bookended by two large gates, one of which was open. The sound of tires on gravel filtered through the crisp morning air as an armored SUV screamed through the open gate, coming to an abrupt stop next to them. Dust enveloped the square as the back door opened, revealing Lou Stokes, the silver-haired director for Stop Human Enslavement Now.

"Get in."

Heart hammering in her chest, she shepherded Munira into the back seat. The traumatized look on the young woman's face stabbed Leine in the heart. *No one should have to endure what she's been through.*

Lou barked into the mic. "Hamid, what's your ETA?"

There was no answer.

"Hamid?" he repeated.

Leine's stomach twisted as she checked her watch. *He should have been here by now.* Unease wound its way up her spine.

"I'm going back." She turned and started for the corridor.

"Almost there." Hamid's voice echoed in her earpiece.

Relief swept through her, and Leine let out the breath she'd been holding. She'd never been so happy to hear someone's voice. Hamid staggered through the archway, gripping his shoulder. Blood saturated his left arm.

Leine slid her knife free as she met him and cut the straps holding his pack. It fell to the ground.

"It's just a flesh wound," he quipped, but his pale face and the obvious blood loss told her otherwise. Shouldering the pack, she helped him into the cargo space of the SUV and climbed in beside him as the driver peeled out of the square.

"I've got a surgeon standing by at the safe house," Lou said.

Unzipping the front of the pack, she pulled out Hamid's medical kit. Alert for signs of shock, she applied a tourniquet to slow the bleeding and packed the wound with clotting agent and gauze. Munira peered over the back of the seat, her eyes wide.

"He'll be fine," Leine said, trying to put her at ease. She couldn't imagine the horror she'd been through. Not only had she been taken from her home in northern Iraq by the terrorist group Izz Al-Din and brutally abused by its fighters, when they'd tired of her she'd been sold to sex traffickers.

Satisfied the bleeding in Hamid's shoulder had stopped, Leine repacked the kit and stashed it inside his pack.

Lou studied Leine. "You okay?"

She nodded. "Yeah. No worries. I think I stopped the bleeding." She leaned over and placed a hand on Hamid's cheek. His skin was cool but not clammy, and his respiration was normal. Relieved that he appeared to be stable, she leaned back and smiled kindly at Munira, who was crying softly. "You're safe now. Everything's going to be fine."

But of course things wouldn't be fine. Yes, her body would heal, but would Munira be able to live a normal life? Or would she, like thousands before her, take her own life rather than live with the shame of what had been done to her?

Leine leaned her head back and closed her eyes. She'd been here before. The disturbing image of tears streaming down the young woman's bruised and battered face and the unfathomable desolation that had settled in her eyes would haunt Leine for years to come.

Fifteen minutes after the extraction, they reached the clinic where Hamid's surgical team waited. While they prepped him for surgery, Leine accompanied Munira to an examination room where a kindly nurse attended to the young woman's injuries and prescribed medication for a severe bladder infection. As soon as the nurse signed off allowing her to travel, Munira would be flown to another facility in Turkey, where she'd be reassessed and monitored, and would participate in a psychiatric evaluation that included individual and group sessions.

Leine had pushed for SHEN to include follow-up care for the victims they rescued. The first several months after the mission were critical for successful reentry into the women's family and culture. For a large percentage of rescued women, unacknowledged societal and emotional stressors often proved to be their undoing. With new tools in place to help them cope, tragedy could often be avoided.

She said her goodbyes to Munira and promised to keep in touch. Exhausted from the mission, Leine hitched a ride with Lou to the safe house to get some rest. On the way, she gave her cell phone a cursory glance and noticed a text from Janice, a friend who was working at a refugee camp near the Libyan-Egyptian border. Their unusual schedules made being on the same continent, much less the same country, a rare occurrence, and they'd been trying to figure out a way to get together for the last few days.

Too tired to think of a coherent reply, Leine put her phone away. She'd get back to her after she got some much-needed rest.

CHAPTER 2

Refugee camp, Libyan-Egyptian border

I t **was the** screaming that woke her.

Janice had gotten used to the bombs, could sleep through the sporadic shelling that came within a mile of the camp. But not the screams. She fumbled for her glasses on the makeshift nightstand and lurched to her feet.

Not again.

Steadying herself, she groped to button her pants— she'd taken to wearing her clothes to bed since the last attack—then stepped into her boots. She didn't take the time to lace them. Amorphous shadows danced before her, forming grotesque figures on the walls of her tent.

Fire.

The screams speared her heart, making it hard to breathe. Who'd been hurt—or killed—this time? Grabbing a flashlight from underneath her cot, she tore out of the tent and raced toward the wall of flames to join the others as they scrambled to salvage what they could of the field hospital.

They did it again. The bastards just bombed another refugee hospital.

Dr. Richard Evans, still in his scrubs with a stethoscope dangling from his neck, motioned her over. The calm intensity of the young surgeon's expression belied the panic radiating off him.

"Two patients are recuperating in the triage area. We've got to get them out." Earlier that day they'd run out of space in the recovery unit hidden yards away beneath a still-intact tarp of desert camouflage and left the last two patients where they had room—the surgical unit.

Please let them be all right.

"Here—take this." The doctor handed her an empty fire extinguisher and started for the blazing structure.

"Wait—" Janice grasped his arm as fire billowed from beneath the tent roof. Sections of tarp were fast becoming skeletal remains of what had once been a serviceable operating room. Camp personnel edged closer with fire extinguishers and buckets of water, but the intensity of the flames held them back. Ordinarily shelling didn't produce so much fire. The bomb must have destroyed one of the oxygen units. Janice glanced toward the east. Eyes wide with fear, a group of refugees stood nearby, watching.

Just then, one of the patients staggered from the blaze and collapsed to all fours. Hacking and choking, his hospital gown slid off his shoulders to reveal his bare back. Two medics rushed to help him.

Dr. Evans broke from her grasp and raced toward the operating tent.

"*No,* Richard. The oxygen tanks—"

An explosion shook the ground and a plume of smoke rocketed skyward, blotting out the stars and illuminating the bleak landscape of row upon row of white tents, sand, and more sand.

"Correction," the doctor replied, his tone bleak. "What oxygen tanks?" His shoulders sagged as he watched the voracious flames consume what was left of the structure.

Someone shouted as the burning effigy of a man appeared at the far end of the tent pushing a gurney holding one of the patients. He staggered a short distance before he collapsed to the ground. Janice sprinted to him as the doctor rushed to check on the patient. Someone handed her a blanket and she threw it over the man, rolling him in it to suffocate the fire.

"It's Ahmed," she said to the person beside her, her voice catching. Ahmed was the Egyptian liaison and translator who doubled as an administrative genie, dealing with the forms and red tape thrown at them by their host country. He was also Dr. Evans's good friend.

"Jesus. Quick, take him to my tent," Evans said. "I've got supplies. We can work on him there." He nodded at two men dressed in scrubs standing nearby.

"Do you need me?" Janice had trained as an emergency medical responder and usually did triage.

The doctor nodded at the patient on the gurney. "He's stable, but you need to get him to a safe area." He turned to the two men, both senior trauma nurses. "Let's go." The three of them grasped the edges of the blanket and hoisted Ahmed, now mercifully unconscious, and carried him away.

Janice pushed the patient to the camouflaged recovery section and checked his vitals. He'd survive, as long as the shelling stopped. She alerted on-duty

11

personnel that he was there before racing to help the others transfer buckets of brackish river water in an attempt to douse the raging inferno.

Half an hour later, nothing remained of the operating tent except the misshapen, blackened metal of what had once been a generator. Janice and the rest of the group watched in silence as the remaining structure gave way and collapsed into a smoldering pile of ashes.

"Why target us?" Marcy, fresh from an internship at a prestigious hospital in San Francisco and the camp's new recruit, stood nearby with her arms crossed, a deep frown creasing her pretty features. Janice had been glad when Marcy joined the group—in a male-dominated organization such as this one another woman with whom to commiserate was a welcome change.

Janice shook her head. "I don't know. I want to believe it was a mistake, that someone got the coordinates wrong, but after three years in this place I doubt it." What earthly reason would either side in this endless, brutal conflict have to demolish a medical facility that only took care of refugees? In all the time she'd been with the group, they hadn't helped anyone even remotely connected to the Libyan National Army or the terrorists. Not that they would have turned away someone who was injured, but treating them would have been the exception.

"Whatever happened to international law?" Marcy asked. "Don't sick and wounded people have rights?"

"You mean the Geneva Conventions?" Janice scoffed. "They don't mean shit in this part of the world."

Janice was about ready to hang up her long-held dream of helping the victims of war. No matter how hard she tried to convince herself that she made a difference, the incessant doubts erased whatever positive feelings she garnered from doing the work. It was hard to stay upbeat and positive when three-quarters of patients treated at the hospital were sick and starving children, or amputees who'd been on the wrong side of an improvised explosive device.

"I'm going to check on Ahmed. See if Dr. Evans needs anything." Marcy gave Janice a brief smile and started for the doctor's quarters. Janice watched her leave and then turned to the smoking destruction in front of her. With a deep sigh she joined the others cleaning up.

A few hours later, after the last of the garbage had been taken to a holding area for pickup, Janice made her way back to her tent, hoping to grab a few hours of rest before her next shift. Everyone else not on night duty had retired to their respective quarters to do the same.

She stopped for a moment, admiring the clarity of the night, marveling over how wars, famine, death, and disease could rage on, yet the sky never changed. Every morning the sun rose, and every evening the moon and stars. Janice inhaled deeply before continuing on to her quarters. As she passed the mess tent, the sound of breaking glass made her stop.

Probably a refugee looking for food. Better go and check.

Janice reached the entrance and hesitated. The distinct silhouette of a man stood just inside the tent. With his back to Janice and dressed in the clothes of a local, she couldn't be sure who it was. She cleared her throat, not wanting to startle him. The figure froze and slowly raised his hands in the air.

"I am unarmed," the silhouette said in heavily accented English. His voice was raspy and undoubtedly Russian. He turned slowly to face her.

A black headscarf with white Arabic lettering framing a face with broad cheekbones and a thick beard set alarm bells off in her head. Dressed in a faded knit shirt, baggy black pants, and a pair of heavily used black boots, his attire resembled the uniform of the terrorists in the area, although the Russian accent threw her. Her gaze shifted to a Kalashnikov rifle propped against a table nearby. The man glanced at the gun and then back to her.

"I thought you said you were unarmed." Blood rushed to her face and she stepped back.

His hands still in the air the man moved with great deliberation away from the gun. "I will not hurt you," he said. The light from the glow of an outside security lamp revealed a dark stain on his shirt.

"You're injured." Janice started toward him but thought better of it and stilled. The man's gaze followed her. He made no move.

"Yes."

His respiration increased, evidenced by the rapid rise and fall of his chest. Sweat trickled down the sides of his face and his arms drooped, as though he found it a chore to hold them up. He winced and raised his hands higher.

"I can help you, but you must tell me who you are and what you're doing here."

"I am Mikhail."

"You're Russian?"

Mikhail nodded.

"Then why are you dressed like Izz Al-Din?" She glanced at his head covering. Although she hadn't come into contact with a member of the terrorist group fighting the Libyans, she'd been through enough briefings to know they wore the same black headscarf to signify their solidarity with other jihadists.

Mikhail swayed slightly as he reached for the scarf and slid it off, letting it fall to the ground. "I am not...I cannot..."

His face contorted in pain and he lowered his hands. His eyelids fluttered and his legs buckled. He crashed into the table behind him, knocking it over as he slid to the ground. Janice rushed to his side. His eyes flickered open, then closed.

"Mikhail. How were you hurt? Stay with me now."

He frowned and opened his eyes. "I wish to surrender. I—" He stopped, the words dying in his throat.

"Here. Let's take a look at that."

He watched her through slits as she carefully raised his shirt to reveal a gunshot wound to his left side. Gently, she felt around his torso, searching for the exit point. The hole in his back was larger and slightly lower than where the bullet entered. Blood seeped from the wound. She climbed to her feet.

The man's gaze tracked her as she crossed the room to the kitchen. She returned with two towels, which she folded into fourths and pressed to each wound.

"Can you hold these in place?"

He nodded. She guided his hands, showing him how much pressure to use. "Is that the only place you were shot?"

"I think so."

Janice checked his pulse. It was fast, but steady. "You need a doctor."

"No, no doctors—"

"You're not in a position to argue," she said. "We've got QuikClot in the supply room but I need to go get it. Will you be okay if I leave you for a minute?"

He nodded. Pain obvious on his face, he shifted slightly before rearranging his hands for a better grip on the towels. She rose to leave but he seized her arm in a surprisingly firm grip. The towel he'd been holding slid from the wound. She picked it up and repositioned it, guiding his hand to hold it in place before she leaned closer to hear him.

"I am not terrorist," he insisted. "I am Russian soldier. My superiors ordered me to join Izz Al-Din."

"You're working undercover?"

The corners of Mikhail's mouth pulled downward in a grimace. "At first, yes. Now I am *helping* terrorists."

Janice narrowed her eyes. "But your government is backing Libya against them. How—"

He shook his head. "This is ruse. My country fights America's allies through Izz Al-Din."

Startled, Janice slid her hand free of his. "You aren't serious." Izz Al-Din's brutal tactics and inhumane treatment of prisoners and civilians was well documented. No sane government would ask its soldiers to willingly fight alongside such butchers.

"*Da.* As you people say, serious as heart attack." A deep, racking cough punctuated his words, and pain arced across his face. Janice got to her feet.

"But—that makes no sense. Egypt and Libya are working against the terrorists, not each other."

"*Maskirovka.* You understand this word?" When Janice shook her head, Mikhail explained. "*Maskirovka* is deception. In beginning, Russia supplied my unit with false information to give terrorists. Izz Al-Din acted on this false information and we win."

"What's wrong with that?"

"Is different now. My superiors now give correct information on United States allied movement. All so US

16

will commit ground troops." Mikhail winced as he tried to get more comfortable.

"But that puts Izz Al-Din in a stronger position. US-backed allies would be decimated."

Mikhail leaned his head back, holding her gaze. "This is why I am no longer interested in helping my country." Another cough seized him and he squeezed his eyes closed against the pain. "Do you think I will die?" he asked.

"Not if I get that clotting agent, you won't."

"I must get message to my father. Information is there." He dipped his chin toward a medallion he wore around his neck.

Janice touched the bronze figurine of a saint. "This?"

He nodded. "*Da*. Is flash drive. Please to send message to him? His contact information is there. Anatoly Sakharov. Tell him I am alive."

"Of course." She pulled the necklace over his head and studied the medallion. The two ends came apart, revealing a USB connector. She snapped it closed and put it in her pocket. "I'll do it later this morning. We'll have satellite hookup then."

"If I am alive in morning, please to give back?"

"Of course." Janice straightened and started for the door. "The QuikClot is in the supply unit. I'll be right back."

Mikhail closed his eyes, pain evident in the white, straight line of his mouth, the pinched eyes, the deep V of his brows. Janice slung the Kalashnikov over her shoulder and hurried from the tent, headed for Dr. Evans's quarters. It didn't matter if the man was Russian or Izz Al-Din, he needed a doctor, now.

CHAPTER 3

SHEN safe house, Tripoli

Leine finished packing her carry-on bag and checked the spacious, well-appointed room one last time for anything she might have missed. The house would be considered luxurious by anyone's standards, but especially when compared to SHEN's usual base of operations. The Libyan businessman who offered his residence as their base for rescuing Munira would be returning the next day, and she wanted to be long gone before then. The fewer people that recognized her, the better. With the increase in sex trafficking they'd been seeing, she had a feeling she'd be back in the region before long.

Hamid's surgery had gone well. Now stable and resting in a hotel room a few kilometers away, the SHEN operative would be transferred to a medical facility in Spain for the remainder of his convalescence. The prognosis for recovering the use of his left arm and shoulder was good, although it would take considerable time and therapy. Lou suggested an extended beach vacation, assuring him that relaxation would be the best thing for him.

Leine grabbed her bag to leave, but then remembered she hadn't replied to Janice's message from the day before, and set it back on the bed. She thought she might be able to get away to see her old friend, but that was before she learned that she could snag a seat on military transport due out of Libya that afternoon. The thought of going home had won out over sticking around in the hot desert.

Hey there, she wrote. *Much as I'd love to see you, I've got a ride out of here that I can't refuse. Let me know when you're back in Vancouver and I'll come visit for a few days. We'll talk smack about old boyfriends, go hiking, and drink wine. Leine.*

Leine had met Janice during the early days of the US war in Afghanistan—Leine had been on a job, and Janice had been working for a non-governmental organization that provided emergency medical care to civilians. Over the years they'd kept in touch, but because of their wildly divergent schedules had only managed one face-to-face meeting.

She pressed send as memories of Afghanistan came flooding back. Considered the agency's premier operative, Leine had been sent to eliminate one of the country's most ruthless warlords with strong ties to the Taliban.

The operation went as planned until she arrived at the extraction point. Someone had tipped off the local Taliban sympathizers and they captured her translator who'd gone ahead to secure the site. They tortured him until he broke, and then dragged his body through the streets behind a dilapidated pickup truck as a warning to others. Dressed in a burqa, Leine was able to elude the gunmen that surrounded the safe house and then get a message to Eric, her boss. But not before she'd seen what they'd done.

Though she didn't know it at the time, that job had been the beginning of the end for Leine. Over the next few years each mission would cost her more and more emotionally, leading to her decision to leave. Her last job for the agency involved a betrayal so deep, the nightmares still haunted her.

An hour later, at an airstrip outside Tripoli, Leine stood in line waiting to be processed to leave when her phone vibrated. She checked the screen. It was a message from Janice. The time stamp told her she'd sent it several hours ago. A message lost in cyberspace, again. Leine figured with the spotty reception she'd encountered in country that she'd been lucky to send and receive messages at all.

I'm sorry we weren't able to meet this time, Janice wrote. *The idea of leaving Libya sounds really good right now and I can't blame you for going. Things here are sketchy. Although the camp has recovered from an "accidental" bombing that occurred several months ago, the hospital is still vulnerable to attack. Dr. Evans refuses to move the facilities to a safer location. His reasoning is that the people won't have as far to go to receive treatment. But what if those people are killed? All I can do is hope and do my work. Safe travels, J*

Leine stared at the screen for a moment. Janice's tone had changed from upbeat to bleak in the course of twenty-four hours. Had something happened to make her outlook change so drastically? The line began to move forward to the last checkpoint. She lifted her bag and moved along with the others. *I should find out what's bothering her.*

That sounds pretty bleak, she typed. *What's going on? Something I can do?* She pressed send and glanced at the phone of the guy standing next to her. Breaking news on one of the 24-hour news outlets showed images of a recent bombing.

"Where is that?" she asked him, nodding at the screen.

"The border, near Egypt," he answered. "Looks like the assholes shelled a refugee camp."

She stiffened. "What news site are you on?"

"BBC."

Leine brought up the story on her phone. Less than an hour before, the terrorist group Izz Al-Din had shelled Janice's refugee camp, destroying their field hospital. There were no reports of casualties. Yet.

Leine looked up from her phone to see that the line had moved on without her. She switched to a dial pad and tapped in the number for Lou's burner phone. Still in country, he'd keep the same number until he left.

"Lou Stokes."

"Lou. It's Leine. I'm taking a detour. I need to get to the Egyptian border."

"What the hell are you talking about? I thought you were going home."

"Izz Al-Din just shelled a refugee camp where a friend of mine is working. I've got to make sure she's all right."

"Jesus. And you want to go there? Do I need to remind you that you just finished an operation for SHEN? You've got to be exhausted." Lou sighed. "How many casualties?"

"None reported yet. We were supposed to meet somewhere between Tripoli and the camp, but I opted to head home."

"Which is the sensible thing to do."

Leine rolled her eyes. "I just called to let you know that I won't be on the flight this afternoon." She scanned the room for a likely contact to hire her own transportation.

He sighed again. "Give me half an hour. I should be able to find you something."

"You're a peach, Lou." Leine ended the call and texted Janice.

Heard about the bombing. Are you all right? Am working on finding transpo there. Stay safe.

She slipped the phone into her pocket. It was going to be a long wait.

CHAPTER 4

Refugee camp, Libyan-Egyptian border

S everal hours later, Leine touched down on the outskirts of the refugee camp. A combination of Lou's contacts, Leine's persuasiveness, and plenty of cash had scored her a flight out of Tripoli on the Mi-8. She'd worry about getting home later.

A large depression where the field hospital had been located scarred the ground, giving the area the appearance of a moonscape. Cleanup efforts appeared to be winding down, and an evacuation was under way. Patients, some on gurneys and others in wheelchairs or on crutches, were lined up, waiting their turn to board a transport helicopter. A group of men, women, and children—mostly refugees—clutched their belongings as they waited nearby.

"Where are they taking them?" Leine asked a man walking by.

"Another camp south of here," he said over his shoulder as he hurried past.

Ignoring the sweat trickling down her back and the scorching midday sun, Leine continued toward a small group of what appeared to be camp personnel. In the center stood a man with dark hair and intense blue eyes, who appeared to be issuing instructions. He looked up at her approach.

"Can I help you?" he asked. His green scrubs were well-worn and splotched with sweat and bloodstains, and the weariness on his face spoke of sleepless nights and more than a passing acquaintance with lost causes. His nametag read *Dr. Richard Evans*.

"My name is Leine Basso. I'm looking for Janice Olson." Leine braced herself for bad news. If Janice had been anywhere near the blast site she wouldn't have survived.

Dr. Evans frowned as he signed a sheet of paper on a clipboard held by another man. "And you just happened to be in the area?"

"Tripoli," she said. "We're old friends. I wanted to make sure she was all right."

The man with the clipboard left and Dr. Evans turned his attention to Leine. Although somewhere in his late thirties, the deep creases and sagging skin around his eyes gave the impression of a much older man.

"She was lucky." He waved his hand, indicating the camp. "We all were. We didn't lose anyone, although I've got a patient in critical condition with third-degree burns over half of his body." The doctor sighed. "This is the second time we've been bombed. Why they keep targeting us is a mystery, but we keep coming back."

A mixture of relief that Janice was all right and sympathy for the doc swept through her. "I'm so sorry," Leine said.

Evans nodded behind him. "I think she's in her tent. Third one on the right." A few yards away, a young blond woman called to Evans.

"Doctor? We're ready for you."

"Coming, Marcy," he answered. "One more thing to tidy up before we close shop," he said to Leine. Resignation flickered over his features as he turned to go. "Then it's time to beg for more money."

"Good luck," Leine called after him before making her way toward Janice's tent. Hesitating at the entrance she called, "Anybody home?"

"Hold on a minute," came the reply. A moment later, Janice poked her head out. At five-feet-five with shoulder-length hair the color of caramel and penetrating hazel eyes, she had the intensity of a person who'd been through more than most. Her face lit up. "Leine!" she said and threw her arms around her in a warm hug. Leine returned the embrace. Janice stepped aside so Leine could enter, a tired smile tugging at her lips. "God, it's good to see you. How long has it been? Five, no, six years?"

Leine smiled back. "At least," she said, and entered the dark interior. "Istanbul?"

"Sounds about right."

Although the tent was open on both ends and captured what breeze could be had, the temperature inside was well over one hundred degrees. Janice followed her in and walked to her cot where she secured the top of her rucksack and set it on the ground.

"Sit, please." She indicated a plastic chair next to a makeshift nightstand. Leine obliged and Janice sat across from her on the cot. "I thought from your last text that you were on your way home."

"I sent you another message as soon as I heard, but it must have gotten lost. The bombing's all over the news. They're saying it was Izz Al-Din."

Janice grimaced. "We've been trying to get the news outlets to cover this conflict for months. *Months.* I guess all it takes is a terrorist bombing in the middle of the desert, eh?"

"You know what they say, 'If it bleeds, it leads.'"

"Yeah. Too true." She frowned and shook her head. "I'm not convinced it was Izz Al-Din."

"Why is that?"

"Early this morning, after the bombing, I came across a man dressed like a jihadi in the mess tent. He'd been shot and had lost a lot of blood."

"And you called security, right?" Leine said.

"Well, here's the thing. He had a Russian accent and said he'd been given orders to join Izz Al-Din."

"Russian soldiers infiltrating a terrorist cell? Not much of a stretch."

"Yes, but he insisted his mission changed from passing along bogus intelligence to actually passing along the *right* information to help them."

"Really." That was interesting. Relations between Russia and the US had warmed recently. The newly elected Russian administration had reached out to the US with offers of friendship and cooperation. Both countries were cautiously optimistic. "Where is he now? Did he survive?"

Janice nodded. "He's recovering from surgery on the other side of camp." She reached into her pocket and pulled out a medallion on a chain, which she handed to Leine. "He gave me this. It's a flash drive."

Leine pulled the two sections apart. "What's on it?"

"A letter and a bunch of photographs. He asked me to contact his father to let him know he was all right." She nodded at the medallion. "I checked the files. The letter's written in Russian and is addressed to Anatoly Sakharov. The jpegs look like vacation photos. I sent a message to the email address listed on the letter a little while ago, but no one's replied yet."

"Did you attach the letter?"

Janice shook her head. "I wanted to make sure it was a valid address before I did, in case the document contained sensitive information. My Russian is pretty dismal."

"Would you like me to translate for you?"

"That would be a big help." Janice opened the front compartment of her bag, pulled out her laptop, and turned it on. She inserted the flash drive, clicked on the document, and handed Leine the computer.

Leine read aloud, interpreting as she went.

To: Anatoly@Sakharov.com

Dear Father,

Sincere apologies for not contacting you sooner, but I was expecting to secure a transfer from my unit. Uncle Roman assigned me to a clandestine operation and for security purposes I could not contact anyone. I hope to take leave next month and will try to visit then.

Please give my love to Grandmother—I know she is in ill health and not expected to last the winter. I think it would be a good idea to transfer her to the medical providers in the US that you and I discussed last summer. It is my belief that the current doctors are not to be trusted and do not have her best interests at heart. It would not surprise me if your generous donations to the medical center had been diverted in some way to line their pockets. You must insist upon a report from their accountants.

Give also my love to my beautiful mother and sister. I am looking forward to seeing you all again soon.

With love,

Your son, Mikhail

Leine glanced up from the screen. "It sounds innocuous enough. He doesn't say anything about fighting on the front lines with Izz Al-Din, although I'm sure he wouldn't in the event that he was captured or killed." She clicked on a couple of the photographs. One showed an image of an oasis surrounded by date palms, and another a lush courtyard with intricately designed tile work. "I don't think you have to worry about sending these. The letter might be some kind of code between them, but unless the person intercepting the files knows that, I doubt they'd think anything of it."

"Good to know." She closed the files and shut down her computer. "How long are you here?"

"However long I need to be. My main concern was making sure you were okay."

She smiled. "That means the world to me, Leine. Thank you."

"Any time."

"So that means you don't have transportation out of here yet?"

"No."

"I'll add your name to the list. The refugees and our patients are priority one, but as soon as they've been evacuated we can catch the next flight to Cairo. Probably later tonight."

"Your doctor doesn't waste time, does he?"

"We've been through this before. It's assumed whoever did the shelling wanted to take out our surgical unit, which they did, so the chance of another attack is slim. All the same, we're packing it in. There's not enough money left to operate until Dr. Evans does his thing with the donors, and no one wants to hang here while he sorts that out." Janice's expression brightened. "Which means we'll have time to catch up."

"Sounds like a plan." Leine couldn't help but smile. Janice always had the capacity to bounce back in spite of obstacles. It was one of the many things she admired about her.

Janice gave her a sly look. "A little bird told me where to find two lukewarm bottles of beer," she said in a conspiratorial whisper. "But first, I need to look in on Mikhail. He asked me to bring him his phone, which is in the supply tent with the rest of his things. Then I'll be back." She rose from the cot. "I shouldn't be too long. I doubt he'll be in the mood to chat. Feel free to walk around the camp. These people are dedicated, hardworking individuals. I think you'll find some like-minded souls here." With that, she left.

Leine walked outside, squinting in the bright sunlight. She pulled a pair of sunglasses from her pocket and slid them on before she set off to explore the rest of the camp. With the evacuation underway, there wasn't much to see. She stopped and helped a couple of camp personnel pack up their equipment before moving on to another area.

A while later, she followed the perimeter back to Janice's tent. She hadn't returned from visiting Mikhail yet. Leine scanned the rest of the camp, searching for her. She turned to go inside when a shockwave of heat and sound and percussion slammed her to the ground. Bits of metal, glass, and dirt rained down like a sadistic storm.

Ears ringing and unable to breathe, Leine lay immobile on her back, staring at a bright blue sky. A creeping darkness clouded her periphery. She blinked, eyes watering as her confusion and vision slowly cleared.

What the hell?

Then, *breathe, Leine. Breathe.*

A split-second later, her lungs caught up with the rest of her and her mouth yawned open. She heaved in a lungful of dusty air as her abdominal muscles contracted and she jackknifed to a sitting position.

Hands, check. Legs, check. Arms, check. Eyes, torso, and anything else she could think of—check, check, check.

Ears still ringing, she climbed to her feet, only then registering the other people who had gathered nearby, alarm and confusion obvious on their faces. She pivoted, searching for the recovery unit where Mikhail had been, but it no longer existed. Instead, a debris field stretched for yards in every direction, the center a deep, jagged depression in the earth where the tent should have been.

Janice. Heart in her throat, she stumbled toward the blast site. Stunned and frightened people mobbed the transport helicopter as camp personnel struggled valiantly to push them back. It was an exercise in futility. Unable to handle the incoming mass of humanity, the ramp began to close. Desperation seized first one and then another refugee and people began to climb on, hoping to be let on board.

"You're hurt." Marcy, the blond woman who'd called for the doctor earlier, hurried up to Leine.

For the first time the pain registered and Leine touched the back of her head. Blood covered her fingers. Marcy produced a small flashlight and shined it into Leine's eyes. She squinted at the bright light for a second and then looked away.

"I've got to find Janice."

"How many fingers am I holding up?" Marcy asked.

"Seventeen," Leine answered and started for the blast zone.

Marcy followed. "Where did you see her last?"

"She was going to check on the Russian."

Marcy stopped, her face white. "The recovery unit," she said, more to herself than to Leine.

Leine nodded and continued to walk, the certainty of her friend's death growing with each step. She ignored the chaos erupting around her and barely noticed when Marcy handed her a wad of gauze for her wound.

Why would terrorists bomb a recovery unit and not the doctor's makeshift operating tent? Surely they'd made their point. If they had eyes on the camp, they knew personnel were packing to leave.

Dr. Evans stood next to the bombsite, staring into space. Leine walked over to join him. He barely acknowledged her.

"Janice was inside." His voice caught.

Leine ignored the impulse to grieve for her friend. Out of necessity, as an assassin she'd learned to compartmentalize her emotions. She'd have plenty of time to process Janice's death once she got back to the States. Right now she needed to act.

"Were there many other casualties?" Leine asked.

Evans shook his head. "Everyone else had already moved to the staging area. We were waiting to transport Mikhail to a hospital in Cairo." He turned to Leine. The expression in his eyes conveyed defeat. "I'm sorry. I know she was a friend."

"I'm sorry for the world. It lost a caring soul."

Leine returned to Janice's tent, her thoughts racing as she tried to work out the reasoning behind the attack. *How can you assign reason to an unreasonable enemy, Leine?*

Seething with anger at the senseless waste of life, she closed her eyes, allowing her rage free rein. Anger she could work with, much more so than grief.

She picked up Janice's rucksack and hoisted it over her shoulder. She'd personally deliver Janice's things to her mother in Vancouver. Janice would want that.

Leine turned to leave when she noticed Janice's computer where she'd left it on the cot. The medallion containing the files was still plugged into the USB port. She pulled the drive free and started to put both the computer and the drive back in the bag but hesitated. If the Russian had told the truth about fighting *with* Izz Al-Din rather than *against* them, there had to be more to the story. Leine slid the medallion into her front pocket and put the computer into the bag.

Perhaps Mikhail's father could shed more light on things. At the very least, he deserved to know what happened to his son.

CHAPTER 5

Cairo, Egypt

Two days later, Leine still hadn't been able to contact Anatoly Sakharov. The man had heavier security than most presidents, which spoke of powerful enemies.

The kind you didn't want as your own.

Leine leaned back in her chair and took in the view of downtown Cairo from the balcony of her hotel room. The smog-filled haze lent the city a sepia-toned, nostalgic air. With a little imagination she could picture herself as a spy during World War II, awaiting a message from Allied command...

What was it like when the entire world hung in the balance between good and evil—when one person alone could mean the difference between success and annihilation? She shook her head, allowing the fantasy to recede. *Back to reality, Leine.*

The idea of spies operating during World War II brought to mind microdots, dead drops, and other means of moving information clandestinely. What if Mikhail had intended to tell his father what his superiors had ordered him to do? Wouldn't he have used some kind of code that only his father would understand? Maybe she could glean additional information from the letter that hadn't jumped out at her before. She retrieved her laptop from the table next to her and turned it on to have another look at the files.

The photographs were innocuous landscapes and still-lifes. Why would a Russian operative who had infiltrated a terrorist network carry vacation photos on a hidden thumb drive?

Unless he'd hidden another file within the photograph itself.

Curious, Leine went to a secure website SHEN often used in sex-trafficking cases and downloaded a program designed to detect invisible files within a digital photograph. She then ran each picture through the cutting-edge software. In a matter of seconds, the program extracted several images embedded within the pictures. Three of the photographs didn't appear to have files embedded in them. Perhaps Mikhail had intended to use them later.

Her heart beat faster at her discovery, and she leaned forward in her chair. The first scene revealed a group of black-clad jihadists gathered around a stack of rectangular containers. The lid of the uppermost container had been thrown open to display several Stinger missiles. One of the terrorists held a missile aloft, a jubilant expression on his face. Leine enlarged the photo to read the logo stamped on the side of the container.

Sakharov Industries. Anatoly Sakharov's company.

The next few images were a brutal chronicle of the slaughter of men, women, and children, and showed a number of jihadists, all wearing black headscarves, aiming weapons at the victims as though having just mowed them all down. Her left eye twitched as she closed the files.

She moved to the last file and paused as she read. The image appeared to be a cell phone picture of an end-user agreement to import munitions into Libya.

The Libyan government had been listed as the end-user, with Sakharov Industries as the supplier. Leine was pretty sure Mikhail hadn't been fighting alongside the Libyans when he took the picture. The date stamp said it had been taken just two weeks before.

Why would Sakharov supply munitions to Izz Al-Din? Leine got to her feet and paced the balcony, sorting through what she knew. A shipment from Mikhail's father had been diverted from the Libyan army to the terrorists, unless someone staged the picture. She discarded that possibility. With what she knew, it served no purpose. What she didn't know was where the photographs had been taken, or if Sakharov intended for those weapons to fall into terrorist hands.

The discovery of the hidden photographs made contact with Anatoly Sakharov crucial. Was he aware that his shipment had been diverted? If so, then Leine would have to tread carefully. Alternatively, did Mikhail intend to warn his father about the diverted shipment by showing him the photographs on his next trip home? No legitimate arms dealer wanted to be identified as supplying weapons to terrorists—sanctions against such illegal activities were too great. The contents of Mikhail's letter to his father made more sense when read with the veiled attempt to alert Sakharov to the possible theft. She'd bet Mikhail's grandmother wasn't dying.

Leine studied the three other photographs. Apparently the program she'd used to ferret out the hidden photographs had been unable to detect additional information within the files. She sent them to Lou through an encrypted app, asking him to see if he could find anything. She also asked him to locate the elusive billionaire.

Less than twelve hours later, Lou delivered a fount of information on Sakharov and his wife, gleaned from reports given to him by an old contact in the CIA. Apparently, Anatoly and Katarina Sakharov left their home in Odessa three years prior to sail the Greek Isles on their magnificent yacht, the *Black Swan*. By the time Leine finished reading Lou's report, she knew where Katarina Sakharov shopped (Gucci, Prada), her favorite brand of shoes (Christian Louboutin), where she and her two children went on vacation (the French Riviera and New York City—Anatoly rarely took a holiday), and her favorite restaurant for brunch (the exclusive Black Pearl Café near the Acropolis in Athens). He'd also sent Leine a recent photograph of the couple.

Somewhere in her late thirties, Katarina Sakharov had a smooth, olive complexion and delicate features, with long, brownish-black hair and dark, intelligent eyes. She was quite a bit shorter than her husband, coming to just above his elbow. She'd look positively tiny standing next to Leine's five-foot-ten-inch frame. Her makeup and clothing were flawless, as if orchestrated by the head of *Vogue* herself. A gold chain with a cross and several other expensive-looking charms adorned her perfectly tanned décolletage.

Anatoly cut an imposing figure in a crisp white shirt, blood-red tie, and charcoal-gray tailored suit. Dark, wavy hair framed Slavic cheekbones and a prominent nose; his intense, raptor-like gaze suggested predatory instincts.

A yacht on the Aegean Sea would be a great place to conduct business, especially if that business included shipping arms to Libya. There was the added benefit of being able to disappear among one of the many tiny islands in the Cyclades when the wrong people got too curious about those business dealings. Locating a moving target would make things interesting. Lou had identified the general location, although the Aegean Sea was a vast area in which to search.

After she finished reading the report, she messaged Lou and asked him to locate the last port of call for Sakharov's yacht. As usual, he hadn't asked why she needed the information. From the beginning as they resumed their former business relationship from their agency days, she'd been able to come and go when and wherever she wanted with the added plus of being able to pick Lou's prodigious brain about the latest and greatest spy gadgets and protocols.

Good to his word, the next day Lou called back with the last known port for the super yacht. The *Black Swan* had taken on fuel in the small port of Milos in the Cyclades two days before and had returned to Athens that morning. He then gave her the contact information for an old acquaintance of his who worked as a security contractor in Greece.

"Art's not the easiest guy on the planet. He's old school, and doesn't think women should be in the field. But he's got a boat in case this becomes a seagoing venture. He's also well connected to the security community. Be gentle with him, Leine."

"When have I not been gentle?"

There was a long pause before he changed the subject. "Will this be a long trip?"

37

"Shouldn't take more than a week. I'll give you a call as soon as I get back. Did you find anything on those photographs I sent you?"

"Not yet. I've got people working on them, though, so it shouldn't be long now. If there's anything these guys'll find it."

Leine thanked him for the information and ended the call. Then she booked a flight to Athens and reserved a small apartment near the harbor. Since it was close to the off season, she got a surprisingly good rate. Her arrival in Greece this time of year meant air and ferry service to the Cyclades would be virtually nonexistent. If the *Black Swan* left Athens before Leine touched down, she'd have to make some kind of arrangement with Lou's friend to find Sakharov.

If all went well she shouldn't need the help.

CHAPTER 6

Athens, Greece

Leine touched down in Athens that evening, rented a car, and drove to the apartment she'd rented.

The sights and smells of the city rekindled memories from an earlier time, and she stared through the windshield at the familiar terrain, feeling like a prodigal daughter. She'd completed assignments in Greece, but it had been a while since she'd been back. Those jobs, assassinations ordered by Eric at a time when he'd been using agency assets for his own ends, still weighed heavily on her conscience. How could she be certain the targets she'd eliminated had been actual threats to national security and not just jobs that would help line her boss's pockets?

There'd been changes to the city most referred to as the Cradle of Western Civilization. Ever since economic collapse and the resulting austerity measures, the difference between "tourist Greece" and "real

Greece" had become much more pronounced. Walls covered in graffiti dotted the landscape where earlier there'd been none. Once-thriving shops were now either shuttered or operating illegally out of someone's home, and protests against the government and transportation strikes had become more frequent. From what little she'd seen so far, the people of Athens still retained their friendly manner and zest for life, although an underlying strain appeared to dampen their enthusiasm.

Leine picked up the key to her apartment from a woman who lived two doors down and dropped her bag in the front room. Before driving to the marina to find the *Black Swan*, she filled a daypack with several items she'd brought with her. She wore light-colored capris and a black camisole under a long-sleeved sweater in anticipation of the warm weather predicted for the next day. Her all-terrain sandals were comfortable and gave her sufficient coverage, and she'd stuffed a weatherproof jacket in the bottom of her daypack in case the forecast turned out to be wrong.

Fifteen minutes later she turned onto a steep side street perpendicular to the Artemis Marina, found a space to park facing the water, and turned off the engine. Several vehicles parked along the street allowed her rental to blend in. Down the hill to her left, kitchen staff sat outside the back door of a busy restaurant having a smoke. To the right, a vacant lot overgrown with vegetation stretched into the darkness.

Harbor lights arced across the Aegean as waves gently lapped the shore. The faint clank of lines against metal masts and the sound of boats thumping against the dock accompanied a light wind blowing through the quiet neighborhood. Air redolent with garlic and onions and fresh grilled fish from the restaurant mixed with the briny scent of the gulf.

A quick glance through the windshield with the night vision goggles affirmed the location of the *Black Swan*. In addition to a pair of sunglasses and the NVGs, she'd packed high resolution infrared binoculars, a computer tablet, bottled water, a first aid kit, and a cell phone, which she used to call Lou.

"Hey, Lou. Checking in."

"I figured you'd be calling. There's been some activity on the *Black Swan*. Looks like they might be getting ready to move. The crew's been offloading suitcases and boxes and taking them to a van parked nearby." Lou had been keeping tabs on the super yacht via one of hundreds of satellites orbiting the earth. This one happened to be owned by a private European communications firm. Lou had searched for and found the CEO's son, who'd been kidnapped and held for ransom by an extremist group, and the two of them had been close friends ever since.

"Makes sense. The weather's turning and the season's winding down. Anyone matching Katarina Sakharov's description?"

"I've seen her twice. She's usually flanked by two big guys in dark suits."

"Good to know."

"By the way," he continued. "Those three photos you sent? Keira found a way in." A brilliant software engineer, Keira freelanced for the agency for several years but had gone off grid after she quit. Lou tracked her down and convinced her to do occasional side work for SHEN.

"And?"

"Two of them were recruitment videos for Izz Al-Din. One showed a couple of Russian soldiers complaining about their mission."

"Can you send them to me?"

"Comin' atcha. Are you going to need any bait while you're there?"

Bait was one of their code words for weapons. "Couldn't hurt. I hear the fishing's amazing this time of year. Minnows and a box of night crawlers should do it." Minnows stood for a semiautomatic, and night crawlers meant ammunition.

"What size container?"

"How about a number nine?" A nine millimeter should be all she'd need.

"No problem. You know the address."

"Thanks, Lou. I'll send pictures if I catch anything."

"Please don't."

She ended the call and found the message from Lou containing the videos. She retrieved her tablet and downloaded them.

Leine opened one of the files and immediately dimmed down the brightly lit outdoor scene. The video had the narrow screen and quality of a cell phone video. Three masked men wearing black headscarves and holding huge knives stood at attention behind the same number of unmasked prisoners. Wind ruffled the prisoners' hair. A nondescript landscape of buff-colored sand and rocks stretched behind them.

The prisoners, two men and one woman, knelt in front of the masked men, hands behind their backs. The man on the left appeared resigned, his features slack, while the one in the middle rocked back and forth and prayed aloud, his eyes squeezed shut. In contrast, the woman's rigid posture and angry expression communicated defiance and white-hot hatred.

One of the masked jihadists began to speak in Arabic, directing most of his diatribe toward the US and the allies fighting against Izz Al-Din. His chilling last words sealed the victims' fates:

"These traitorous dogs have aided the infidels in their fight against Allah. Their sentence is to die at our hands and burn in the fires of Hell. *Allahu Akbar.*"

The other two parroted the speaker's last words before each of the three masked men stepped forward, grabbed a prisoner by the hair, exposing their throats, and raised the knives to each of their necks. Leine stopped the video before the beheading. She'd seen enough.

The next video opened with a shot panning a barren landscape. Bright sun and unbroken, flat terrain hosted the occasional dust devil eddying across the ground like a whirling dervish, disintegrating as quickly as it formed. Gusts of wind buffeted the microphone, punctuating the videographer's even breathing. A few seconds into the recording, the camera zoomed in on what looked like the edge of a large pit. The person recording the video walked steadily toward the crater, the sound of crunching gravel competing with the wind.

The picture bounced with each step before coming to rest at the edge of the hole. The videographer paused, his breath catching before the camera panned down. At the bottom of the massive excavation lay hundreds of bodies covered in filth and beset by flies. Arms, legs, torsos, and heads sprawled across the bottom as though a janitor had disposed of a pile of trash. Men, women, and a disturbing number of children made up the horrifying tableau.

Somewhere off camera an engine caught, choked, and rattled to life. The camera panned back to take in the lumbering mustard-yellow bulldozer pushing a wall of dun-colored earth toward the gaping gravesite. Black smoke belched from the dozer's exhaust as it pushed the huge pile of dirt closer to the edge of the pit. The machine lurched forward the last few feet, dumping sand and dirt onto the bodies, partially burying them. A dust cloud rose from the bottom of the picture and enveloped the scene.

Leine leaned back in her seat. *Right out of the Nazi playbook.*

Finding the bodies would take a miracle.

With a feeling of dread, Leine double-clicked the next file. In a dark room two men sat on a cot, facing the camera. The low angle of the shot suggested the person recording the video didn't want his subjects to know they were being filmed. A time and date stamp told her the scene had been recorded several weeks earlier. She turned up the volume.

"This whole thing is shit," the man on the left side of the screen muttered in Russian. He glanced behind him before continuing. "I want to fight for my country, not help these barbarians."

The man on the right nodded. Keeping his voice low he said, "But if we disobey, we will be shot. The general—"

Off camera another voice interrupted, "No matter what happens this does not end well. The terrorists could kill us at any moment."

The man on the left leaned in as if to say something else, but the man on the right stood, turning his back to the camera as he spoke Arabic to someone Leine couldn't see. A second later the screen went black.

Leine took a deep breath and let it out slowly. There was no way to prove who these men were or where they were at the time of the recording. The man who recorded the video, Mikhail, was most likely dead, and the others could be anywhere and from anywhere—mercenaries tended to go where the highest bidder sent them. The clips didn't constitute enough evidence to show the files to anyone who mattered—whoever presented them would be summarily ignored, if not viewed as a conspiracy nut. She could take her chances and leak them, but in the current climate of fake news and dubious sources, getting anyone to take them seriously would be a crapshoot.

If it turned out that Sakharov had nothing to do with diverting the arms shipment, he might agree to back up her story to keep his company from being dragged through the muck. Then she might be able to get a meeting with someone in a position to do something. She ran through names in her head, discarding all but one: Scott Henderson.

Henderson, the boss of her former boss, Eric, still ran the black ops agency Leine worked for all those years ago and had direct access to the vice president. There was just one problem: Leine's *persona non grata* status. As it was, Scott Henderson wasn't too happy with her, hadn't been for a long time, and scheduling a meeting with him would most likely be difficult. She supposed it was because she outed one of his favorite directors for going rogue several years prior.

Maybe "outed" wasn't the right word. "Caused to be dead" was more accurate.

The culture at the agency had been such that Henderson preferred to handle "problem employees" internally. The real cause of the explosion in a rundown LA neighborhood had been covered up sufficiently so that it couldn't be traced back to Leine or the shadowy agency. But Henderson had never forgiven her for her role in events surrounding the shakeup. Leine couldn't have cared less.

Until now.

She hadn't foreseen the need to be on Scott Henderson's good side. True, burning bridges was never a good idea, but Leine had been left with no choice. If she hadn't revealed her former boss's misdeeds to his superiors, agents sympathetic to the agency would have hunted her down for her role in Eric's death. She'd already been a target.

At the time it was a no-brainer. Now she wished she had Henderson's direct line.

Life was funny that way.

Leine shut down the tablet and put it away. She leaned her head back and stared out the windshield, looking at nothing.

Everything hinged on finding Sakharov.

CHAPTER 7

The morning dawned clear and bright with the occasional scudding cloud in an otherwise flawless sky. The sun hadn't yet crested the horizon, creating a violet display that would soon turn orange, then yellow, and end in brilliant white sunlight reflecting off the glassy smooth Aegean. Yearning for an espresso, Leine stretched her arms and cracked her neck, shaking off the last vestiges of a cat nap. The front seat of the car had been somewhat comfortable, although her body would pay later.

A delivery driver and two fishermen were going about their business, but the surrounding neighborhood hadn't yet fully awoken. Two ambitious crewmembers dressed in matching polo shirts were hosing down one of the yachts, but it would still be the better part of an hour before the area came alive.

Leine trained her binoculars on the section of the marina where the larger yachts were berthed. The *Black Swan* was tied stern-first to the long concrete dock, with a black Mercedes Benz sedan parked nearby. Three men could be seen patrolling the decks. She made a note of several neighboring yachts and their country of origin, and settled in to wait.

The sun crept skyward and slowly the marina and surrounding neighborhood began to stir. An older man driving a small delivery van pulled up to the back of the restaurant, got out, and unlocked the door leading into the building. A stray dog trotted by and slowed near the garbage bin, but finding nothing to eat resumed its original course.

At nine thirty, two black Mercedes Benz SUVs pulled up to the marina's guard house and stopped. The window of the first SUV rolled down and the driver's arm materialized. The guard poked his head out, said something to the driver, and laughed. A moment later the gate swung open, granting both vehicles access. They continued past the yachts before stopping next to the sedan opposite the *Black Swan*. Moments later, a woman wearing oversized sunglasses and a sleeveless white, knee-length dress stepped off the yacht onto the dock and into one of the waiting SUVs. She matched the photographs of Katarina Sakharov.

Leine started the car. She allowed the two vehicles a slight head start before she nosed into the street to follow them.

She tailed the SUVs onto a busy freeway and drove until they reached Kifissia, an upscale suburb in northern Athens. The difference was startling. Where the majority of Athens had been hive-like, filled with graffiti and sound and chaos, the tree-lined, shade-dappled, park-adorned boulevards of Kifissia brought instant calm.

Interesting. With her tastes, I'd have expected her to go to Kolonaki. High-end luxury shops like Gucci and Prada clustered together within a few blocks of each other at Kolonaki, the Rodeo Drive of Athens. In contrast, Kifissia was upscale, but much more low-key.

The SUVs pulled to the curb next to a well-appointed outdoor mall of white stucco buildings with roofs like nipples rising from the wide, immaculate sidewalks. Leine pulled into a parking space two cars down and turned off the engine. A muscular man with massive shoulders exited the lead vehicle and did a perimeter check. He wore mirrored sunglasses, an earpiece, and a dark suit, and didn't smile. Apparently satisfied with their surroundings, he turned back toward the SUV and held out his hand, saying something to the person inside. A delicate hand grasped his, and a moment later Katarina Sakharov emerged. Another man dressed identically to the first exited the vehicle from the opposite side. A telltale bulge near the men's armpits completed the ensemble. A perfect pair of bookends.

Leine stepped out of her rental and slid on the sunglasses before following the small group into the mall's courtyard. Even though it was early in the day there were quite a few people shopping. Taking her time, Katarina Sakharov walked into each shop and out again before disappearing into a boutique specializing in eveningwear. Leine stayed back far enough so she could continue to monitor them but remain inconspicuous.

Pretending to window shop, she glanced behind her. Another man dressed similarly to the other two bodyguards stood several yards away. Leine continued to walk, feigning interest in a rack of clothes outside the boutique. Apparently, Katarina Sakharov had found something she liked—her security team took up posts on either side of the entrance.

Leine smiled as she walked between them into the store. Their expressions granite-like, the only indication they registered her presence was a slight shift in their stances when they made their threat assessment. Evidently she'd passed. Once inside, she slid her sunglasses onto her head and let her eyes adjust.

Artfully designed racks filled the small shop with haute-couture evening gowns sporting astronomical prices. Lute and violin music played gently over invisible speakers. The only other customers in the shop were two women who appeared to be in their late thirties. Leine greeted the shopkeeper as she perused the merchandise, all while listening to them chat.

Most of the women's conversation centered around where they were going to have dinner that night, how a piece of clothing worked or didn't, and the changing weather, which meant it was time to return home. Leine detected a hint of sadness from the smaller woman's tone, but the other seemed ready to go back to wherever she'd come from.

"Aren't you tired of the endless partying, Livia?" the taller one with red hair asked in a clipped British accent.

"How can you even ask such a thing?" replied the other woman. "Going home means dreary skies and a dreary life. London's so tedious. I'd live here year-round if Barry would agree."

The redhead scoffed. "That'll be the day. Your husband is married to his job. I'm surprised you were able to talk him into going on holiday at all."

"If it wasn't for you two, I'm afraid I'd be sentenced to live in *jolly old England* every day for the rest of my life."

"Oh, get out the violin. Listen to you. You've got a gorgeous flat and two beautiful children, yet here you are complaining about having to go back to live in *London*, for

God's sake." The redhead clucked at her in mock sympathy.

Chagrined, the other woman smiled. "Oh, I know, I know. An embarrassment of riches."

"Does this mean you won't be attending the party at the museum Saturday?" The redhead stopped sorting through the clothes and looked at her friend.

Katarina Sakharov glanced at the two women.

"No," the one named Livia lamented. "Barry says we *must* leave Friday."

"You mean to say you're going to miss the biggest bash of the season?" The redhead's expression held a mixture of disbelief and sympathy for her friend. "I'm so sorry." She resumed looking through the clothes on the rack in front of her. "From what I hear, it's going to be absolutely smashing."

The other woman looked crestfallen. The redhead gave her a quick smile and said, "Don't you worry, sweetie. There'll be other parties."

Katarina Sakharov put back the dress she'd been looking at and moved on to the next rack.

The redhead glanced at her and raised an eyebrow as she discreetly elbowed her friend. "I couldn't help noticing, but aren't you Katarina Sakharov?"

"Yes," Katarina replied in English, her tone frosty. "I'm sorry, do I know you?"

"Oh, no. But I know you. This benefit we've been on about wouldn't be happening without the generous donation from you and your husband," she gushed. "Will you be at the benefit?"

"I believe so." Katarina's tone was cool and noncommittal.

The redhead's smile grew wider. "Oh, fantastic. You must come and say hello. I'm Barbara, and this poor, unfortunate woman is Livia." She nodded at her friend, who gave her a mock scowl. "Are those your men out there?" she asked, indicating the two bodyguards outside.

Katarina nodded, her interest squarely back to the clothes in front of her. "Yes."

"I see." Barbara gave her another warm smile. "Well, then, Katarina, until tomorrow night."

"Yes. Until then."

Barbara picked out a saucy little number and brought it to the clerk.

"This should work perfectly." She turned to Livia. "Oh, go ahead and buy something, why don't you? It's not like Barry can't afford it. Call it a consolation prize for making you leave Athens."

"You know what? I think I will." Livia took a turn down the aisles and pulled something off of each rack, then brought the items up to the counter.

"Would you like to try them on?" the clerk asked.

"No," Livia replied. "If they don't fit, I'll give them away."

Katarina smirked as she caught Leine's eye. Leine raised an eyebrow and returned her attention to the dress in front of her.

A few minutes later, Katarina appeared to lose interest in the offerings and headed for the door.

"Goodbye, Katarina," Barbara called out. "Hope to see you Saturday!"

Katarina gave her a wan smile and walked out of the shop. Barbara turned to Livia and gushed, "Do you know who that was? That was the wife of Anatoly Sakharov—one of the richest men in Russia."

Livia glanced out the door as the two bodyguards left their posts to follow Katarina. "She seems a bit of a cold fish, if you ask me. And what's with the two big thugs?"

Barbara rolled her eyes and started in about judging a book by its cover. Not waiting to hear the rest, Leine slipped out the door to follow Katarina and the bookends.

"Excuse me," she called.

Katarina turned around. Flanking her, the bookends clasped their hands and stilled. The third bodyguard had taken a position several feet behind Leine.

"Yes?"

"You are Katarina Sakharov?"

Her eyes narrowed. "I am."

"I have information for your husband. It's about your son, Mikhail."

Uncertainty mixed with a hint of worry replaced the wariness on her face and she stepped forward. The bodyguards stiffened and closed ranks. Leine kept her hands relaxed at her sides. No point in making anyone nervous.

"What kind of information? Is Mikhail all right?"

Leine switched to Russian. "It's important."

Her eyebrows rose upon hearing her native tongue and she considered her for a moment. Then she said, "You must tell me. I am his mother."

"It's more complicated than that. I need to speak with your husband. In person, preferably."

Katarina shook her head. "That is impossible."

"Then I will try another avenue." Leine turned to leave. The third bodyguard stepped in her way.

"Wait."

Leine stopped but didn't say anything.

"I will call him and you can speak with each other. This way, we will let my husband decide if the information is important."

"Thank you." It was better than nothing. She couldn't tell Sakharov much over the phone. The Russians had been known to keep tabs on their own people, especially the rich, powerful ones. Leine studied the third bodyguard. She'd have to make the conversation count without giving anything sensitive away.

Katarina rummaged in her Gucci bag for her phone. She turned away, making it difficult to hear what she said. A moment later, she faced Leine and held out the phone.

"He says he will speak to you. But you must be brief." She waited as the third bodyguard stepped forward and took the phone from her. He then handed it to Leine.

"Anatoly Sakharov?"

"Yes." The annoyed tone told Leine he was indulging his wife and to make the conversation quick.

"I have news about your son, Mikhail."

"What news? And why didn't you tell my wife?"

"I'm afraid I can't tell you over the phone. We need to meet."

There was silence on the other end. Then, "Is my son all right?"

"When can we meet?"

"Who are you?"

"My name is Eve Mason, and I've been asked to contact you." Eve Mason had been one of the aliases she'd used when she worked for Eric. When she started contracting for SHEN, Lou obtained a passport, driver's license, and credit cards with the same name, and created an uncomplicated legend of sorts for her undercover work with the anti-trafficking agency.

"By whom?"

"I really can't say."

Anatoly Sakharov sighed. "This is ridiculous. What news do you have of my son?"

"I can tell you that you have not heard from Mikhail in at least two weeks, and that he promised to visit you and your wife next month."

"And?"

"And that you have a mutual friend he calls Uncle Roman."

Anatoly Sakharov paused before he said, "You are American?"

"Yes."

"Your Russian is very good."

"I'll tell you why when we meet."

A second sigh came from the other end. "Have my wife take a picture of your passport information. If you pass a security check, I will obtain a ticket for you to a gala my wife and I are attending tomorrow night. We will meet there." Leine was about to hand the phone to the bodyguard when he added, "And you had better have something worthwhile." The implied threat was obviously meant to intimidate.

Leine ended the call and handed the phone to thug number three.

"Looks like I need to find something to wear."

CHAPTER 8

Moscow, Russia

General **Roman Tsarev** scowled as he set the phone down on his impeccable desk. The caller, a carefully placed informant the general trusted implicitly, had just advised him of a troubling development with one of his clandestine operations.

It seemed a woman had contacted the wife of his childhood friend, Anatoly Sakharov, claiming to have information regarding Anatoly's son, Mikhail. Anatoly had tasked a member of his security detail to run an extensive background check on her. Apparently, whatever she said had sparked Anatoly's interest enough that he was considering meeting with her.

Up to that point the operation had been working better than expected. The soldiers embedded within Izz Al-Din had been passing along intelligence alerting the terrorist organization to US-allied positions in the region. As a result, the allies had suffered heavy casualties.

All according to plan. He could almost taste victory. It wouldn't take much, not in that incendiary part of the world. Tsarev would be more than happy to strike the match that sent everything up in flames.

Let the Zionists and Islam fight it out on a dusty, barren battlefield in Libya. Extremists from both sides seemed to think it was God's plan that one destroyed the other. He would just direct their hatred to a different setting.

Idiots.

The so-called edicts from God himself were taken from two antiquated tomes written by ignorant men from another time, for another conflict. It would take very little to stage the last, great war between the zealots of the two religions somewhere other than Dabiq, the so-called battlefield of Armageddon. Tsarev had only to push them toward each group's belief in their sovereignty, their God-given right to wipe out an entire religion.

Brilliant.

His plan was much like what earlier political operatives had accomplished in America on a smaller scale decades before; by introducing cheap, addictive drugs to the streets and fueling the fire of segregation with turf wars that spilled over into fringe groups, the American ruling class was able to stoke unrest between minority factions. This ruling class kept them manageable by creating deep rifts between agitators and groups within the minorities, turning their attention away from what was really happening. He laughed at the prevailing belief that America was a classless society.

Social manipulation and experimentation. Sleight of hand and obfuscation. Look over here—it's so much more interesting than what's really going on. Ancient Romans used it. So did Hitler, as did most governments operating today. Pure genius.

People were so malleable.

Tsarev had learned well from his study of history. Lesser men refused to make the connections. This is what differentiated him from the others, the ones who would ultimately fail. The study of the past was humbling, yes, but also an amazing trove of what to do and not do when it came to building his masterpiece.

Most people were intellectually inferior. They had no idea of what went on beneath their noses. They didn't want to know.

So it was with surprise and an increasing sense of dismay that Tsarev had listened to his informant. Finely honed instincts from years of working in Russian intelligence were pricking at him, telling him he needed to pay attention to what his source had told him. At best, the woman represented a slight wrinkle in the carefully constructed tapestry Tsarev had woven. Even so, the wrinkle set ugly red flags fluttering in his mind.

The woman could be nothing, merely a loose sheaf in the pages of his magnum opus. One easily plucked out and disposed of. But she could also signify an unraveling, something for which he hadn't planned.

Of course, he was tempted to ignore the possibility. Was he not General Tsarev, one of the most decorated Russian soldiers in modern times? A master counterintelligence officer and brilliant strategist? His complexity and cunning unrivaled, he'd gone over his plans with painstaking attention to detail, following each thread to its most likely conclusion until he'd exhausted all probable scenarios. Then, he'd done it again, this time substituting improbabilities. Later, when the operation concluded, he'd be remembered as the genius who brought Russia back to her former glory. They'd hail him as a humble student of history, a man of unmitigated bravery and intelligence. They'd write about him in books, hold parades, name a holiday after him.

He allowed himself a tiny smile. If only his beloved mother could see him. He looked at the ceiling and crossed himself. She'd have been so proud of her only son.

Roman Tsarev shook his head, shoving the memory away. Now was not the time to lose himself in daydreams. Now was the time to bring to bear his iron hand on this insignificant problem before it became significant.

Had he missed something crucial? If so, then this woman might represent an opportunity to fine-tune the operation, possibly bringing even greater success. As Tsarev had learned, what might first look like a problem could be viewed as an opportunity to strengthen the structure of a plan. That's how he'd survived. How he'd gained the trust of the president and upper echelons of Russian leadership.

Although, having been childhood friends with the acting prime minister certainly helped.

The image of the current leaders of the Russian Federation brought a sneer. Weak men, all of them, and too conciliatory to the West. How they'd come to power was beyond his understanding. He hadn't been part of the election process then, but he'd soon remedied that. Apparently, he needed to control everything or it would all come crumbling down.

The proof of the leaders' intent to bring Russia to her knees was evidenced by what they were now doing with their old enemy, the United States. Tsarev grimaced as he swallowed, trying to eliminate the bad taste that had formed in his mouth. How had such a young, spoiled country so filled with opposition remained a super power—actually *gained* in power? Yet another question for the ages.

Tsarev shook his head to clear it as he picked up his phone and punched in a familiar number. He would soon know if this woman represented a problem.

CHAPTER 9

Athens, Greece

Leine ascended the steps to the entrance of the National Archeological Museum, careful to keep the shimmery floor-length gown out of the way of her stylish heels. No sense ruining the hem—she was just going to return the dress after the gala. The day before, she'd located a small boutique that provided haute-couture eveningwear for short-term use, with a steep deposit via her credit card. The gold jewelry she wore was also on loan from the same place. She fit right in with the other arrivals. Most were elegantly attired—the women in floor-length evening gowns and shimmery wraps, the men in crisp black tuxedos.

She stepped across the threshold of the sprawling neoclassical building and came face-to-face with the brilliant gold "Mask of Agamemnon." Its empty eyes had a haunting, slightly unnerving quality.

An attendant took her wrap and offered her a glass of champagne, which she accepted with no intention of drinking. The bag she carried had been exactly the right size for the 9mm semiauto. She'd swung by the shop on her way to the gala to pick up the weapon and ammunition. It was a fine leather goods store in the heart of Athens that she'd used previously in her work as an assassin, and the original owner had handed the business down to his son, Other than the change of ownership, everything remained much the same. While there, she'd picked up some additional tools she thought would come in handy. One was an ornamental hair comb that sported two wicked three-inch blades. She wore it now, as part of an elegant updo. No one would know it could double as a lethal weapon.

She moved with the rest of the attendees toward the main event, held in one of the larger halls. Twenty-five-hundred-year-old marble statues depicting Greek gods and goddesses shared the tasteful, high-ceilinged, well-lit space with the affluent guests. The drone of conversation and the occasional clink of glasses undercut a calming soundtrack of soft violin music.

Leine stood next to an image of Zeus and surveyed the crowd. Anatoly Sakharov had told her to wait in the main room with the other guests, and would send for her as soon as he arrived.

Everyone appeared to be having a good time. Efficient, white-coated waitstaff wove their way through the various groups of patrons, offering hors d'oeuvres and champagne. Animated conversation and laughter from attendees filled the air. For the most part, the women were perfectly tanned, fit, and surgically sculpted, while the majority of men showed telltale signs of rich food, too much wine, and years of inactivity: thick waists, pallid complexions, and sagging skin. Barbara, the redhead from the boutique, was there in a brilliant red gown with a plunging neckline.

A man dressed in non-tuxedo designer wear who looked like he'd rather be anywhere else stood on the fringes surveying the crowd. His gaze flickered past Leine and then returned for a moment before continuing on to the rest of the room. She scanned the space for more security and was rewarded with a taller, similarly dressed gentleman who appeared more relaxed than his partner.

Sakharov's advance team?

Leine glanced at her watch. Five minutes past the time Sakharov had said he would arrive. Absentmindedly, she took a shallow sip of her champagne, wondering when and how he'd make contact. The Russian had been adamant that he not be seen speaking with her, citing vague security reasons. Leine assumed there was more to it than that but agreed to a private audience prior to his and Katarina's entrance.

Just then, a young woman walked up to Leine. Smiling, she placed her hand gently on Leine's elbow and steered her toward the back of the room.

"Come with me, please," she murmured. "Mr. Sakharov would like to see you."

Leine allowed herself to be led through a doorway and into the next room, filled with smaller figurines from another era in Greece's long and storied history. They veered off from the main exhibits and walked through several more rooms and down hallways until they came upon what looked like a conference room.

The two men she'd seen scoping out the party flanked the door. The woman asked Leine to stand still and hold her arms out to the side.

"I have a gun in my purse," Leine said and opened the clutch to show her. The woman removed the 9mm and handed it to one of the men, who slid it under his jacket.

"It will be returned once the meeting is concluded," she said. "Do you have anything else?"

"A lighter and some cigarettes." She showed her those, too. The woman flicked the cover off the old-fashioned lighter, lit it, and then opened the pack of cigarettes. Seeing nothing of concern, she replaced the items and continued to pat her down.

Satisfied that Leine had no additional weapons, she told the two men to step aside and allow their boss's guest to enter, which they did. Leine walked through the door into a well-appointed conference room adorned with framed Greco-Roman sketches illuminated by track lighting. The two security guards followed her inside and took up their same positions on either side of the door.

Arms folded, Katarina Sakharov stood near one of the floor-to-ceiling windows, staring outside at the spot-lit landscape. She wore her dark hair swept up in a chic coif, and a sapphire blue, off-the-shoulder gown with long white gloves á la Audrey Hepburn. Seated behind a massive table was her husband, the commanding figure from the photograph with broad shoulders and black, naturally wavy hair shot through with gray. The photograph hadn't done him justice—his tanned face and prominent cheekbones, nose, and chin practically shouted Slavic ancestry, further emphasized by a salt-and-pepper goatee. A widow's peak dipped onto his high forehead like an exclamation point, accentuating the raptor-like gaze.

"Sit, please," he said, nodding at a chair across from him. Katarina turned to face Leine. At first glance she appeared calm, but a pinched expression betrayed her distress.

Leine glanced at his men and gave Sakharov a pointed look. "I said alone."

Anatoly Sakharov shrugged and waved at his men. "Leave us." Without a word they exited the room, closing the door behind them.

"This is about my son," Katarina said unnecessarily. "I will stay."

Leine wondered if the words were for her benefit or her husband's. She walked over and set her champagne on the table.

Sakharov studied her with cold indifference. "I am here as you requested. What information do you have of my son?"

She glanced around the space. "May I ask if you've swept the room?"

Sakharov scowled. "Of course." He waved impatiently at her to continue.

"Then you won't mind if I do?" At his shrug, she reached into her clutch and brought out the lighter. She flipped the cap up and pressed a small button on the bottom. A tiny green indicator light blinked on. Leine walked the perimeter of the room, watching the light. At no point did the green glow change, which told her the room was clear. She returned the tool to her handbag, removed the pack of cigarettes, and sat down in the chair across from Anatoly Sakharov.

"I would prefer that you don't smoke," he said, eyeing the pack in her hand.

Leine opened the box and removed the decoy cigarette filters, revealing three folded pieces of paper.

"Who do you work for?" he asked.

"If you're asking whether I'm a spy, the answer is no. I'm here on behalf of a friend." *And for my piece of mind,* she thought. She unfolded the first paper and handed it to him. She'd decided earlier that it would be best to get things out in the open quickly. To do otherwise seemed cruel. "There's no good way to say this. Your son is dead."

Katarina Sakharov made a sound like air escaping from a tire and gripped the back of her husband's chair. Anatoly's hand froze, but his mask of impassivity never slipped. A second later he accepted the paper from Leine.

"This is a copy of a letter written to you from your son. One of many files he saved to a flash drive."

Anatoly Sakharov scanned the letter once and then slid it toward his wife to read.

"How do I know you are telling the truth?"

"You don't. But I have a feeling that you didn't know your son had been embedded in a terrorist cell in Libya."

Katarina gasped and looked at her husband. "Is this true?"

Anatoly narrowed his eyes. "I didn't know that my government had infiltrated the enemy, but the information isn't surprising."

"Did you know that your son was tasked with passing along US-allied movement to Izz Al-Din?"

Sakharov shrugged. "I'm sure if this is true, it was meant to mislead."

"At first, maybe, but not now. The last intel contained actual allied positions. In effect, your government is working with the terrorists. Your son believed it was so that the US would have no choice but to become involved in the conflict."

Anatoly snorted. "You don't know what you are talking about."

Leine pulled out a second paper from the pack of cigarettes, unfolded it, and slid it across the desk. "Does this look familiar?"

He glanced at the copy of the end-user certificate. Again, he showed no reaction.

"Of course," he replied. "This is paperwork generated for a shipment of weapons to the Libyan government. May I ask where you obtained this?"

"From your son's flash drive. He also had several videos of atrocities committed by Izz Al-Din. I believe Mikhail was gathering evidence to prove that he'd been ordered to infiltrate the group and pass along information to sabotage US-Egyptian efforts."

His eyes steady on Leine, Anatoly said to his wife, "Leave, Katya."

She gave him a sharp look. "But—"

"Now."

At her husband's commanding tone, she clamped her lips closed. Head held high, her spine ramrod straight and anger oozing from every pore, she marched out of the room.

The door closed behind her and Leine handed him the last document—the photo showing the crate filled with missiles surrounded by triumphant jihadists. "You can see by the date stamp on the two photos that this took place on the same day that the Libyan government supposedly accepted delivery of your shipment. I can only surmise that your son saved these images to prove to you that the weapons were diverted." Leine leaned forward. "What I need to know before we go any further is if that was your intention."

Sakharov's eyes flashed with anger. "Of course not. Those butchers are a threat to my country. I would not help them if they were drowning in a pile of steaming shit."

"Not knowingly," Leine said. She studied the Russian. The momentary blip of anger had disappeared, replaced by an implacable expression. He would have made a formidable poker player. "I'm sorry to have brought such bad news," Leine continued, softening her voice. "If it helps to know, you were the last person your son spoke of before he died."

Anatoly Sakharov blinked. "How did it happen?"

"A direct hit from an enemy shell. He died quickly. Prior to the bombing he sustained a gunshot wound to the abdomen before he made his way to a refugee camp with a hospital on the Libyan-Egyptian border. The camp had been shelled earlier that morning. The official version is that both attacks were instigated by Izz Al-Din."

"But you believe differently." His question was more of a statement.

Leine nodded. "Yes, I do. I think Mikhail was the sole target of the second shelling. Although one other person died in the blast, I believe she was collateral damage. The first bomb took out the camp's operating facilities, which everyone assumed to be the original target. Your son was recuperating in an unmarked area far from the temporary surgical unit, but ended up being at the epicenter of the second blast. If the group that ordered the first bomb were surveilling the camp, they would have known this."

"Then how do you think they pinpointed his location? A transmitter?" Sakharov shook his head. "This is not possible unless this transmitter had somehow been secured to his body. You yourself said he was recovering from surgery."

"I think his cell phone had a locator. The person who died with him in the second bombing brought his personal effects to him right before the attack, most likely including his cell phone."

"Did you speak with my son before he died?" he asked.

"No."

"Did you see him while visiting this refugee camp?"

"No."

"I see." The temperature in the room dropped several degrees. Anatoly Sakharov stared at Leine, his jaw and shoulders rigid. "Then you have no proof of his death."

"The surgeon and attending medical personnel would be able to corroborate the story."

"How would they know if their patient was my son? This letter states he was on a clandestine operation. If true, he would not have carried identification. If he had, then the bombing would have wiped out any credentials."

"I will tell you that I trust the person who gave me this information. I should also tell you," Leine continued easily, "that if I don't call a specific number at regular intervals, the contents of your son's flash drive will be made public. The people who release the information will make sure it is viewed as your company's intentional diversion of arms to the terrorist group that Russia is supposed to be fighting. I assume that wouldn't sit too well with your government. Or the world, for that matter."

"Understood." Anatoly Sakharov held her gaze for a moment before continuing. "Now we have come to the part of the meeting where you tell me what it is you want."

"I want you to back me up when I go to my government with this information. You need to go on record that you had nothing to do with diverting the shipment to Izz Al-Din and that you believe someone with ties to the Russian government is trying to lure the US into a ground war. As it is, there's not enough actionable intelligence. With information this potentially explosive, I need corroboration from one of the principal players or it won't be taken seriously. Although damaging to you and your company, releasing the information without your verification will likely do nothing to stop the deception from going forward. At best, my government will look at the leak as an interesting possibility to be followed up at some point. At worst, they'll chalk it up to some sort of conspiracy theory."

"And my country will collectively roll its eyes and assume the information is more of your fake news." Anatoly Sakharov stared at Leine. "If what you have told me is true, then it places my company in a very dangerous position. Whoever is behind this will not be happy if they find out I have helped put an end to their ruse."

"That's certainly something to consider."

Sakharov stretched his neck first one way and then the other. "Is there anything else you wish to tell me?"

"There is a cell phone video ostensibly taken by your son of two Russian soldiers who speak of not wanting to be part of their unit's campaign aiding Izz Al-Din. There's a date stamp but no way of knowing where it took place or who the soldiers are. I can't stress strongly enough that your son's files alone aren't sufficient proof for me to go to my government." Leine closed the cigarette pack and put it back in her purse. "The détente between our countries has been good for both sides, wouldn't you agree?"

"Of course."

"The details on the flash drive tell a vastly different story than Russia's official line. I'd hate to think that your president is trying to deceive the US. I'm also sure you would agree that releasing this information could seriously damage relations between our two countries. Where that might lead one can only guess."

He nodded. "I will check out the veracity of your story."

"Be discreet. I'm not certain who we're dealing with."

"Of course." Anatoly Sakharov stood and came around the side of the table. "I believe our business has concluded."

"Here's my mobile number." Leine wrote it on a notepad on the table and slid it toward him. "I need to hear from you by this time tomorrow. If I don't, then I will assume you're part of the deception and I'll release your son's files to the major news agencies, whatever the cost." She picked up her clutch and rose from her chair. "May I have my gun?"

If he was surprised she had a weapon, he didn't show it. He clapped his hands and the door opened. The taller of the two bodyguards looked into the room.

"Return Ms. Mason's weapon to her."

The man reached in his jacket for the gun and handed it to Leine. She slipped it inside her handbag and walked to the door.

"Enjoy the party," Anatoly said.

After Eve Mason left, Anatoly Sakharov motioned to his two guards to come into the room.

"Follow her and report back," he said to the taller one, pinning him with a hard stare. "Don't lose her, Yevgeny."

"Do you want me to detain her?"

"Only if she attempts to leave the country."

Yevgeny nodded and left. Sakharov turned to the other man. "Remain outside the door. Let no one inside."

"Your wife is waiting—"

"Yes, I know," he snapped, cutting him off. "She will have to wait."

The guard did as he was told. Sakharov reached into his pocket for his phone, hit speed dial, and waited for the other party to answer.

"Hello?" The deep voice of Anatoly's childhood friend, General Roman Tsarev, rumbled across the line.

"We need to talk."

"I do not hear from my old friend Anatoly for weeks and this is how he greets me?" Roman Tsarev sighed. "What have you done now?"

Bristling, Sakharov bit back a sharp retort. Roman had a way of getting under his skin—had done so since they were children. "Where is my son?"

"You know I can't tell you that. He's on special assignment."

"Just tell me one thing. Is Mikhail still alive?"

"Yes, of course he is. Why would you ask such a thing?"

Sakharov closed his eyes as relief washed over him. "Never mind. It's important that I contact him."

"I'm afraid that's impossible. As I said, he's on special assignment. Tell me what's wrong. What has happened that you are so desperate to speak with him?"

"It's nothing. Would you get a message to him for me?"

"Of course."

"Tell him to contact me as soon as he can. Tomorrow, if possible. Something has come up that I need to discuss with him."

"I will be sure to have the request forwarded. Is there anything else I can do?"

"No."

"Well, something has gotten you excited. If there's anything I can do to help, you know all you need do is ask."

"Of course. Thank you, my friend."

Roman Tsarev chuckled. "Anytime. And Anatoly?"

"Yes?"

"Please don't worry. Whatever the problem, I'm sure everything will be fine."

CHAPTER 10

Leine wound her way back through the crowded party to the entrance and stopped at the coat check to retrieve her wrap. As she put it on, she felt a light tap on her shoulder. She turned to see Katarina Sakharov, her ever present security detail hovering nearby.

"Leaving so soon?" Katarina asked.

"I'm not really one for parties," Leine answered.

"I wanted to speak with you before you left." She nodded toward the entrance where attendees still streamed in. "Walk with me?"

Leine finished putting on her wrap and picked up her purse. "Of course."

With her security guards trailing, Katarina Sakharov led her outside and down the steps. At the bottom they turned right and continued walking. After they'd gone a short distance, Katarina stopped and said something to the two guards before indicating that she wanted Leine to walk with her. The guards stayed where they were. Conversation and the occasional peal of laughter from people arriving at the gala faded to the low murmur of background noise. There was no one else within hearing distance.

"Why did you come here?" Katarina asked.

"I told you and your husband. Because of your son."

Katarina shook her head. "No. You misunderstand. *Why* are you here? What do you want?" She glanced at the moon, still low on the horizon, its beams illuminating the museum's grounds. "If it's money, I will tell you right now that my husband will not pay."

Leine sighed. "Mrs. Sakharov, I am not here to extort your husband. I'm here to gain his cooperation."

"I don't understand."

"Your husband sells weapons to the Libyan government."

"Yes," she replied, nodding her head. "But what he does is legal."

"That may be. But some of the files on your son's flash drive tell a different story."

"What are you saying?"

"I'm saying it appears that one of your husband's shipments headed for Libya was diverted to Izz Al-Din. I think your son was trying to gather information to give to his father as proof." She turned to face Katarina. "It appears Mikhail did not believe that your husband knew what had happened. I'd like to think that's the case. That's why I made the effort to contact him. Otherwise I wouldn't have risked my life coming here." She glanced behind them, gauging the time that had elapsed since she'd left her meeting with Anatoly Sakharov.

Katarina stared at Leine. "So he is dead, then."

Leine nodded. "I'm sorry."

Tears welled in her eyes and she angrily wiped at them with the back of her hand. "My husband assured me that Mikhail would not be in any danger when he was assigned to Roman's unit. In fact, it was supposed to be the other way around. Roman promised to look after our son." The tears fell freely now. Katarina pulled a tissue from her bag and blotted beneath her eyes.

"Roman is the name of your son's superior?"

"Yes. *General* Roman Tsarev." The sarcasm in her voice was hard to miss. "He's Anatoly's childhood friend. I never liked the man."

"Do you believe your husband had anything to do with diverting the shipment?"

Katarina shook her head vigorously. "Never. He *hates* Izz Al-Din with a passion. This is why he agreed to provide weapons to Libya."

"That's what I thought. I'm sure I don't have to tell you that if this information gets out and your husband is implicated, he could be facing international condemnation, possibly prison."

"Then why should I let you go? A word to my men…"

"Do you really think I would go into a meeting with your husband without some kind of fail-safe?" Leine frowned. "I'm not stupid. Look. I don't want to see your husband go to prison, but if he doesn't agree to officially confirm my reports then I'll have no choice but to release the information. It's that simple."

Leine glanced back at the museum's entrance. The taller of Anatoly Sakharov's bodyguards was standing on the top step, scanning the parking lot.

"I need to go. Do you have your phone with you?"

"Yes." Katarina reached into her handbag and pulled out her mobile.

"Put my number in your contacts. In case you remember anything you think might help. I need to hear from you or your husband by this time tomorrow."

Leine noticed the tail after the third maneuver. She lost the SUV a few minutes later, but continued to watch in case more than one team tracked her. Soon, a suspicious looking sedan took the place of the first vehicle. This one stuck and she found herself relying on a series of counter surveillance moves that she hadn't used since she worked for the agency. She'd checked the undercarriage of her car for a tracking device before she left the gala, but found nothing suspicious.

Twenty-five minutes later, she deemed herself surveillance-free and continued toward Athens International Airport. Her carry-on bag was in the trunk with a change of clothes easily accessible in the top zipper compartment. On the way, she stopped at a restaurant and changed in the restroom, putting the gold dress, shoes, clutch, wrap, and jewelry together in one box. She took out the silver comb and shook her hair loose, then placed the weapon inside her bag. A quick detour brought her to the small boutique where she'd rented her outfit. The shop was closed for the evening, so she dropped the sealed box into a depository located next to the door and walked back to her rental car.

As she reached for the car door handle a thick arm snaked around her neck. Instinctively, Leine grabbed her attacker's forearm with both hands and shifted her body to the right. The larger assailant leaned back, tightening his hold, and her feet came off the ground. She brought her knees up, and using as much momentum as she could, straightened her legs, arched her back, and swung her feet down, landing hard on the sidewalk, forcing him to jackknife forward.

Still holding on, the man tightened his grip, nearly strangling her. She dropped to one knee and forced him to lean farther, pulling him off his center but worsening the chokehold. Black spots appeared in her periphery and she battled for breath. With one last surge of energy she twisted and managed to slip her left leg behind his right. This created a narrow opening near the crook of his elbow and she wrenched her head through. At the same time she grabbed his right hand and bent it at a painful angle before she straightened, jerking his arm up between his shoulder blades.

Before he could counter, she kneed him in the groin multiple times. He gripped his crotch and collapsed to the ground with a groan. She brought the heel of her hand down fast and hard, smashing him in the sensitive area near the back of his head. He pitched forward and sprawled facedown across the sidewalk. Gasping for air, Leine staggered back and scanned the street for more attackers.

Hers was the only car visible in the deserted neighborhood. She moved to the fallen assailant and shoved him onto his back so she could see his face.

She didn't recognize him. She felt for a pulse. He was still alive. Keeping an eye on him for signs of recovery, she rifled through his clothing and found a .45 snugged in a shoulder holster. She pocketed the gun and looked through the rest of his pockets. He carried nothing else except for a cheap mobile phone. Leine checked the screen, but it was locked. She pocketed the phone without removing the battery in case a tracking device had been installed. No sense letting whoever was after her know their guy had been compromised.

Yet.

Why didn't he use the gun? If he was one of Sakharov's men, he didn't send him to kill her or she'd be dead. Was he going to take her somewhere? If so, why and where? She'd thought her warning to Sakharov not to harm her would have been sufficient. He didn't need the weight of the international community coming down on him for supplying arms to known terrorists. Especially when they were enemies of Russia. Even though well-connected, the intense scrutiny would at the very least put a damper on his business dealings.

She hadn't noticed the tail. Then it hit her. She opened the passenger door and reached under the drivers' seat for the 9mm. She jacked the slide, ejecting the chambered cartridge. The brass pinged as it struck the sidewalk and skittered away, and she leaned over to pick it up. It looked and felt like the same ammunition she normally used. Then she removed the magazine and inspected each round. When she got to the third one, she stopped. The weight was wrong. She moved under a streetlamp to take a closer look. In comparison to the other rounds, the metal jacket had a slightly different color and the whole thing felt too light.

Holding the brass between her thumb and forefinger, she twisted the lower section of the casing with her free hand. The bottom screwed off easily, revealing a miniature circuit board connected to tiny wires.

Sakharov's people had substituted a tracking device for one of the rounds in her gun. Anger boiled inside of her—anger at Sakharov, but also anger at herself for not being more astute.

You're getting soft, Basso. Whether the result of her tamer, domestic life in California, she wasn't sure. All she knew was she'd lost her edge and made what could have been a deadly mistake. In the old days she would never have missed something like that.

She dropped the device into her pocket before pulling out her phone to take a picture of the man's face. Then she slid underneath her rental car and checked once more for signs of tampering she might have missed.

Satisfied her vehicle was clean, Leine climbed to her feet and gave the neighborhood one last scan. Then she slid in the driver's seat, started the car, and headed for the airport. Once she was there, she'd flushed the tracking device down the toilet.

She'd deal with Sakharov later.

CHAPTER 11

Moscow, Russia

S he's what?" **General** Tsarev gritted his teeth. He had to consciously release his fingers one by one from the phone before he damaged the plastic cover.

"She's gone."

Georg, his top security man, had lost Eve Mason. Anatoly Sakharov had provided the perfect cover for her abduction by having his bodyguard Yevgeny follow her, although he'd been ordered not to approach the woman. The general's mole in the billionaire's security detail had reported Yevgeny's actions, and hidden a tracking device in the woman's gun. Tsarev had instructed Georg to pick her up and take her to a safe house for questioning.

Somehow she'd been able to escape—no, escape wasn't the correct word—somehow she'd been able to *outmaneuver* Georg in the field before she disappeared. Not only that, but he'd found no record of her leaving Greece, either by plane, train, or boat, even though she'd checked out of her apartment and returned her rental car at the airport that same evening. According to his sources she hadn't rented another.

"Remain close to your phone. I will need your services once I locate this woman."

"Yes, sir."

The general ended the call and sat for a moment, staring into space. He had to admit his confidence in Georg had been badly shaken. Such a shame. All of the preparation and training for nothing. Tsarev heaved an internal sigh.

Time for a fallback plan.

Once the pounding in his temples eased, he mulled over his options.

Obviously, there was more to this woman than her background suggested. What information he had been able to glean in a brief background check held no clues as to how she could have done what she did to Georg. She had no record of military service—her life was as blasé as they come. She might have learned self-defense by attending classes, but that didn't explain the evasive maneuvers she employed as Georg tracked her. That suggested she knew she was being followed.

Initial inquiries had returned information giving only her age, her birthdate, and her occupation as an adjuster for a large insurance company in Los Angeles. She had no prior arrests, no online social media accounts, a single email address on one of the free email providers that she rarely used, and few friends. If the report was to be believed, she lived alone in a small rental in Pasadena and had no known relatives.

It was too vague. The dossier read like a legend for an agent. And not a very convincing one, at that. Tsarev ordered an expedited and extensive security check on the woman. He'd get to the bottom of who she was, and who she really worked for.

There was also the question of what she told Anatoly about his son. Tsarev had been able to put his old friend off for a time but sooner or later he would have to come up with a workable story for Mikhail's death. The general experienced some remorse for putting Mikhail in such a dangerous position—he wasn't a monster—but when the young Russian began collecting information that put Tsarev's plans in jeopardy, his friend's son had sealed his fate. The noble cause the general sought to strengthen was much too important to allow one individual to bring it all down.

The homing device in Mikhail's phone had been a good safeguard. In actuality, the general used the same locator program for all his troops. None of the soldiers knew they were being tracked. They were glad to get the government-issued device, no questions asked. The general had installed software that could transmit conversations even while powered off, which was how Tsarev first learned of Mikhail's information-gathering exercise. The software also gave him the information that Mikhail survived the first attempt on his life and sought help at the refugee camp.

He'd checked to ensure all of the young Russian's files saved on the flash drive that hung around his neck had been obliterated in the bombing. The investigator had told Tsarev's contact that there wasn't sufficient material left for a DNA sample.

Perfect.

How much did the woman know? And what had she told Anatoly? It was imperative that he locate and question this Eve Mason to find out the extent of her knowledge. Had she spoken to Mikhail before he died?

Possible. If so, then what had she been doing on the Libyan-Egyptian border?

From his conversation with Anatoly Sakharov it was obvious her argument hadn't convinced him of her veracity—but that didn't make her any less dangerous. Tsarev understood well a father's reasoning. If the news of your offspring is unpleasant, why not put off the inevitable? Live in that gauzy world between lying to yourself and the truth. Only when the facts become too obvious to ignore would decisive action be taken.

The general picked up the phone and dialed a number he'd memorized from an earlier life. A life where he'd had to use dramatic solutions.

THE LAST DECEPTION

CHAPTER 12

Athens, Greece

Anatoly Sakharov closed the file he was reading and rubbed his temples. The low-grade headache had made its appearance shortly after the woman delivered the news about Mikhail and the possible shipment diversion to Izz Al-Din. Was his son really dead? He pushed aside the horrific thought. It couldn't be true. The army would have notified him. Roman wouldn't lie about that.

Would he?

If he had, and the woman was telling the truth, then Sakharov would need proof. If his son had been the victim of a bombing, evidence of his death would be hard to come by unless his DNA had been recovered from the bombsite. And since his son's superior was denying his death, Anatoly assumed this evidence would not be forthcoming.

He gazed out the window at the brilliant sun reflecting off the calm waters of the harbor. Seabirds wheeled in the sky, vying for scraps tossed from the yacht tied up next to the *Black Swan*. He didn't want to go back to Moscow, would much rather winter in Greece, but if he wanted to find out more he had no choice. He would have to be careful when he spoke to his contact.

And he needed to see all of the files on his son's flash drive. Perhaps there was something Eve Mason had missed.

The night before, Yevgeny had lost her. Sakharov checked his Rolex. Over twelve hours had passed since she disappeared. He would call her soon enough.

His frustration at Yevgeny's incompetence had boiled over and he'd almost let him go. But when the bodyguard expressed his surprise at the woman's ability to evade his surveillance, Sakharov held back. Yevgeny was no slouch when it came to surveilling a target. He'd learned it well during his employment with Global Secure, one of the largest and most highly rated security companies in the world. Indeed, Sakharov had hired him away from them, promising to double his salary. The information helped explain the woman's fearlessness, as well as her nonchalance at possessing a firearm.

She was a spy, certainly. Or she had been, which meant she lied when she told him she wasn't, putting the veracity of her story in question. Who did she answer to? The US? A mercenary group? A competing arms dealer?

And where was she now? The evening before, Yevgeny paid a visit to the apartment she'd been renting. He learned from a neighbor that she checked out that afternoon, before the gala.

Sakharov's mind raced with the possible implications of what he'd learned. He needed to take a step back and look at things methodically.

Had Roman set him up? He couldn't think of another reason for his old friend to betray him by linking Sakharov Industries to a diverted arms deal. But why?

Shipments seized by the enemy were always a risk. Up until now, Sakharov's successful deliveries topped out at well over ninety percent. Except this time he'd left security measures to Roman.

If Roman had diverted the shipment to Izz Al-Din, then Sakharov would need to tread carefully. The general brokered the deal with the Libyan government, orchestrated the deliveries, and provided proof that the Libyans took possession of the shipment. But as Sakharov well knew, the paperwork could have been forged. He opened his desk drawer and stared at the documents Eve Mason delivered the night before.

He reread the letter from his son and again tried to parse his words. Mikhail's grandmother, though elderly, was not in any immediate danger of dying. His words didn't fit the truth, and Sakharov assumed his son had intended an underlying meaning to the letter. He closed his eyes as the possibility of his son's death loomed in his mind. Why would this woman, a complete stranger, risk her life to tell him his son had died if it weren't true? Mikhail's survival meant nothing to her.

For her, the news of his son's death would be secondary, merely a reason to meet face-to-face with him, to find out for herself whether he was involved. The diverted shipment was what concerned Eve Mason. This gave more credence to his belief that she was indeed a spy.

Be that as it may, it still left the likelihood that his old friend Roman Tsarev had deceived him, was deceiving him still. The possibility wasn't a stretch. Roman had clawed his way up the ranks of the GRU, Russia's powerful intelligence agency, by being the best at subterfuge and deception, and had taken over more and more operational duties. He was now considered one of the most influential and powerful men in Russia's intelligence apparatus, second only to the director. Along with that power and influence came an inordinate amount of money as well as unprecedented access.

Anatoly Sakharov was as well connected as the general, albeit through different channels. Plus, they were both on a first-name basis with the new Russian prime minister, Ian Fedorov, had been since the three met in school. Sakharov still kept in touch with another friend from university, Sergei Gorev, now a general in the SVR.

Was his government actively trying to engage the Americans in a proxy war? Again, not a stretch. Proxy wars had occurred many times before: Vietnam, the Arab-Israeli conflict, Afghanistan. But were they truly backing Izz Al-Din? If so, his country had gone too far.

Sakharov glanced again at the photocopy of the crate filled with Stinger missiles surrounded by black-clad terrorists. He squinted at the grainy picture to bring the details into focus. The bold Cyrillic lettering on the wooden box was unmistakable: Sakharov Industries.

A slow burn began in Sakharov's belly and traveled to his chest. Either the shipment had been purposely diverted to the terrorists by someone within the Libyan government, or Roman was responsible. Either way, if the information got out, the scrutiny of the Russian government and the international community would be trained on Sakharov Industries—a precarious position for an arms dealer—even one who worked within the law. Was his son's letter warning him not to trust Roman? If that was the case, then the truth was inescapable. The general had lied and was covering up his son's death.

Sakharov would get to the bottom of this deception, this *maskirovka,* and find the truth if it was the last thing he did.

A knock sounded, breaking into his thoughts. Scowling, Sakharov hit the hidden button under his desk, unlocking the door. Katarina and their daughter, Olga, walked in, followed by Yevgeny and another bodyguard. His second wife was beautiful but his daughter could have been Aphrodite herself. Perfectly proportioned, Olga wore a short, metallic dress that showed off her long, shapely legs. Her glossy black hair fell straight past her shoulders to the middle of her back and curled gently at the ends. Both women wore oversized sunglasses and carried matching purses, making it obvious that a shopping trip was imminent.

"To what do I owe this welcome visit?"

Katarina set her purse on his desk and turned to Olga. "Our daughter has something to ask of you."

Their daughter smiled, revealing two perfectly placed dimples and a set of dazzlingly white teeth. The dental work had cost him a fortune but had been well worth it. Sakharov couldn't help but smile back. How could she be eighteen years old? To him she would always be the adorable toddler clinging to his leg, demanding that he walk with her.

"Daddy, I know you need to leave Greece and go back to Moscow for business, even though you don't want to." She came around the desk to sit on the arm of his chair and plucked at his sleeve. "Wouldn't it be wonderful if you had an apartment in Athens? Then you could always have a home here."

Sakharov snorted. "And of course you would make the ultimate sacrifice by staying on to keep an eye on my property, right?"

Olga widened her eyes and put a hand to her chest. "Me? Oh, Daddy. Of *course*, I'd be honored." Before he could protest, she threw her arms around his neck and gave him a dozen kisses. "I *knew* you'd agree. Thank you, thank you, thank you."

In between his daughter's happy kisses, Sakharov peered at his wife. Something was going on behind those lovely dark eyes. He gently extricated himself from Olga's enthusiastic embrace and patted her arm. "We'll talk about it later, all right?"

"Of course, Daddy," she said, her gleeful tone indicating she was sure of the hold she had over him. She walked back to join Katarina. "Ready to go?"

"In a moment," Katarina answered. "I need to speak to your father."

Olga gave her an inquiring glance but when an answer wasn't forthcoming casually shrugged a shoulder and beamed at them both. "I'll wait for you outside," she said, and walked out of the office. The other guard followed her, while Yevgeny stayed.

Katarina turned to her husband. "Well?"

Sakharov shook his head. "There is nothing more to say."

Lifting her chin, she squared her shoulders. "You mean to tell me that our son might be dead, but you've done nothing to verify this?" Her clipped tone told him her anger waited close to the surface. She handed him her phone. "Call her. Now."

"Not yet. I'm not convinced she tells the truth." He didn't want to say that if Eve Mason's story was true, then not only was their beloved son Mikhail gone, but everything would change. He would have to hire heavier security and she and Olga would need to curtail their

91

movements—in effect go into hiding—until he straightened things out.

"But you *must*. I spoke to her before she left the gala. She was adamant that our son had been killed. Why would she tell me this if it wasn't true? She asked for nothing in return but the truth." Her eyes glistened and her voice cracked, the stress of holding back tears obvious. She took a moment to compose herself. "You *promised* me Mikhail would be safe."

"We don't know that he isn't. I spoke to Roman last night and he assured me that he is still alive. In fact, he is going to have Mikhail contact me as soon as he can."

Katarina crossed her arms and gave him a disbelieving look. "So you would believe your friend, who has much to lose, over the woman who risked her life to speak with you? She asked for *nothing*." She shook her head in disgust. "You are a fool."

Heat flooded his cheeks. Sakharov leaned forward and fixed her with a hard stare. "You will never refer to me that way again, Katarina."

"Oh? And what will you do? You are a man who wouldn't see the truth if it bit him on the ass. Why do you not stand up to Roman?" Anger radiating off her like heat from an incinerator, Katarina picked up her purse and turned to leave.

"Be careful, Katarina." Firm warning permeated Sakharov's words as he glanced at Yevgeny. The protection supervisor looked as though he'd like to disappear into the woodwork. "Speaking this way in front of anyone but Yevgeny may cause your pot of gold to disappear."

Her hand on the doorknob, Katarina hesitated but didn't turn around. "I know how to live without money,

Anatoly," she said in a quiet voice. "But not without my son."

She opened the door and walked out, leaving him alone with his bodyguard.

CHAPTER 13

Leine checked her watch. Less than an hour remained until Sakharov's deadline to call her. She was still pissed off that he'd had her followed and especially that he'd used one of his goons to attack her. She'd expected the tail. Not the physical altercation.

His distrust was understandable. He didn't know her and of course he hadn't found out much about Eve Mason with a background check. Out of nowhere, a woman he knows nothing about just shows up speaking fluent Russian with a cache of files purportedly from his son, sweeps the room for bugs, and delivers news of his son's death and the diversion of one of his shipments to a group of bloodthirsty terrorists. She would have been suspicious, too.

She would have detained her for questioning, as she suspected the man who attacked her had been ordered to do.

He should've asked first.

She fervently hoped he'd call. She didn't want to release the files from Mikhail's flash drive into the Wild

West of cyberspace—not without corroboration from a credible player. If she took the information to Henderson, it wouldn't have nearly the impact without Sakharov's backing.

She'd try once more to get through to Henderson before she released the files. If she didn't succeed, then she'd upload the incriminating photos and videos and send a link to a reporter she knew at one of the news agencies. Under attack from both the right and the left for not checking their facts before breaking stories, news agencies were being overly careful before relaying anything without a credible source. With uncharacteristic shortsightedness, Leine hadn't cultivated many reporters to whom she could leak information, except for the one. And with her background as a government assassin scrubbed from official records, there was no way to back up her bona fides.

She might be able to get Lou to help her, but she hated the idea of dragging him into what could soon become a hot mess. A Russian arms dealer and a top GRU operative who had the ability to divert arms shipments from Libya to Izz Al-Din and subvert US-backed allies were not people you wanted to be involved with if you could help it.

Just then, her cell phone rang. The screen read *Private Caller*. She glanced at her watch. Right on time.

"Eve Mason," she answered.

"Anatoly Sakharov." His deep voice reverberated in her ear.

"What's your decision?" Leine was in no mood to play nice. Or waste time.

"I have called you back at your request. This is how you treat those who do as you ask?"

"Listen. I don't appreciate being followed—"

"It was a precaution. Besides, you lost him. What's the problem?"

"Lost him? He practically broke my neck. I do not take well to being strong-armed." Heat flushed her cheeks as her anger spiked. *Calm down, Leine. Being angry will get you nowhere.*

"I don't know what you are talking about. My security man told me he lost you last night—that you acted as though you knew you were being followed. He was impressed with your abilities."

"Then who attacked me on the sidewalk next to my car?"

"I have no idea." Sakharov paused. "What did he look like?"

"Big. And deadly. The photograph I took doesn't do him justice. Let me send it to you and you can tell me who you think it is." She texted the picture to him and waited.

"I've never seen him before."

Leine sighed. Was he telling the truth? "Look, if you didn't order him to rough me up, then who did?"

"I did not order anyone to 'rough you up' in any way. I asked Yevgeny to keep an eye on you for my own peace of mind, but I specifically instructed him not to approach you."

"Last night someone replaced one of the rounds in my gun with a tracking device. If you say it wasn't one of your people, then you've got a problem within the ranks, and someone else knows why I'm here. Have you told anyone of our conversation?"

"No, I have not. My wife says you and she spoke outside of the gala last night. Could someone have overheard you?"

"Not a chance. We were far from the other guests and her security contingent wasn't within range."

"You needn't worry about her security detail. They've been vetted, as have mine. I trust them with my life and the life of my family."

"If you say so. In my experience—"

"And what exactly is your experience, Ms. Mason? If that really is your name."

"I'm not sure I understand the question."

"You come to me with news of my son's death and tell me that he was gathering information regarding one of my shipments. You speak fluent Russian, carry a gun and a bug detector in your purse, and know how to elude surveillance. What do you imagine I think?"

"That I'm a spy. I told you last night, I'm not."

"And I am supposed to believe you?"

"You're going to have to take me at my word. I am no danger to you or your family. In fact, the opposite is true. I'm only trying to sort the truth from the lies. And I need your help to convince my government to take my concerns seriously."

"I need more time."

"What does that mean? That you'll help me eventually? Or are you putting me off so that I won't release the information before you've put some kind of safeguards in place?"

"I must dig deeper into this before I will commit to helping you. My reputation and the reputation of my business are at stake, as may be the lives of my family."

"How much more time do you need? I'm trying to head off a much larger problem and time is in short supply. You claim you didn't have anything to do with diverting that shipment of missiles. Fine. If that's true, then someone in either your government or the Libyan regime is working against the US and I need to find out why, who, and how so we can avoid more serious complications."

"Yes, I understand. But first I need to discover who diverted the shipment. As far as I know, our countries have been working well together. Both sides benefit. Why would my government be interested in causing another rift between us? It makes no sense, unless Libya is responsible."

"I agree. It doesn't. Which is why I need to take this information to my government. But I need you to back me up when I do. How do you propose to find out the rest of the story?"

"I have a contact within the Russian government who is in a position to help me uncover the truth."

"Obviously you're not talking about your dear friend, the general."

"Obviously."

Leine sighed. This was going nowhere. "I'm going to ask you again, how much time do you need?"

"Give me seventy-two hours."

"Fine. If you haven't contacted me by then, I'll give the information to my contact at the Associated Press."

"Understood."

CHAPTER 14

Moscow, Russia

General Tsarev stared at the email he'd received from his source at the Federal Bureau of Investigation and wondered two things. First, why would a woman who worked for an anti-trafficking agency need a fake passport and an entire legend surrounding a false name, and second, which American intelligence agency was using SHEN as a front? His contact could find no credible evidence of the latter, but Tsarev was certain this Basso woman was a covert operative.

Who are you, Madeleine Basso? And why are you meddling in things that are not your concern?

She probably worked for the CIA. Although it could very well be the DIA, or maybe even the NSA. Lines between the agencies had blurred in recent times, with many of them doing redundant work. It amazed him that the US was able to coordinate anything. Certainly, 9/11 had brought about change, but in Tsarev's view this change had muddied the waters even more, making the acquisition of actionable intelligence difficult for such an onerous and sprawling entity as the United States intelligence system.

Russia's intelligence apparatus was much more nimble. Although competition between agencies was fierce, at least sharing intelligence was more competent than in the US. Yes, there were problems, but they weren't insurmountable. Russia's GRU still operated with little oversight, which he vowed to maintain once he was in charge. After all his hard work, as soon as Russia was back to her pre-perestroika strength he would be appointed head of Russian Military Intelligence—the ultimate culmination of years of sweat, sacrifice, and hard work, all in service to the greater good.

The email went on to say that Madeleine (Leine) Basso had at one point worked security for the now-defunct reality show *Serial Date*, and briefly for an A-list actor by the name of Miles Fournier. Since then, she'd been working with Stop Human Enslavement Now, or SHEN, a non-profit anti-trafficking agency based in Los Angeles. She lived in a modest apartment near the beach with one Santiago Jensen, a homicide detective for the Los Angeles Police Department. They were not married. She had one child, a twenty-three-year-old daughter named April, who was currently attending classes in New York City in hopes of becoming a playwright.

The daughter was a potential vulnerability. A way to get to Basso if she refused to cooperate. Tsarev filed it away in the back of his mind for later use.

He scanned the rest of the report, which contained information detailing her four-year marriage to Frank Basso, an Italian-American businessman from whom she was now divorced, and other semi-pertinent facts. She had a checking and savings account at a local banking institution that contained several thousand dollars, a credit card with a balance of $1,790 for which she received air miles, and various investment accounts. She was quite well off, financially. He doubted working for a non-profit paid well, and wondered where the rest of her wealth came from. On rare occasions she used a FaceMe account, ostensibly to keep in touch with her daughter, and a generic email account. Tsarev's source had hacked into her internet service provider but found nothing unusual in her search history.

He studied the photograph the source had forwarded to him. She was good-looking, if you liked women with dark auburn hair, high cheekbones, and riveting eyes. Personally, Tsarev preferred blue-eyed, buxom blondes. There was just something so pure about them, unlike brunettes, who always seemed so ethnic. Immensely proud of his Russian ancestry, he preferred to associate with other members of such. He copied and pasted the photograph into an email, encrypted it, and sent it to Dmitry with a short note.

With a deep sigh, the general closed the email and leaned back in his chair. The lies the Basso woman told his old friend Sakharov would be enough, he thought, to steer him away from dealing with her. Then, Tsarev would ensure she didn't contact him again. His initial decision to dispatch Dmitry had been a good one. He picked up his phone and dialed Anatoly Sakharov. It was time to set the hook.

"What is it, Roman?" Anatoly's voice held a hint of annoyance.

"I thought you would like to know. I just received a report on a woman named Eve Mason. I believe she contacted Katarina recently?"

"And how would you know this?"

"A colleague saw your wife speaking with her outside of the National Museum of History in Athens the other night. I believe he said you both were attending a charity gala? He mentioned that what she said appeared to greatly upset your wife, so I did a little checking."

"How astute of you."

Tsarev noted the sarcasm in Sakharov's reply. *Curious.* "I was only looking out for my oldest friend. During our last conversation you seemed upset."

"About that conversation. Have you been able to contact my son?"

Tsarev shifted in his chair. "Not yet. But I have heard from his commanding officer that he is to rotate out of his current undercover unit, so you should be hearing from him soon."

"Good. I look forward to it." There was a pause. "Well? Are you going to tell me what is in this report of yours?"

"Of course." Tsarev pulled up the email on his screen. *And now to reel him in.* "Her name is Madeleine Basso, but she goes by Leine. She lives in Los Angeles and works for an anti- trafficking organization. According to my sources, prior to 2006 her past is practically non-existent. No job, no credit cards, nothing."

"Which means what, exactly? That you think she's a spy?"

Tsarev chuckled. "I can't say for sure, but it does give one pause, does it not?" He waited for Sakharov's reply, but there was only silence. He cleared his throat. "Before joining the anti-trafficking organization she worked as a security specialist for various entities in the Los Angeles area."

"Is that all you have? Because frankly I'm surprised, Roman. I would have expected a more in-depth report, given your access."

Tsarev bit back an angry retort and continued. "Before coming to Los Angeles, she lived in a one-bedroom apartment in Seattle, Washington, and was employed as an insurance adjuster. Before that she was married to an Italian-American businessman for four years. The relationship ended prior to her moving to Seattle. There was no reason given for their separation beyond irreconcilable differences."

"Ah."

"Does this information not give you pause? The woman lied to your wife. Whatever her reason for seeking Katarina's counsel, it could not have been in your wife's best interests. I also believe the organization she works for is a front for another agency. A *government* agency, if you understand me."

"I appreciate your concern, Roman, but I conducted my own background check and found much the same information. My wife's emotional reaction was due to a misunderstanding."

"A misunderstanding?" Tsarev was stunned. He had expected Sakharov to be indebted to him for uncovering such a blatant attempt at using his wife to gain access. Or at the very least be angry at Basso's deceit. Creating suspicion regarding her employer in the States was inspired genius, something he'd just added for a little extra tension. Like seasoning to a savory dish.

What had she told him? For a moment, the image of trying to make his way in the dark without a source of illumination filled his mind. Unaccustomed to the sensation, he bit back yet another angry retort and shook it off.

"Apparently it was a matter of mistaken identity," Sakharov added.

"I see. Well, I'm glad to hear that." Tsarev would have to pursue another option. Then he added, "In your business, one can't be too careful." There was nothing like a veiled threat to put a subject on edge.

"You're so right."

Did he detect yet more sarcasm? He would have to step up surveillance of Sakharov and his wife and daughter. One never knew when compromising information would come in handy. Now, though, he needed to repair the small rift he sensed had formed between them.

"Please accept my apologies for taking action where none was called for. I had only you and your wife's welfare in mind."

"No apology necessary."

The clipped assurance didn't sound like Sakharov had accepted his apology, but Tsarev decided to let it go for now. He'd get to the bottom of this woman's role in Anatoly Sakharov's life. He was sure she'd raised doubts about his son's welfare, but how did she come by the information?

And what else had she told him?

CHAPTER 15

Athens, Greece

I**t didn't take** Leine long to find the boat. The *Cyclops* was one of the least conspicuous vessels in the harbor. Nestled among a parade of gleaming white pleasure yachts, the rugged fishing boat looked like a child's toy in a sea of grownup ships. As Leine drew closer, she corrected her first impression. It wasn't that the *Cyclops* was small, just that the other boats were immense.

She paused near the stern of the *Cyclops* as a barefoot man wearing faded jeans and a blue plaid shirt with the sleeves rolled up finished spraying the side decks with a hose. A triangle of white T-shirt peeked out above the plaid.

"You must be Art."

The man pivoted at her question and looked her up and down, his impassive expression giving no clue to his thoughts. Leine returned the stare. Powerfully built, he looked to be in his mid-sixties with long, ropey veins popping out along his forearms and large, calloused hands. His steel-gray hair was closely cropped and the muscles of his neck strained against his collar. Startling blue eyes gazed out from a weathered face bearing a five o'clock shadow that looked like four in the morning.

After a moment, he nodded and went back to his work. "And you must be Leine." He finished spraying and made his way toward her, coiling the hose as he did, then sprang with an agile grace onto the dock, where he deposited the hose.

He was a good three inches shorter than Leine but carried himself as though he was the tallest man in the marina. *Ex-Special Forces,* she thought. In her experience, the men who'd worn the Green Beret walked with a purposeful stride and an alert, quiet watchfulness that came with their specialized training and experience. Especially the older ones, who never lost the look even when they retired. The younger types tended to have more swagger that would inevitably be "experienced" out of them, once they'd put in their time. Lou had been sketchy on his friend's past history, saying only that Art had helped him out on occasion and that his word, like his abilities, was rock solid. Art currently worked as a part-time security contractor, and when he wasn't working he was fishing.

Leine pulled an envelope that contained their agreed-upon fee from her pack and held it out. Art took it from her, glanced inside, and then slid it into the back pocket of his jeans. He untied the mooring lines before climbing back on board.

"You coming?" he asked over his shoulder.

She followed him onto the boat and stowed her pack in a locker in the pilot house. The trawler was Spartan in its accommodations. Everything had its place. The bright work gleamed, and the space was so clean, a speck of dirt wouldn't dare show itself. A small galley with a kerosene stove stood to Leine's left, with a couch and a pair of captain's chairs to starboard. A table sandwiched between two bench seats covered in dark blue canvas was next to the stove. Several built-ins lined the walls, with the steering console at center stage, beneath the windscreen. Two steps below led to a short companionway and to what Leine assumed were forward berths. Outside, a stainless steel ladder offered access from the deck to the flying bridge.

"Head's down there, to the right." Art motioned toward the bow. "Beer and ouzo are in a cooler on deck. Water's over there." He pointed to a pallet of plastic bottles next to the gimbaled stove. "Help yourself, but keep your paws off the Jack."

"Thanks. I appreciate you taking me on such short notice."

Art shrugged. "Long as your money's good, you can do just about anything you want short of taking a shit on my deck."

Charming. Leine had contacted Art the evening before and asked him if she could rent his boat for a few days, with him staying on as captain. She figured if she was a moving target she'd be safer when she started digging into Mikhail Sakharov's death and the diverted shipment of Stinger missiles. Art quoted her a reasonable price and told her to come by the next morning. She'd spent part of a restless evening at a small, all-night diner near the marina, concerned that whoever had her under surveillance the night of the party was still tracking her.

Another reason why I quit that life. She wasn't in the mood for rekindling the stress of her time as an assassin. Constantly being on edge and looking over her shoulder made her downright cranky. Back then Carlos had given her a hard time, telling her she wasn't cut out for the life. She'd practically bitten his head off before she realized he was kidding. Sort of. She'd always needed some way to burn off the stress and tension. Running or swimming or kickboxing or sex would usually do the trick.

The weather at this time of year wasn't exactly swim-friendly, but if her tenure on the *Cyclops* ran long she'd have Art take her somewhere with a deserted beach where she could get in a punishing workout. The short run she'd managed that morning wasn't nearly enough. And she was tired from lack of sleep.

"Where to, boss?" Art called down from the flying bridge.

"Wherever you want. What's the Wi-Fi password?"

"It's on the list next to the console."

Leine took her tablet over to the console and typed in the password. *Cyclops* had a dedicated satellite connection, something Art said he made sure to have before deciding to live on board the sturdy fishing boat. "Certain people need to be able to find me," he'd said.

She logged into an online database Lou had "borrowed" when he retired from the agency. He'd given Leine access on one of her jobs for SHEN that had the earmarks of a state-sponsored kidnapping. The database was a list of all known intelligence operatives, domestic and foreign, and was a joint effort to share intel between the FBI, the CIA, the DIA, and the ever-secretive NSA. Although the other alphabet agencies grumbled over whether the NSA was at all forthcoming with regard to its own intel, the list had proven to be most effective in identifying operatives friendly—and not—to the mission of the United States.

Leine quickly scanned the list for General Roman Tsarev, finding mention of his rise in the GRU several pages down. She clicked on the link attached to his name, and it took her to a page with everything that had been acquired on his background. Tsarev was the poster boy for Russian intelligence. He'd started his career with the army, attaining the rank of general, then moved to intelligence analysis for the GRU. He was eventually promoted to his current position, and it was well known that he had designs on moving higher.

The liner notes mentioned he was a hardline hawk who didn't agree with current Russian policy regarding foreign relations. On more than one occasion, he'd tried to convince the Russian president to take back the Balkans by force, citing Russia's need for sovereignty over the region. The president had refused, believing correctly that the US would not pursue détente with a country bent on turning back the clock to the glory days of the Soviet Union.

That would explain his diversion of Sakharov's arms shipment and of passing along intel detailing allied positions to embedded soldiers. The American people strongly opposed committing ground forces to the war against the terrorists, a position that Blackwell, the current US president, had echoed in a State of the Union address several weeks before. Air strikes and advisers were fine, but no one wanted to risk an American life to fight what was seen as someone else's war.

It looked like Tsarev aimed to take the fight to the next level and engage the US by making it impossible to say no to troops on the ground. Leine didn't think that President Blackwell would fall for the ruse, but just the fact that Tsarev risked his men and his reputation to lure the US into a ground war with Islamic terrorists was enough to give her pause.

The gentle rocking of the *Cyclops's* path through the calm, blue waters of the Aegean Sea worked its magic and Leine's shoulders inched down as her body relaxed. Putting the tablet aside, she leaned her head back and closed her eyes. Sometime later, she woke to a dark cabin. Shaking off the vestiges of sleep, she got up and walked out to the stern where Art sat smoking a cigar in a deck chair, a glass of amber liquid in his hand. Seeing her, he raised his drink in a toast and took a sip.

"Sleeping Beauty awakens."

"How long have I been out?" Lights from shore winked against a backdrop of shadows, and a smattering of stars had made an appearance against the deep indigo sky. A slight breeze ruffled her hair. She took a deep breath in, tasting the briny sea on her tongue.

"Couple of hours. Figured I'd let you sleep. Looked like you could use some shut eye."

Leine smiled and sat down in the deck chair next to him. "Got any more of that?" she asked, nodding at the drink in his hand.

"Yes, ma'am." He reached beside him and brought out a bottle of Jack Daniel's.

"I thought you told me to keep my paws off the Jack."

Art studied the bourbon and then fixed her with a wry gaze. "You see anyone else's hand on this bottle?"

"Point taken."

"Glasses are in the cupboard above the stove."

A minute later she was in the other deck chair and sipping her drink. She leaned her head back to look at the stars. "So where are we?"

"Near the island of Hydra. Thought since you were looking for a place to hide out we'd come here."

"It's quiet."

"Yes, ma'am."

They let the silence rest between them for a while, enjoying the stillness of the evening. The temperature had barely cooled off from the heat of the day, so there was no need to get her jacket.

"How did you meet Lou, if you don't mind my asking?" Leine took another sip of the bourbon and rolled it around her tongue, savoring the warmth.

Art shrugged. "Oh, you know. It was one of those things. He needed someone like me for something off-book, and I needed the cash."

"Someone like you. I'm afraid Lou didn't tell me very much about you."

Art nodded. "That's Lou. He's one of the good guys." He set his drink down on the cooler between them and gave her a hard look. "As a matter of fact, he didn't tell me much about you, either."

She stared out at the twinkling shore lights. Music from a taverna onshore drifted toward them. "No, he wouldn't. Like you said, he's one of the good guys." She thought about what she could tell him. "We worked together for a few years at a place you've never heard of. He was my support system when I was on the road."

Art nodded again, but didn't say anything, giving her the space to talk.

"Then something happened and I left. He retired soon after."

"Sounds ominous. You work for SHEN now?"

"Yes."

"Are you trying to locate someone?"

"No."

"Then who's after you?"

Leine glanced at him. "Why do you think someone's looking for me?"

He swept his hand in an arc, indicating their remote location. "This ain't your average resort." He cocked his head at her. "And I'd guess you ain't your average female."

"I'm not sure, exactly. Maybe no one."

Art snorted as he picked up his drink and took another sip. "You're gonna have to do better than that. Boat rules. I don't take on anyone or anything that could get me killed."

It was Leine's turn to set her drink down. "Fair enough." She stared at a spot on deck as she worked out what to say. "How familiar are you with Sakharov Industries?"

"Anatoly Sakharov was the client of a company I worked for back in the day. In fact, he tried to hire me for his personal security contingent."

"And?"

"And I declined. Politely, of course. Not many people say no to Anatoly. He ended up grabbing two of Global Secure's finest. A Russian and an Albanian. They thought they'd won the lottery." He shook his head. "I didn't have the heart to tell 'em they'd bought a ticket to their own funeral. That guy has more enemies than there are ducks on a Minnesota pond."

"Apparently so," Leine agreed. "One in particular."

"Which one are you talking about?"

"General Tsarev."

"Shit." Art leaned back in his chair and clasped his hands behind his head. "That's one crazy-ass Russian there."

"Oh? Why do you say that?"

"He's ambitious as hell, for starters."

"That much is evident. Go on."

"He's also shrewd and ruthless. Not a good combination for an enemy. He'd as soon drop his own granny where she stands than give up an iota of power." Art shook his head. "If Sakharov's made an enemy of Tsarev, then he's not long for this world."

"They were childhood friends. Sakharov's son referred to him as Uncle Roman."

"Huh. Well." Art leaned forward. "From what I understand, the general's not real family-oriented. How'd they fall out?"

"I don't know if they have, exactly. But logic points toward Tsarev meddling in Sakharov's affairs in order to push his own political agenda."

"Oh?" Art lifted a brow.

"Lou said you could be trusted. That your word's solid, and you're a good man. I'm going to assume that I can trust you with sensitive information." Leine was going against everything she'd been trained to do, but she figured Art deserved to know the potential shit storm he might be walking into. And, he was a friend of Lou's.

"What do *you* think?" His penetrating gaze told her all she needed to know.

"One of Sakharov's arms shipments was diverted to Izz Al-Din."

Art whistled. "You mean to say that Tsarev had a hand in that? What the hell for?"

"That's not all. Sakharov's son was serving in the military under Tsarev and embedded with the terrorists. He was gathering information that proved he and his fellow soldiers were ordered to pass along US-backed allied positions to the terrorists to draw the US into a ground war in Libya."

"You refer to the son in the past tense. Am I to understand he's no longer with us?"

Leine nodded. "Somebody dropped a bomb on him at a refugee camp. There was nothing left to identify."

"Jesus." Art scrubbed his face and grimaced. "Then how did you come by the information?"

"He gave his flash drive to a friend of mine before he was killed and she showed me the files. That friend died in the bombing with Mikhail."

"Have you contacted Sakharov?" He leaned back, studying her. "I see that you have."

"I met him and his wife at the National Archaeological Museum last night at a charity event. I told them what I knew. He didn't believe me, of course. Even after I showed him the documents from his son's flash drive."

"And Sakharov contacted his friend the general to find out if you were telling the truth." He crossed his arms. "Tsarev's after you, isn't he?"

"I think so, yes. Sakharov had one of his men follow me, but I lost him. Then I picked up another tail. He jumped me on the street near my car, but I neutralized him. He wasn't interested in killing me, or I wouldn't be here."

"It wasn't one of Sakharov's bodyguards?"

"He insists he only sent one guy and he didn't order him to physically restrain me. The man who attacked me wasn't at the benefit. At least, I didn't see him there. Someone replaced one of the rounds in my gun with a tracking device, so it looks like there might be a mole inside Sakharov's security."

"Christ. You're in it up to your eyeballs, aren't you?" He rose from the chair and began to pace. "You say you were able to neutralize him. Did you kill him?"

"He was still breathing when I left him."

He turned to look at her. "You worked for Eric at the agency?"

Leine was stunned at his knowledge. Not many people knew about Eric or the agency. *Did Lou mention something?* "Why do you ask?"

"Because one, you're in the middle of a shit sandwich. Two, you have certain, shall we say, *qualities,* that contract employees there have, and three, you know Lou. It doesn't take much to connect the dots." Art's tone had turned from curious to pissed off in a matter of seconds.

"I'm not sure why you're getting angry. I no longer work for them. And you may not have heard, but Eric's dead."

Art slammed his fist on the gunwales and glared at the water. "Doesn't matter where I go or what I do, that shit follows me."

Leine stood and walked to where Art leaned against the port side of the *Cyclops*. "What are you talking about? I told you, I'm no longer part of the organization. This isn't agency business."

He narrowed his eyes. Anger radiated off him. "Tell me you've been able to avoid getting sucked back into that cesspool they call government work." He folded his arms. "Go on. Tell me."

Leine started to insist that he was wrong, that she'd been successful in staying out of the trap that so many operatives had fallen into. But had she really? She'd been working for SHEN, looking for missing women and girls who'd been trafficked, and eliminating the people responsible in an attempt to atone for her past sins. But here she was with a powerful Russian operative after her who would more than likely torture her to gain whatever knowledge she had, and then kill her once she'd outlived her usefulness. Not only that, but over the years she'd had several run-ins with old "friends" who would've sold her out for the price of a cup of coffee.

Art was right. She'd never be completely free.

"I see by the look on your face that you get my point." Art had calmed enough that he stopped pacing and sat back in his chair where he poured himself another three fingers of Jack. He waved the bottle near her glass, but she shook her head. She needed to be clear. Art's little outburst reminded her of something she'd tried to forget. If she was going to talk Sakharov into backing her story when she went to Scott Henderson, then she had to be ready for anything. Just like the old days.

This is it, Leine. If you go forward from here, you're not in Kansas anymore.

Leine returned to her deck chair. "I can see you're not interested in being a part of this. I don't blame you." She looked at the twinkling lights in the bay. The dark sky had deepened to a midnight blue and the stars were coming out in force. "If you could let me off somewhere on the mainland so I can get back to Athens, I'd be much obliged."

Art snorted. "I'm not leaving you off anywhere. You obviously need my help. One woman can't take on Tsarev and his wannabe KGB thugs."

"But what about the cesspool and the shit sandwich and all that? Was that just a performance?"

Art's lopsided grin gave Leine the feeling he was further into the bottle of Jack than she first thought.

"Lady, I was born for this kind of work." He rubbed his hands together, clearly ready to bust some heads. "Especially since it involves General Tsarev."

"Don't tell me you miss the Cold War?"

"Hell, yes I do. At least then you knew who your friends were. And your enemies. Now days, shit, you're lucky if you can tell right from wrong."

He had a point.

"Well, if you're serious, then I'm glad to have your help. My contacts in this part of the world have either died or disappeared."

"Tends to happen in your line of work. We've got a loose conglomeration of folks in the private security sector that I can contact, so I'll be able to find out some specifics. We'll have to be careful whose chain we yank."

"That's an understatement. What do you suggest?"

"Not sure yet. I've got some ideas, though." Art lifted his glass in a toast, and then took a sip. "Let's give this little problem a think. I'll bet we come up with something."

They stayed up late into the evening, talking strategy. Art had the mind of someone who'd planned hundreds of covert operations. Leine appreciated his ability to see all sides of a problem, and welcomed his input. By the time the bottle of Jack was gone they'd covered several scenarios and had a plan of action for each—even though the odds were low of any plan working flawlessly, especially since there were so many unknowns.

"I think I'm going to call it a night." Leine stood and stretched.

Art waved toward the bow of the boat. "Sure, sure. You take the port side bunk. I think I'll sit up a while longer."

"See you in the morning."

Leine rinsed her glass at the galley sink and left it to dry in the rack before grabbing her pack and making her way forward. She opened the door to her berth and stepped over the threshold. The small room was serviceable enough, not luxurious by any means, but Leine had slept in worse. A single bunk lined the far wall, with a built-in desk and heavy metal chair to one side. A white porcelain sink stood in the corner, with a mirrored medicine cabinet above it. She leaned closer to get a better look at herself. Her eyes were roadmap red from lack of sleep, and small dark bags had formed under them. She sighed and shook her head.

Such a glamorous life.

CHAPTER 16

Moscow, Russia

Anatoly Sakharov buttoned his overcoat and braced himself against the icy wind. Moscow was unseasonably cold for late October, although the last two winters had been long and bone-chillingly arctic, so he shouldn't have been surprised. It was one of the main reasons he preferred to do business from his yacht in the Aegean, and why he'd given the green light to Katarina and his daughter to find an apartment in Athens. Maybe this way they would stop hounding him to work less. Working less meant less money, which meant fewer shopping trips for them.

How did they not see this?

With a sigh, he continued to the main gate of Gorky Park to meet his contact, Sergei Gorev. Roommates at university, they had shared a passion for jazz and Paris's Latin Quarter, although with perestroika they'd each gone their separate ways. Like Roman, Sergei saw opportunity in climbing the ranks of the military, while Sakharov took advantage of the lucrative black market that sprang up in Moscow, earning a small fortune in a short span of time.

Sakharov glanced at his Rolex. His friend wasn't usually late. He attempted to check his email on his phone, but Eve Mason's warning regarding a mole within his security detail played like a loop in his head and he couldn't concentrate. If her suspicions were correct then he had a far larger problem than he'd first thought.

As a precaution, he'd let the majority of his security contingent go and hired fresh blood. He didn't have the time or patience to find a mole. Yevgeny and Farid had both retained their positions—the two men had been with him the longest and were the only people he trusted with his family. He'd vetted several new bodyguards for the trip to Moscow and added additional security to watch over Katarina and Olga. Two of the new hires followed him now, at a discreet distance. The unexpected turnover would alert the person running the informant. What would stop them from trying again?

Moments later a red-faced Sergei huffed his way toward him through the small crowd of people who had gathered nearby. Sakharov pushed his worries to the back of his mind and turned to watch his old friend approach.

"Anatoly! It's been far too long. How are you? And how's Katarina?"

The two men embraced warmly. Sergei's dark brown hair had grown thin and was sprinkled with more gray than the last time they'd seen each other. The lines around his eyes and between his brows spoke of the stressors experienced by many in the employ of the SVR.

"I'm well. Thank you for taking time out of your busy day to meet with me." Sakharov broke contact first and gestured for Sergei to walk with him.

"It was no hardship, believe me. I don't get into the fresh air often enough," Sergei said.

Sakharov eyed the other man's ample midsection and raised an eyebrow. Sergei laughed and patted his stomach.

"You know how much I love French food. So many sauces."

"We've come a long way since our days at university," Sakharov said.

Sergei smiled at the memory. "What was the name of that club we used to go to in Paris? The one in the Latin Quarter on the Rue des Lombards?"

Sakharov closed his eyes as he thought. "The Duc."

Sergei snapped his fingers. "That's right. Le Duc des Lombards. How I miss those days. Everything was a discovery."

"Especially discovering girls who liked jazz."

"Especially that," Sergei agreed. He rubbed his hands together and blew on his fingers to warm them. "The weather has turned early this year. I fear Muscovites will be in for a long winter." He stopped rubbing and shoved his hands inside his coat pockets before giving Sakharov a sidelong glance. "So, to what do I owe this happy occasion?

Sakharov frowned. "I have a favor to ask."

"Yes?"

"I've received news that my son has been killed."

Sergei stopped and narrowed his eyes at Sakharov. "I'm deeply sorry. How did this happen?"

"That's not important. What is important is that our mutual friend Roman Tsarev has told me that Mikhail is still alive. I need proof of the circumstances of his death. Or, if what Roman says is true and Mikhail is still alive, then proof of his continued good health. Can you do this?"

"Of course. But there is a larger problem here."

"You mean my distrust of Roman." Sakharov nodded. "What little research I've done points to his deception and I need to know why."

"I see." Sergei frowned as they resumed walking. "Finding this information should not be difficult. As it involves our friend Roman, I will go through less obvious channels."

"Thank you."

Sergei waved his thanks away. "What are you doing for dinner this evening? I know a place that serves the most exquisite bouillabaisse. I'll bring Nataly. She'd love to see you."

"I'd like that," Sakharov replied. Good food, good wine, and old friends would take his mind off of Mikhail and the Basso woman.

And Roman's lies.

Athens, Greece

Dmitry Romanov checked his bank account balance with his phone. It was all there. He enjoyed seeing the long string of zeroes. Money gave him a surge of power, greater even than sex. And that was saying something— he had a voracious appetite for women, although they had to be small and demure or he wouldn't bother. No brash career girls for him, which left out most of the women living and working in and around Moscow—and Athens, for that matter. Besides, the smaller ones were easier to control and easily discarded. He'd had his fill of demanding princesses who expected to be treated like Catherine the Great.

The money was all well and good, except for one tiny detail: Dmitry was unable to locate his target. With help from the general, he monitored the ports and border crossings in Greece, as well as various online venues. She'd surface eventually. He just had to be patient.

After what the general's security man had revealed about her evasion techniques and fighting abilities, as well as the lack of personal information prior to 2006, Dmitry was convinced he was dealing with a member of a clandestine American organization. He relished the opportunity to pit himself against an intelligence operative from the United States. Although he shared the general's contempt for the American intelligence community, when confronting one of their operatives he would need to be at his best.

He made his way along the busy boulevard, smiling at the women who gave him the once-over. With his dark good looks and the rakish scar along his jaw, Dmitry prided himself on being every woman's bad boy. He stayed in exquisite shape and had perfected a confident, lazy smile whenever a woman gave him the eye. One of his many lovers had complained that he had the look of one who recently left the warm bed of one woman while contemplating the next.

He couldn't argue with that.

His thoughts turned to his target. Was she a member of Special Operations? He didn't think the US Army allowed women to serve in that capacity, although it probably wouldn't be long before they demanded equality. Dmitry rolled his eyes at the thought of a woman operative doing what he did. Yes, they often made good snipers as long as they could hold their emotions in check, like Pavlichenko and Shanina, but war was an unusual circumstance. He doubted many could last through the rigorous physical training.

You can't take this one for granted, Dmitry. He was an expert at determining what kind of adversary his quarry would be. His own training had been as an elite killer for a group in Chechnya. A secret arm of the Chechen Republic's government designed to carry out assassinations, kidnappings, and torture, as well as fomenting unrest and revolution in countries on the brink, the group's exploits were never alluded to in reports. No one knew they existed, except for the head of the Chechen Republic and General Tsarev, who worked closely with the group against the wishes of the new Russian Federation leaders. As he explained to Dmitry, "Ask for forgiveness, never permission."

In a stroke of brilliance, Tsarev had been able to redirect funds to the secret agency, veiling the expenditure as "Community Outreach" and "Infrastructure Repair." No one had been the wiser. Unfortunately, a few years into the program, some peon in accounting discovered the redirect and mentioned it to an auditor in the accounting chamber who mentioned it to the head of the budget committee. Fearful of the fallout should the world discover the sordid link between Russia and Chechen "Death Squads," the president cut off funding for the secret organization before anyone found out the true reason for the redirect, although he'd given a wink and a nod to the general, suggesting Tsarev create his own operation and the funds would follow.

Once the dust settled, Tsarev had personally asked Dmitry to leave Chechnya and work for him on a contractual basis, which he was happy to do. Being a lone wolf appealed to Dmitry much more than taking orders from an organization. It was quite a bit more lucrative, too. Dmitry now had a home on the shores of the Black Sea thanks to his expertise and the largesse of the general.

He stopped next to a low, sleek McLaren coupe parked next to the curb, admiring its lean lines and how the sports car appeared to be in motion while still. *That would look good in my garage.* He'd have to order the newest model and have it delivered as soon as this job was finished. He dragged his gaze away from the piece of automotive artwork and brought out the keys for his rental from his pocket. Although still a high performance vehicle, the black Mercedes wouldn't draw attention like the McLaren.

Inside the car, he retrieved his phone and ran a search to see if Eve Mason, aka Leine Basso, had made an appearance anywhere. Her name or passport hadn't pinged any of the general's bots, which meant that either she slipped across the border undetected or she was still in country and hiding. Anatoly Sakharov was in Moscow on business, and according to recently accessed aviation records was due back in two days. Basso/Mason had been in contact with him and his wife, so the best bet was to keep an eye on Mrs. Sakharov and the daughter while waiting for the Basso woman to surface.

Not that watching the daughter would be a hardship. Dmitry was willing to suspend his "no princess" rule, at least for one night with Sakharov's daughter. Such a sweet young thing.

He sighed and shifted in his seat, the growing evidence of his fantasy becoming obvious. There'd be plenty of time for that. Perhaps Tsarev would have him apply for a position in her security detail. He'd heard that she and Sakharov's wife were looking at a luxury villa near the water. Apparently the youngest wanted to spread her wings in Athens. He'd certainly be happy to help her spread something.

Shaking off his carnal thoughts, Dmitry accessed the encrypted email account he used with the general in case there were any new developments. There was an automated message from one of the intelligence sites where the general had a virus embedded in his dossier in case someone accessed the information. He clicked on the message.

Someone bearing the username SHEN1 had accessed the general's page the evening before on a secret database used to track foreign intelligence operatives. The automated message included SHEN1's longitude and latitude at the time of access. Dmitry entered the coordinates into an app on his phone and was rewarded with a little flag in the Saronic Gulf near the island of Hydra.

It has to be her. Who else would be in Greece and use the name of the anti-trafficking agency to access intelligence files? Obviously, she was *in* the gulf which meant she was on a boat of some kind. That made things interesting. He took out his phone and called a nearby marina to rent a skiff.

Smiling to himself, Dmitry put the keys in the ignition and started the car. *How can one man be so lucky?* Money, cars, luxury villas, fast boats, and interesting sexual conquests, along with a job he enjoyed. In an article he'd run across online, he read about how successful CEOs often exhibited psychopathic tendencies—no conscience, no empathy, hard to read, sexually insatiable. Dmitry mused that those qualities, although not held in high regard in most occupations, were exactly what an assassin needed to be good.

And Dmitry was good.

CHAPTER 17

Anatoly Sakharov unfolded the copy of the end-user agreement and laid it on the desk in front of him. The name of the person who received the shipment was illegible. Sakharov called his assistant, Felix.

"Get me the supply depot in Benghazi. I want to speak with whoever signed for this shipment." He read off the invoice number and ended the call.

After a protracted wait, Felix called him back. "I've got Khaled Ali in procurement on the line."

Sakharov waited as Felix connected him. "This is Anatoly Sakharov of Sakharov Industries."

There was silence on the other end followed by a muffled cough.

"You know my name?" Anatoly asked.

"Yes, yes. Of course, Mr. Sakharov. What can I do for you?" The man had finally found his voice.

Sakharov continued. "I need to check on a specific shipment. I heard there were some complications." He rattled off the certificate number and waited while Khaled looked it up on his computer.

"I have no record of any complications, sir. From what I can see, the shipment arrived several weeks ago and has been disbursed to our ground forces through the proper channels. If you could be more specific, perhaps I might be of better service?"

"So each of the components has been accounted for?"

The sound of tapping on a keyboard could be heard. "Yes, sir. All components have been received. I remember signing for the shipment myself. Has there been report of a problem?"

Sakharov reined in his anger. *Yes, there damn well is a problem,* he thought. Instead he replied, "I was only confirming delivery. Thank you." He ended the call and stared at the picture of jubilant terrorists surrounding the cases bearing his name.

Mikhail, why are you not here to tell me yourself what you found? The pain of losing his only son lay like an anvil upon his chest. How could it be that he would never see Mikhail's mischievous smile, or hear his voice as he tried to convince him of some theory or another? He didn't want to believe that Roman had a hand in Mikhail's death. He also didn't want to believe that his country had resorted to working with the terrorist butchers. Sakharov considered himself a patriot, comfortable looking the other way when the Libyans sent bombs raining down upon its people—men, women and children alike—all in a bid to rout the enemy. Such was the cost of war. Innocents were collateral damage. If civilians wouldn't leave their war-torn neighborhoods, nothing could be done to save them.

But if Russia was aiding the terrorists by providing weapons and soldiers, and using *his* company to do it, then his country had gone too far.

Sakharov checked his watch. It was almost time to meet Sergei for dinner. Besides Katarina, Olga, and Mikhail, Sergei and his wife, Nataly, were two of the only people with whom he could be himself. He pushed the thought of Mikhail aside. Tonight he would eat too much rich food, laugh, and drink too much wine. Tomorrow he would deal with the pain of losing his son.

And his childhood friend.

Khaled Ali hung up the phone and stared at his computer screen. This wasn't supposed to happen. The general had assured him there would be no chance of anyone finding out about the diverted shipment. Cold sweat rolled down his face. His hand shaking, he wiped his forehead with his shirt sleeve. His superiors would never understand.

And why should they? Tsarev's vision for Russia's future aside, the money Khaled earned as a procurement specialist barely paid the bills, and his were mounting. His boyfriend was pushing for him to leave Libya and join him in Paris, but had been happy to take the money Khaled sent to pay for the apartment and groceries while he looked for a job. Khaled had been like a drowning man, desperately hoping for a miracle to keep his lover happy, when the general approached him and offered a lifeline in the form of a one-time payment with the alluring promise of more to come. All he had to do was sign his name to the end-user certificate, alleging that the full shipment had reached its intended destination.

Simple.

Khaled squeezed his eyes shut, trying to block the thoughts that crowded his mind. What should he do? Obviously, he needed to call the general to let him know that Sakharov was nosing around, but should he then disappear? Tsarev wouldn't like that. He'd said repeatedly that this special arrangement between them was exclusive and long-running—that he expected him to remain in his current position for the foreseeable future or he'd let his superiors know about his secret life. But what if his superiors launched an official inquiry? He'd be in deep trouble if his relationship to the Russian general was exposed, not to mention the relationship with his lover in Paris.

If he left for France, what would stop Tsarev from tracking him down to take the fall if the ruse was discovered? He'd have to change his name and obtain forged documents so he could travel. That could get expensive. Once he'd managed that, if he could, he'd be looking over his shoulder the rest of his life wondering what Tsarev would do when or if he found him.

The cold sweat spread to his armpits and down his back. No, the prudent thing to do was call Tsarev, tell him about the phone call from Sakharov, and let him handle things. The man was Russian intelligence. He'd know what to do. He eyed the jacket he kept on a hook near the door to his office. He kept the burner phone the general supplied in the right front pocket. *You must wait until the end of the day, to keep the conversation from being intercepted.*

Then he'd call Paris.

CHAPTER 18

Moscow, Russia

Sakharov checked his watch. Sergei was thirty minutes late. He sipped his wine and glanced at the front of the restaurant, expecting to see his friend walk through the door, an apologetic smile on his face. The hushed conversations of the four-star eatery only added to his somber mood. Two of his security guards stood near the entrance, with no attempt to blend in with the well-heeled crowd.

Fifteen minutes later when Sergei still hadn't materialized, Sakharov pulled out his phone and dialed his number. The call went to voicemail. The waiter walked by and asked if he needed anything. Irritated at the intrusion, Sakharov waved the man off.

Where was he? It wasn't like Sergei to be late and not call. He heaved a long sigh and nibbled at a caviar-slathered toast point and sipped his drink. The wine tasted bland, even though it was vintage Petrus, and the caviar smelled fishy. He dropped the toast back onto the side plate and checked his watch again. A faint keening could be heard outside, ramping up in decibels until it was hard to ignore. Sakharov stood along with several other patrons and craned his neck to look out the glass doors onto the street. Several diners gawked out the windows, straining to see.

Gripped by a sudden realization, Sakharov dropped his linen napkin onto the table and rose from his chair. His security guards fell into formation—one in front and one at the rear—as he exited the restaurant. Multi-colored lights from an ambulance and two police cars lit the street in a garish display halfway down the block.

"Go. Find out what happened," he ordered one of his men, nodding toward the chaotic scene. As the guard raced away, Sakharov hastily retreated to his Mercedes S-600, with the other bodyguard close behind. Several minutes later, the first bodyguard returned and slid into the front seat.

"It's General Gorev," he said. "He and his wife are dead." He slid his finger across his throat, indicating the method used.

"Are you sure?" Sakharov demanded.

"I'm sure. He wore the same overcoat when you met with him this afternoon."

"Take me back to the hotel," Sakharov snapped at the driver. The Mercedes pulled away from the curb and merged into traffic.

Anger boiled in his chest replacing the initial shock of his friend's death. *Roman. It had to be.* Somehow, the general had learned of their meeting. Sakharov hit speed dial and attempted to tamp down his rage as he listened to the phone ring, barely registering the urban landscape through which they drove. Finally, the person on the other end picked up.

"What can I do for you, my friend?" Roman sounded as if he were mentioning the weather. Sakharov wanted nothing more than to reach through the phone and strangle the bastard. He'd enjoy watching him claw at his hands, begging him to let go.

"What game are you playing, Roman?"

"I'm not sure I know what you mean," he replied, wariness replacing the friendly tone.

"You know exactly what I mean. You diverted my missiles to the terrorists. To what end, I don't know but I assure you, I will find out." Sakharov squeezed the phone, glad for the feel of the hard plastic pressing into his hand. "And now, because of this...this *whatever* it is that you have set in motion, Sergei is dead. Nataly is dead. *Mikhail* is dead. Where will you draw the line? Will you not stop this madness until *I* am dead, too?"

"Calm down. Have you been drinking? Where do you come up with this nonsense? What do you mean Sergei and Nataly are dead? What happened?" Concern laced Roman's voice, but Sakharov knew it for what it was—subterfuge, lies, *maskirovka*.

"When I find out what you're planning, I *will* stop you."

"You don't know what you're talking about. Stop this foolish talk and meet with me. We can work out whatever it is you think I've done."

Sakharov's chuckle held a bitter edge. "No, Roman. I will not make it easy for you. You may think you know me, but you don't. You have no idea what I'm capable of. As of this morning, I have halted shipments to the Libyan army. There will be nothing more from my company to prop up your ambitions in that region."

"Be careful, Anatoly." Roman's voice dripped menace. "I have a contract with your signature at the bottom. A contract to supply the Libyan army with a specific number of weapons. To break this agreement could have...unfortunate consequences."

"Is that a threat? How things have changed. Only a few days ago you offered your help in finding my son. But you can't help me with that, can you? Because my son is dead." He took a deep breath, attempting to calm his thudding heart. When he next spoke, his voice shook with fury. "I will tell you this—if anything happens to me, there are people who will know it was your doing. And believe me, Roman, you don't want these people to know who you are."

Before he said anything further, Sakharov ended the call. With the utmost control he placed the phone in his coat pocket.

He had just declared war on his oldest friend. Strangely, the thought calmed him. He would need to hire even more security, especially for his wife and daughter. Thankfully, she and Olga were staying at a leased apartment in Athens with no ties to him or Sakharov Industries, which Roman knew nothing about. Still, it wouldn't hurt to ramp things up for the foreseeable future.

He didn't know yet how he was going to do it, but General Roman Tsarev was going to fall.

The general wiped his forehead with an already damp handkerchief from his pocket. His blood pulsed heavily in his ears and sweat rolled down the sides of his face. He caught his reflection in the mirror on the wall across from him. His eyes were wide and wild, and his cheeks flushed a deep shade of purple. His respiration came in uneven and rapid bursts. Alarmed, he fumbled in his top desk drawer to pull out a small vial, popped the top, and drank its contents. Then he sat back and closed his eyes, waiting for the drug to work its magic.

Anatoly Sakharov had threatened him, a highly decorated general and member of the GRU. Not only that, but his old friend had tipped his hand when he told him that he knew his last shipment of missiles to Izz Al-Din had been diverted. Obviously, the Basso woman was more of a threat than he first realized. How did she come by this information? She must have been in contact with Anatoly's son, Mikhail. It was the only explanation.

That complicated things.

His heart slowing to a more manageable level, Tsarev checked his watch. Dmitry was fully engaged in neutralizing Basso, if he hadn't already done so. He would have to give this new task to one of his other operatives—one who called Moscow home.

Messy. Things were getting messy and that was something Tsarev always tried to mitigate. Hence the meticulous planning before he executed even one step to his grand plan. He sighed and opened a lower desk drawer where he pulled out a large legal pad and pencil.

He would have to rework his masterpiece.

CHAPTER 19

Hydra, Greece

The sun had barely poked over the horizon when Leine woke the next morning. She'd put on a pot of coffee and was just finishing her 500th sit-up when Art made his appearance, squinting against the brilliant sunshine.

"Huh. I wouldn't've pegged you for an early riser." He shrugged and scratched his chin as he walked back inside the pilot house to pour himself a cup of coffee. A minute later he returned, sipping from a cracked mug with a cluster of penguins depicted in suggestive poses on the side.

"Looks like you slept well."

Leine climbed to her feet and nodded. "Best in a long time."

"Yeah, the boat rocks you to sleep like your mama. Can't hardly live on land anymore."

Leine poured her own cup of coffee and joined him on deck. There wasn't much activity in the small harbor.

Even though it was the end of the season, a few yachts anchored nearby. Orange-tile roofs, perched atop whitewashed buildings, crowded the harbor and climbed up the dun-colored hillside, with little space between. Leafy green trees grew next to the buildings here and there, giving the dry locale some verdant relief. A couple of fishermen cruised by in a low skiff headed out to sea, their boat filled with nets.

"Half the fish in the Aegean are threatened." Art scowled as he watched the fishermen grow smaller in the distance. "Pollution and overfishing. It's a shame. I remember when fish were plentiful in this part of the world. Didn't take long to fuck *that* up."

"I'd like to come back here sometime." Leine took in the calm scene before her and sipped her coffee. "I've given some serious thought to the possibility that Anatoly Sakharov isn't going to want to play," she said. "Even though his reputation is on the line, it's not like he can't rebuild. There's no proof of his wrongdoing or that something's going on. If I release the information, no one will believe me. Or should I say, the people who matter won't believe me because they have more to lose if it's true than if it's not."

Art snorted. "Sounds like government types, all right. Got their heads up their asses as far as they can go, just so they don't have to see the truth."

"I'm still going to try. My old boss at the agency will probably shunt the information off to some low-level administrative grunt to research for due diligence, but if I don't have corroboration of some kind he won't be able to act. That's *if* he even takes a meeting with me."

Art drained his coffee and set the cup down. "Well, then. That calls for a hearty breakfast."

Leine looked at him sideways. "I'm sorry, what?"

"Whenever I'm stuck between a rock and a hard place, I like to eat a big meal. For some reason, the act of eating a shitload of food helps me make decisions when I'm stumped. Whadya say?" He nodded toward a taverna with a green canvas shade next to the harbor. Two of the outdoor tables had early risers at them. "Best food in town."

Leine shrugged. "I could eat. Hell, if it works, I'll buy."

As promised, the traditional Greek breakfast was filling and tasty, but the huge omelet with *graviera* cheese didn't shake any decisions loose for Leine. Perhaps the pancakes with tahini and pork sausage Art ordered would have done the trick. She still wasn't any closer to figuring out what to do with the files if Sakharov wasn't willing to back up her claims.

The two of them hopped into Art's Zodiac and headed back to the *Cyclops*. Leine climbed aboard as Art tied the tender to the stern. As she moved toward the pilot house, she noticed the spear gun that usually hung on the outside wall was missing.

She turned to ask Art where it was when she caught movement in her periphery. Leine pivoted as a dark figure emerged from her left. There was a flash in the sunlight and she dove behind a metal stanchion. Something thudded against the side of the stanchion and clattered to the deck. She came up in a crouch, reaching for the pistol tucked in the back of her waistband.

Gun in hand, Leine shifted to peer around the metal support and get a look at the assailant. She caught a glimpse of a man in a black hooded wetsuit, still dripping with water.

"We've got company, Art."

"Stay where you are, old man," the man warned. Definitely Russian. "This isn't your concern."

Leine moved left, trying to get a bead on the intruder while keeping the stanchion between them, but he was partially hidden behind the corner of the pilot house. He held the missing spear gun, another spear loaded and aimed in her direction. Dark eyes narrowed to slits above a strong chin and nose. A jagged scar dimpled his jawline.

Before she could get off a shot, he disappeared up the steps to the side deck. She dropped to a crouch and took the opposite side, slowly moving forward and focusing on the area ahead of her.

As she approached the bow, the side deck access door exploded open and the man barreled into her. She squeezed off a shot but it went wide as he slammed her onto her back on the deck. Her hand smashed into the side of the pilot house. The gun flew from her grasp and down the companionway.

He reached behind him and brandished a wicked-sharp divers knife. She latched onto his wrist and squeezed, but his grip didn't loosen. Gaze riveted on the knife, Leine doubled her efforts attempting to hit the radial nerve, but he was in the better position and had at least thirty pounds on her. The tight space didn't help.

Finally, her thumb found the nerve and his grip weakened. The knife clattered to the deck. Leine bucked and twisted, throwing him off balance. He captured her right arm and forced her hand backward, trying to break her wrist. Pain shot through her as she raised her free hand and jabbed his throat.

Eyes wide with shock he struggled to breathe, but didn't let go. Leine pressed her advantage and slammed the heel of her hand into his face. He dodged and she missed his nose, hitting his cheekbone. His head snapped sideways. She was ready for the recoil and tried for another throat punch, but at the last minute he pulled back, taking the force out of the hit.

Behind him, something rolled across the deck. Art materialized near the bow, Leine's gun in his hand. He fired at the same time the man threw himself backward and jackknifed over the side. There was a splash as Leine and Art ran to the side and looked over.

A few scattered ripples remained on the surface. He was gone.

"Did you hit him?" Leine asked.

Art shook his head. "Couldn't tell."

She sprinted to the other side and scanned the waterline. "Nothing over here." They kept watch for several more minutes, but nothing moved. Leine joined Art at the stern.

"Probably left his gear on the seabed. He's gone unless he bleeds out." Leine wondered if he had a propulsion system secured to the bottom. That's what she would have done.

"That either took someone supremely arrogant or really stupid to board this boat looking for you. I can't figure which." Art shook his head, still looking for a telltale ripple.

"He wasn't stupid," Leine replied testily. "He got the drop on me. It never should have happened."

"You got a problem with how I handled things? I got there as fast as I could."

"Yeah, well, a second later and you might have had to perform a burial at sea." She closed her eyes and took a deep breath to calm herself. Adrenaline pulsed through her. She crossed her arms and looked at Art. "So the question is, who sent him and why? Clearly he was Russian, but who hired him? Sakharov or Tsarev?"

"And how'd they track you here? That's the real question."

"I don't know, but we should check the hull for explosives, and then get the hell out of here."

Art nodded. "I'll get the submersible rigged up with a camera and drop it in."

"I was going to offer to do it."

"No need. The camera's a high-def model. Saves me from having to go down there and check for barnacles."

"Then I'll keep an eye on things while you're doing that." She glanced toward shore. A small crowd had gathered on the main dock. "They must have heard the gunshots. Do we need to do some triage?"

He shrugged. "I doubt it. Most folks around here mind their own business. We should probably wave and smile, though, to make it look like everything's fine."

They turned and waved. Leine smiled and nodded, and Art did the same.

How the hell did the guy find them? They were on a fishing boat in the middle of the Saronic Gulf. She glanced at Art. He'd been pretty late to the party. Sure, he was a friend of Lou's, but how well did Lou really know him? It had been a while since they'd worked together. She'd have to be careful going forward.

The crowd thinned, leaving the dock empty except for two donkeys tied up next to each other, waiting for the next load.

Art handed her the .45. "You're not safe on board. Let me think a minute where to put you."

"Really, Art, you didn't ask for this. Just get me back to the mainland and I'll be out of your hair."

Art snorted. "You're not blowing me off that easy. Things are just starting to get interesting."

"Sure, when it's my life." Leine gave him a sidelong glance. Until she knew who and what could be trusted, she'd follow the original script. "I can't say I wouldn't welcome the help."

"It's settled, then." Art started for the pilot house.

Leine tucked the gun back in her waistband. "I hope you know what you signed on for."

Or what I did.

CHAPTER 20

Moscow, Russia

Sakharov returned to his hotel and ordered a bottle of scotch from the concierge before heading to his room. As he was boarding the elevator, the desk clerk ran over to him with a manila envelope that had been delivered earlier that afternoon. Aleksei took it from her and checked the contents before handing it to Sakharov.

After sweeping the room, the security team took their positions—Aleksei stood in the hallway outside the door while a second man took a position near the stairwell with a clear view of the elevators. A third roamed the lobby and underground garage.

With his coat still on and envelope in hand, he opened the French doors to his balcony and walked out, grabbing a glass on the way. He stopped at the table and poured himself a stiff drink, then set the bottle and envelope down. Sipping the fifty-year-old scotch, he stared at the lights of Moscow spread out before him, mulling his options.

How far did Roman's influence reach? When Sakharov went to war against him, what and who would he be going up against? No longer the Roman Tsarev he knew from childhood, his old friend's tentacles reached into places that Anatoly Sakharov couldn't begin to imagine.

And what to do about the Basso woman? As it stood, he didn't trust her. What good would it do him to help her? The information from the flash drive would eventually come to light through leaks or some other avenue, and his company would have to weather the storm those leaks would unleash, guilty or not. Besides, she'd lied and used his wife to get to him.

In the distance, the lights of the Kremlin gave rise to thoughts of the former Soviet Union and the way things used to be. Would he be the man he was today if perestroika hadn't happened? Doubtful. The freedom had been intoxicating, and he'd taken advantage of the prevailing "anything goes" atmosphere in the marketplace. Similar to the gold rush, the boldest ones made the most money. No way would he have been able to become as rich and powerful under the old rules. He might have moved into arms dealing no matter what—the opportunity would have been there either way—but he would have had to work the dark edges for far longer to acquire his empire.

With that, his thoughts turned to his family. Katarina may have been his second wife, but they'd been together so long now that their marriage seemed like the only one for either of them. If Mikhail was truly dead, then Olga was now his only child, as his first marriage hadn't produced any offspring. He was hard-pressed to remember much good from the pairing, although the bad taste that accompanied the memories stopped him from thinking about it for too long.

Katarina would wonder about the added security. He turned to go back inside to call her but hesitated when he remembered the envelope the hotel clerk gave to him. He opened it and pulled out three enlarged photographs. Taken from a distance with a telephoto lens, they were obviously surveillance photos.

He studied each one and then set them down. Although Sergei hadn't been able to confirm or deny Mikhail's death before he was murdered, he'd furnished the next best thing—proof of the lengths to which Roman would go to further his agenda.

He slid the photographs back into the envelope, but one slipped from his hand, falling to the balcony floor. As he bent to retrieve it there was a sharp thud against the brick wall next to him. Startled, Sakharov dropped to the floor and ripped his semiauto from his shoulder holster.

Someone was shooting at him.

Another round hit the wall only inches from his head. Heart thudding in his chest, he crawled to the French door and catapulted himself into the room. More shots hit the door, raining shards of glass around him, splintering the carpet and cutting his hands. He scrambled behind the massive divan and heavy wood side table and yanked the lamp cord free of its plug, submerging the room in darkness.

The front door opened and light poured in from the hallway.

"Shut the door!" Sakharov yelled. The door slammed shut and the room was once again encased in darkness. "Aleksei?" he asked. His hands shook from the adrenaline coursing through his veins.

"Yes," his bodyguard answered.

"The shots came from outside. The shooter has a clear view of the balcony."

Without another word, Aleksei low-crawled his way behind the desk next to the broken glass door and raised his rifle to peer through the infrared scope. He did a sweep and then dropped back.

"There are several positions he could be shooting from," he said. "There may be a team—another gunman, someone watching the lobby. Our best bet is to move you via the stairwell." Aleksei murmured into his wrist mic, alerting the others and ordering the car.

Sakharov groped the surface of the side table for his phone. It was a good bet the sniper was using an infrared scope similar to Aleksei's, which meant he would be able to see them move through the room as they prepared to leave. Sakharov brought up the hotel room's automation application on his phone, found what he needed, and pressed a button. The remaining glass instantly darkened, obscuring the interior.

"Let's go." Sakharov climbed to his feet as Aleksei moved in front of him to the door.

They managed to make it to the garage without incident. An armored SUV waited near the elevators. Aleksei took the front seat next to the driver. The other two rode in back with Sakharov. The driver asked where to go and Sakharov replied, "Just drive."

He leaned back and stared out the window. Obviously, his outburst on the phone with Roman had instigated the assassination attempt. The man worked exceedingly fast. Faster than anyone Sakharov had been up against in his years as an arms dealer. In that world, everyone was suspect. The only trustworthy thing was cold, hard cash, and even that could be counterfeit.

Had Roman only meant to issue a warning? The sniper hadn't found his mark. If Sakharov hadn't moved in that instant, would he now be dead? Or had the sniper intentionally missed?

If Tsarev only meant it as a warning, it was the wrong one to send to a man like Sakharov. Seething rage bubbled below the surface. Roman would stop at nothing, it seemed.

Two could play that game. It was time to change the rules.

CHAPTER 21

Must you leave so soon?" A languid smile on her lips, Pearl Kaminski stretched across the satin sheets, reminding Roman Tsarev of a lazy blond jungle cat. The general tweaked one of her nipples and she squealed with delight, desire flaming in her eyes.

"I must." He leaned down to take her breast in his mouth. Pearl groaned with need, but Roman broke contact and rose from the bed. The twenty-two-year-old pursed her lips in mock disappointment before a coy smile curved her lips. Trailing her fingers slowly down her ample chest and taut belly, she slid the sheet down until she was fully exposed. With a glance at his growing erection, she touched herself provocatively before raising her fingers to her mouth and slowly sucking each one.

Maybe he had a few minutes. He checked his watch. He'd be late for his meeting with the prime minister if he didn't leave at once. Stifling a frustrated groan, he turned away and picked up his clothes from the chair where he'd left them the night before. As usual, his wife was on holiday and wouldn't be back for several weeks. He'd have plenty of time with Pearl until then.

"Why don't we meet for dinner at that new restaurant in the city center?" Roman had no illusions as to why such a lovely young woman agreed to keep him company, although sometimes he allowed himself to believe it was because of his prowess in the bedroom rather than the wealth and power that turned her on. Or the money he paid to keep her calendar free. The envious looks from other men when he and Pearl were together were worth far more than he cared to admit.

"But I don't have anything to wear." Pouting prettily, she arched her back and caressed her full breasts.

Roman smiled. "Then you should go shopping." The expense was worth it—a simple way to keep her happy.

He opened the double doors leading to the sitting room of the luxurious apartment he'd purchased for their trysts, and nodded at his security guards. One of them brought him his overcoat, and another his attaché case. Two more waited outside the door. A quick look at the messages on his phone told him it would be a long, arduous day ahead. With a sigh, he headed downstairs to his waiting car.

Stepping out the door he buttoned his coat against the crisp morning air before walking toward the armored SUV idling curbside. Georg opened the back door and stepped aside so he could enter.

"Wait," the bodyguard said, his eyes narrowing. "Where's Boris?"

Tsarev froze, immediately tense. Boris was the general's usual driver. He glanced through the driver's window, but the dark glass made it difficult to see inside. Georg seized the general by the arm and dragged him away from the SUV while the other three guards drew their weapons and closed ranks around him.

Seconds later the general's vehicle exploded. Tsarev and his men were blown back several feet as the force of the blast lifted the SUV into the air and slammed it back down, setting off car alarms on both sides of the street.

Ears ringing and utterly disoriented, Tsarev felt someone grip him under the arms and drag him up the front steps into the building. Halfway to the door, he found his feet and propelled himself and two of his bodyguards inside the marble entrance. A third bodyguard followed and slammed the heavy door shut.

Tsarev sucked in deep breaths to calm the hammering in his chest. "Where's Georg?"

"Outside," one of the guards answered.

"Go get him," he snarled.

Two of the guards scrambled to do his bidding as a budding rage seethed within him. Although he'd made many enemies throughout his career, the timing of this attempted assassination told him all he needed to know. The audacity of a daylight bombing after a visit to his mistress had the hallmarks of someone who was familiar with his schedule. He'd been careful to keep the location secret, had worked diligently to make sure he'd never been followed to this address. Although he bugged the apartment and her phone, expecting to uncover some kind of blackmail scheme, Pearl had been surprisingly innocent in her phone calls and conversations, convincing him her only interest was in the money he paid her and in being the mistress of a powerful man.

No, this bombing had the hallmarks of retaliation for the recent attempt on Anatoly Sakharov's life. Even though Tsarev had sent the sniper as a warning, Sakharov had now become a much greater liability to his carefully laid plans.

It was time to teach him a lesson.

CHAPTER 22

Athens, Greece

Katarina Sakharov watched her daughter purse her lips at herself in the mirror and then blow a kiss at her reflection. The new lip color matched the heightened blush on her cheeks perfectly. She shook her hair back and struck a pose with a sultry look. The lacy minidress set off her dark tan and made the green in her eyes pop. She twirled, giving herself the once-over, and smiled.

The boys at the club would walk on their tongues through glass to be alone with her. As the daughter of one of the richest men in Russia she could get into any exclusive club in Athens, but her high cheekbones, perfect breasts, and long legs were what put her in the top five percent.

Katarina had told her to enjoy this time, that it wouldn't last, but her daughter didn't believe her. Why would she? The young couldn't imagine sagging skin and wrinkles, though their brains told them it was so for all, even with the wonders of plastic surgery. Taking one last look in the full-length mirror, Olga picked up her silk wrap and Prada clutch, and turned for her mother's inspection.

From her vantage point on the couch in the front room, Katarina saw a beautiful and talented young woman, eager to make her way in the world. She sighed, wishing for a younger version who wanted to stay home and keep her company, but that was not to be.

Except tonight. She didn't relish the news she was about to deliver.

She smiled at Olga and said, "You look lovely. Men would fall over themselves to be near you. I'm sorry they won't have the chance this evening."

Her daughter gave her a quizzical look as she walked over to the upholstered settee across from her mother and sat down. "Why not?" she asked.

"Your father called from Moscow. Certain... events have transpired and he's decided to hire more security."

"Is he all right? Are we?" Worry etched Olga's face.

"Yes. For now. But to be absolutely certain of our safety we are not to leave the villa."

Olga's eyes widened in alarm. "What? But I've promised Nalini—"

Katarina closed the magazine she'd been reading and gave her daughter a stern look. "Nalini will have to go clubbing without you. No exceptions."

Olga leaped to her feet, anger sweeping her face. "That's not fair. I have plans for tonight."

"You will have to cancel them."

"I can't. I won't." She lifted her chin defiantly. "I am an adult now. I make my own decisions."

"Not tonight." Katarina sighed. "I'm afraid your father's decision overrules your adulthood." She hated having to rein in her daughter, but she wouldn't take a chance on losing Olga. Especially since Mikhail…She pushed the thought away. There was no proof that he was dead. Yet.

"I'll take Farid with me," she protested, waving her hand at the bodyguard standing near the doorway.

"I'm sorry, Olga." At eighteen, having her freedom restricted must have felt as though it was the end of the world. Katarina softened her voice. "There will be other nights. The boys will wait, my sweet. I promise."

"But—"

"No. Your father's and my decision is final." Katarina injected enough steel into her voice to let Olga know she would brook no further argument.

"How could you?" Olga glared accusingly at her mother. A storm of emotions washed over her face: anger, betrayal, disbelief.

"Your father and I will do whatever it takes to keep you safe."

"You wouldn't have to if he wasn't in such a dangerous business," she said, tears of frustration glistening in her eyes. "Why can't we be a normal family?"

"Are you suggesting that we give up our way of life?" Katarina asked, spreading her arms wide, indicating the well-appointed villa. "You forget it's his business that allows us to live like royalty."

Olga's eyes darkened with anger. "How can I forget?" She nodded toward the gold-lacquered, silk-tufted furniture, and then at the gilt-framed portrait of Katarina hanging over the fireplace. Pieces her mother had moved from the yacht to the villa to make the modern décor feel a bit more like home. "His 'Early Tsarist' taste follows us everywhere. I can't get away from it."

Katarina had had enough. "I'm sorry, Olga, but that is the way things are. You will accede to our wishes, or you will find yourself even more restricted in your activities."

"Fine." Olga turned abruptly, then stalked from the room and up the stairs. Moments later, the door to her bedroom slammed shut.

Katarina sighed, unease snaking its way up her spine. During the best of times, she worried about her children being held for ransom or some other kind of leverage to hold sway over Anatoly and his vast wealth. But now that her husband's childhood friend was working at cross purposes to her family, she had much more cause for concern. Someday, Olga would understand.

Thankfully, they were living in a villa rented under a shell company that, if someone were to dig, would never link back to them. Also, most of their friends and family didn't know that she and Olga had stayed on in Athens and were looking to buy property. The added security had been worrisome, but Anatoly had assured her that as long as they didn't leave, she and Olga were safe.

For now.

Even then, her husband's assurances didn't go far enough to assuage her concerns. True, he'd told her he would no longer ship weapons to Libya, not if it meant they might be diverted to Izz Al-Din. But what if Roman decided to blackmail Anatoly into continuing? How could he refuse? No, something else had happened in Moscow to make her husband take such precautions. She could tell by the tone of his voice.

What have you done, my love?

Roman Tsarev might have been a powerful friend, but he was a much more dangerous enemy.

After texting her friend, Nalini, to let her know she wouldn't be joining her at the club that evening, Olga threw herself onto her bed and stared at the ceiling.

She was eighteen years old, an age recognized as an adult in most countries in the world, and nothing had changed. She'd waited impatiently for the magic birthday, had been excited to enter adulthood, but in one night had been relegated back to child status.

It was so unfair.

Many times she had wished her father was not so wealthy. Well, maybe that wasn't it, exactly—more that he wasn't so well known. The perks of being a billionaire's daughter more than made up for the inconvenience of bodyguards hovering nearby.

Usually.

But what difference did her age or her father's wealth make if she couldn't do what she wanted?

Frustrated, she selected a movie she'd been meaning to watch from her queue and streamed it on the large flat screen at the foot of her bed. Along with multiple texts from Nalini and her other friends, she'd get through the evening, somehow.

An hour later, Olga made her way downstairs to the kitchen for a snack. Her mother had retired for the evening, evidenced by the closed doors to her parents' bedroom, and the sparse lights on in the rest of the villa. She grabbed a carton of milk, a pint of gelato, and a spoon, and sat at the marble counter.

She was three bites into the gelato when Farid walked into the room.

"Want some?" she asked, nodding at the slowly melting pint.

"Sure." Farid walked to the counter and opened the utensil drawer to grab a spoon.

"Are things really as bad as my mother says?" she asked.

Farid shrugged. "It's not for me to say. Why?"

"Because I want to go out. My friends are having such a good time."

"That could probably be arranged," Farid said, his voice low.

Olga's mood brightened. "Really? How?" she whispered.

"I could take you." He gave her a conspiratorial wink. "But you must never, ever tell your parents. Your father would kill me."

"Literally," Olga agreed. Her heart raced with excitement. "It would only be for a couple of hours. I would have to be back before anyone wakes up."

"Easily done." Farid eyed the clock on the microwave. "You have plenty of time before the clubs close." He put his spoon down and rose from his stool. "Meet me outside in fifteen minutes."

Olga leaned back in the soft leather seat and sipped from the flute of Cristal Farid had handed her. She'd texted Nalini to tell her she was on her way to the club. Her heart still raced—sneaking out of the house had been so exciting. Farid was waiting for her outside in his SUV. He'd had her duck out of sight in the back seat, and they'd made it past the guards at the gate with no problems.

She ignored the niggling unease at the back of her mind. She didn't usually defy her parents but she wanted to make a point. Besides, if things were really that dangerous Farid wouldn't have suggested she go out. He was a bodyguard. He was trained to stop threats.

Farid made a left hand turn and the inside of the SUV started to spin. Olga braced herself against the door and the back of the seat. She glanced at the champagne in her hand. Funny, she'd only had half a glass. Maybe she should have had more for dinner than just the gelato.

"Farid?"

"Yes?" The bodyguard glanced at her in the rearview mirror.

"Can we get something to eat before we go to the club? I'm not feeling very well."

"Of course."

Olga put her glass in the drink holder and leaned her head against the seat. The spinning came back, this time much stronger. She opened her window and gulped in the cool evening air.

What was wrong with her? It wasn't like she was starving—she'd eaten breakfast that morning—and she didn't have a fever, so she wasn't ill.

Farid pulled to the side of the road, and turned in his seat to look at her.

"Are you all right?"

His words sounded as though he was talking from inside a deep well. She squinted, trying to bring his face into focus but everything was a blur.

"What's happening...?" She tried to move her arms—they felt like a dead weights. Her legs were the same. Finding it too difficult to remain upright, her head lolled back and her eyelids fluttered.

And then there was only darkness.

CHAPTER 23

Katarina Sakharov woke with a start. She turned on the lamp and glanced at the clock. Two thirty. What on earth had woken her? Then she remembered the dream.

Olga and Mikhail had been much younger than they were now. They'd been playing in the backyard of their old home in Odessa. The rest of the dream was hazy, except that they were sad and waving goodbye.

She threw off the covers and climbed out of bed. Grabbing her robe, she pulled it on and walked into the hall before making her way to Olga's bedroom. She eased the door open and quietly slipped into the darkened room. She needed to see her daughter—needed to make sure she was all right.

She advanced toward her four-poster bed, expecting to hear her heavy, even breathing. But something wasn't right. There was no sound.

Katarina turned on the bedside lamp and her breath caught. The bed was empty.

Don't jump to conclusions, Katerina. She could be downstairs. Anatoly's deep, practical voice echoed in her head.

Tamping down her alarm, she retraced her steps to the hall and made her way downstairs to the kitchen. Two spoons lay in the sink. She checked the living room and the media room. Olga was nowhere to be found.

"Farid?" she called. There was no answer. She returned to the living room, found her phone on the side table where she'd left it, and hit speed dial for her daughter's mobile. Olga's voice came on the line, urging her to leave a message. "Olga, this is your mother. Call me as soon as you get this." Frustrated, Katarina ended the call and slammed the phone back onto the table.

One of Anatoly's new security guards walked into the room. "Is there anything I can do for you, Mrs. Sakharov?" he asked.

"Have you seen my daughter?"

The guard shook his head. "No."

"Olga's missing." Her heart squeezed tight at the thought that her child might be in danger. It was hard to breathe.

"Missing? What do you mean, missing?" His confused look amplified her fears.

"I mean she's not in her room, she's not in the kitchen, she's not *anywhere* in this house." She tried to keep the panic from her voice. Cold dread wound its way from her belly into her chest. "Who's watching the video feeds tonight?"

"Farid."

Katarina led the way downstairs to the security staff room. It was empty.

"Roll back the feeds and fast forward through them," she ordered. The recordings had to show where her daughter went. The guard did as instructed.

Halfway through the second recording, Farid appeared near the entrance. He paused at the alarm keypad, punched in a code, and walked out the door. Another camera picked him up as he got into his vehicle. Katarina frowned.

"Did he tell you he was leaving?" she asked the new guard.

"The last I spoke with him, he told me to cover the east section of the villa."

"Who else is on duty tonight?"

"There are five men patrolling the grounds, and two inside—Farid and myself."

A few seconds later, Olga walked into the shot and slipped out through the same door as Farid. Switching to a different camera, the next frames showed her climbing into the backseat of his SUV.

A mixture of relief and anger flowed through her. Her daughter was safe. She was with Farid. But why did he help her leave? He knew the surveillance cameras were there, would know he'd be fired at once if he was caught helping Olga sneak out. If he wanted to keep his complicity a secret, he would have erased the video.

Unless he didn't care if they knew what he'd done.

She glanced at the guard. "What's your name?"

"Jansson."

"Jansson, call Farid. Now."

He brought his radio to his lips. "Base to Farid."

No answer.

"Base to Farid. This is Jansson, over."

Still no answer. Anatoly had replaced all of his security guards except Farid and Yevgeny—the two who had been with them the longest. She hadn't thought to ask why. Until now.

"I have to call my husband." Katarina sprinted back up the stairs to the living room for her phone. Her hands shook as she pressed the speed dial number for her husband. She needed to hear his voice, needed to know he was all right.

"You're up late." Anatoly's deep voice reverberated over the line.

"Why did you replace all of our bodyguards?" she demanded.

"Why do you ask?"

"Olga's missing."

"She's what?"

Katarina explained what she'd seen on the security footage. "You were trying to get rid of a mole, weren't you?"

He didn't answer.

"Well, you didn't go far enough. It was Farid." Her self-control broke and tears sprang to her eyes. "And now our baby's gone." She sucked in deep breaths, trying to control the emotions sweeping through her. *First it was Mikhail and now this.*

"Don't cry, Katya. Are you sure? You know how headstrong she is. Could she have talked him into helping her sneak out to the clubs?"

"Yes, I'm sure. They'd have been back by now, and Farid would have erased the feeds so they wouldn't be found out. He knows you would fire him. That he didn't do anything to cover his actions tells me he doesn't care if we know what he did." She took a deep breath to clear her thoughts. "It's because of your war with Roman, isn't it? Anatoly, what have you done?"

There was another brief silence. "We *will* get her back."

The resolve in his tone gave her hope. "I-I can't bear to lose another—"

"I know. I will not let that happen, I promise."

"Should we call the police?"

"Not yet. I'd rather not involve the authorities at this point."

"But—"

"No police, Katarina."

"When will he make his demands?"

Anatoly sighed. "I don't know. Soon."

"We're going to need help."

"What do you mean?"

"Can't you call one of your well-connected friends to find out where she is?"

"It's not that simple."

"Why not?" she demanded. Her cheeks flushed with anger.

"You know who did this. We have to be careful."

Katarina blinked. "But why?" Her voice cracked.

"There's something else. Something I didn't tell you. Sergei and Nataly are dead."

Katarina inhaled sharply. "You think Roman—"

"I do."

Roman ordered the assassination of a general in the SVR? "No," she said, fresh tears sliding down her cheeks. It was all too much to process. She sank onto the couch. "How?"

"I'd rather not talk about it over the phone. I think you'll agree it changes things."

"I'm not sure I understand what you mean."

"I'll explain everything when I return. Don't call anyone until I get back."

"Don't—how can I *not do anything*? Our daughter is *missing*."

"I realize that."

"Didn't you tell me that Eve Mason—"

"Her name is Leine Basso."

165

"Fine. Leine Basso. Didn't you tell me that she finds women and children who have been taken by traffickers?"

"Yes, but she lied to us."

"But she didn't lie about Mikhail, did she?"

Anatoly Sakharov hesitated a moment before he said, "No. I don't think so."

It felt like someone had thrust a knife into her stomach. She closed her eyes, absorbing the pain as reality came crashing down around her. Her husband had confessed to believing his only son was truly dead.

"Oh, my God."

"Please don't cry, my love. We must be strong. We must focus on getting Olga back."

She'd never before heard such misery in her husband's voice. Her heart broke at the thought of how anguished he must be. She would have to be strong.

"Yes, my darling. We must be like steel." She pushed away the thought of Mikhail's death. "This Basso woman must have had a good reason to travel under a false name. She risked her life to give you the information on Mikhail's flash drive."

"Yes, she did. But still she lied."

"That doesn't matter. She obviously knows how to find people. And according to your sources she's an expert at finding young women who've been kidnapped. Call her, Anatoly. We need her."

"I will not. I don't trust the woman."

A flame of anger erupted inside Katarina. How could he not be willing to try anything to find their daughter? "You trust the wrong people," she retorted. "What about Roman? You trusted him."

"I'll be home in a few hours." He ground out the words. "We'll discuss it when I return."

"Yes, we will," Katarina snapped. She jabbed the end call button and sank onto the couch as a wave of powerlessness washed through her. Now that she was alone, the real tears came. Tears of frustration, fear, and anger at her inability to do anything to find her daughter.

But there was one thing she could do.

She accessed the contacts on her phone and scrolled through until she found the number she was looking for. The other party answered on the second ring.

"Eve Mason."

Katarina took a deep breath and started talking.

CHAPTER 24

Leine put down the phone and checked her watch. It was three twenty. She'd just agreed to find Katrina Sakharov's daughter.

When Leine asked her why she'd contacted her and not the authorities, Katerina had given her a surprising answer.

"Because your name isn't Eve Mason. It's Leine Basso, and you find missing people for a living."

Leine had paused for a moment, allowing the implication to sink in. Someone, possibly Anatoly Sakharov but more likely Roman Tsarev, had uncovered her true identity. That told her that the man on the boat that morning had ties to the general and she needed to be extraordinarily careful. After the attack, Art brought her to a safe house with heavy security in a nondescript neighborhood in Athens, so in theory she'd be all right for the time being.

As long as she could trust Art.

"I expected to hear from your husband, not you. He needed time before he would commit to helping me. Does he know about this call?"

168

"No. He does not. The last time I talked to him he mentioned that he did not trust you. If Anatoly doesn't trust you, he won't do anything to help you. That's the way my husband works."

"Why doesn't he trust me? I've told him the truth about your son, among other things."

"But you lied about your identity. To him, that makes your motivation suspect."

Then Katarina Sakharov told her that two of their friends had been murdered and that one of the victims, Sergei Gorev, had been a general in the SVR. When Leine probed her about whom she thought carried out the assassination, Katarina refused to say anything over the phone, leading Leine to believe it was Tsarev. Now that the general had become serious about reducing friction to his plans no matter the consequences, Leine reassessed the situation and decided the time had come to escalate.

"I will help you," she'd told her. "But your husband must return the favor by backing me up when I meet with Henderson."

"If you help us find our daughter, I'm sure Anatoly will be much more amenable to providing the proof you need to present your case to your government."

After the call, Leine accessed a secure chatroom where she left an update for Lou and asked for lateral support. Her original task of locating Sakharov and finding out if he diverted the shipment had just morphed into something larger and much more complicated. She and Art were going to need all the help they could get. She checked the time again. Afternoon in Los Angeles. A good time to call Santa.

Santiago Jensen, aka Santa, worked as a detective in the robbery homicide division, or RHD, for the Los

Angeles Police Department. He was also her live-in partner.

"Hey there."

She smiled at Santa's voice—the familiar timbre melted a good portion of her stress. "Hey. You busy?"

"For you, never. Are you still in Greece?"

"Yeah. About that. Looks like things have taken a bit of a turn and I'll need to stay here a while longer."

"By 'a bit of a turn' I assume you mean clusterfuck?"

"It's complicated. I can't go into a lot of detail, but I wanted to let you know not to expect me any time soon."

"You need anything? I've got some comp time on the books." He let the offer hang between them.

"That sounds amazing." She sighed, looking at the four blank walls of her room. "I'd rather be home with you, but you being here comes in a close second. Unfortunately, there's not much you could do at the moment. I'm in wait-and-see mode and I know how much you enjoy that."

Santa chuckled. "My favorite part. Nothing like sitting on your hands, waiting for something to happen. You know, there are things we could do to pass the time..."

"Don't remind me. You'd better save your comp days. You won't be able to get out of bed much less walk once I get back to LA."

"I'm counting on it."

"There is one thing you could do."

"Name it."

"Hire a security detail for April."

"Oh? What's going on?"

"Like I said, it's complicated. Could you make sure she's taken care of?"

"Of course. What kind of security are we talking about?"

Leine hesitated. "Robust."

Santa's silence spoke volumes. "All right, then, robust security it is. Does she know?"

"Not yet, but she will." Leine glanced at the time. "I'd better get going. I've got a lot to do."

"Isn't it three thirty in the morning over there?"

"I couldn't sleep and thought I should call."

"No worries. I'm glad you did. And Leine?"

"Yes, love?"

"Don't take any chances."

"I won't. Same back to you."

They said their goodbyes and Leine ended the call. Touching base with Santa always grounded her in ways she couldn't put her finger on. She wondered what it would be like when he retired. She couldn't imagine him not doing something. He wasn't a "sit in a recliner and watch television" kind of guy. Maybe he'd want to sign on with SHEN? His training as a detective would be a huge benefit to the organization. And working together would definitely be a plus.

But then memories of the last time she worked with someone she loved rose to the surface. Even though she could trust Lou and SHEN, thoughts of what happened with Carlos were hard to shake.

Pushing her feelings aside, she took the chance that Art was still awake and walked downstairs to the kitchen. He was sitting at a table, playing cards with two of the other security guys.

Art grinned as he laid his cards face up on the table. A full house. The two other men groaned and threw their cards down. Chuckling, Art swept the pile of euros toward him.

"Can you guys give us a minute?" Leine asked. They both slapped Art on the back as they left the room.

"What's up?" Art asked.

"I just got a phone call from Katarina Sakharov. Their daughter's been kidnapped."

Art blinked a couple of times, letting the information sink in. "And she wants you to find her."

Leine nodded. "Interested?"

He gave her a look. "What do you think? Having a chit to call in from one of the wealthiest men in Russia isn't something that drops into your lap every day."

"Agreed." Leine pulled out a chair from the other side of the table and sat down. "According to the wife, Sakharov wasn't going to cooperate on the terrorist intel. Said he doesn't trust me."

"Well then. This happened at an opportune time, didn't it? I assume you made a deal for his cooperation if you recover the girl."

"Of course."

"Any demands yet? I assume we're treating this as a ransom kidnapping." Art cocked his head to the side. "Or do you have another theory?"

"One of their long-time guards is involved—a guy named Farid. I'm ninety-nine percent sure he's the mole I told you about, and that Tsarev's behind it. Feels to me like an attempt to get Sakharov to comply with whatever the general wants him to do."

"Then we need to be ready. Where's Mrs. Sakharov staying?"

"At a villa on the north side of town."

"We're going to need access to their phones. I'll bug the place and put a tracker on her vehicle." Art rested his elbows on the table. "So how do you want to play this? I've got contacts at Global Secure I can check with, and I still keep in touch with one of the guys that Sakharov hired away. Should give us a good start." He rubbed his hands together. His eyes had a gleam she hadn't noticed before.

He's enjoying this. Maybe she got his background wrong. Maybe Art was a former—or current—spook. *Well, that should help move things along.* She'd met a few retired CIA field agents in her line of work, groups of former spies who ran clandestine operations for foreign governments as well as operating within the private sector. She could always tell them by the glee with which they planned off-book ops, not to mention their willingness to skirt international law.

"I've got a message in to Lou for lateral support. He's a wizard when it comes to setting me up with whatever I need."

"Great. I'll work on the intercepts. See if you can get the missus to voluntarily give up her phone. Anatoly Sakharov might be a hard sell. I can always go at it from a different angle."

"Then we should probably get moving." Leine checked her watch. "I'll meet you at the Sakharovs in a couple of hours?"

Art nodded. "Should give me enough time."

She gave him the address and returned to her room. She was scheduled to meet Katarina in an hour, but Leine didn't want to waste any time. When April had been abducted she hadn't been able to rest until she'd found her. She assumed Katarina would be the same.

April. She didn't know how far Tsarev would go, but didn't want to take any chances. She texted April, letting her know she would soon have a shadow, and to take precautions before then. She'd rather April moved back to LA where Santa could keep an eye on her, but that would be a hard sell, no matter the danger. April was nothing if not stubborn. But, she was also savvy. Before she'd moved to New York to study, she'd wanted to join SHEN. In response, Leine had taught her self-defense and how to handle firearms, so at least she had some training.

It could come in handy.

She checked with the guy watching the security monitors downstairs to be certain no one was waiting for her outside, then let herself out and headed into the predawn to meet Katarina Sakharov.

CHAPTER 25

Sakharov villa, Athens, Greece

Leine pulled up to the guard shack outside the immense estate and gave the man on duty her passport. Once the home of a reclusive shipping magnate, five years earlier it had undergone a major renovation and been turned into a number of exclusive residences for lease. The guard checked his computer for her name.

"A little early, aren't you?" he asked.

Leine shrugged. "I couldn't sleep."

"I'll notify the residence." He flipped her passport closed before handing it back.

Leine waited as he made the call. A couple of minutes later, he leaned out the window. "Straight back, second villa to the right," he said, and waved her through.

She drove along the pristine driveway, her headlights giving her glimpses of colorful annuals, ancient olive trees, and an occasional palm. Greek statues with up-lights adorned the lush green lawn.

Leine parked in the driveway of the second villa and got out. The outlines of the Acropolis glowed in the moonlight, visible in the distance on its perch high above Athens. In a couple of hours the sky would be awash in deep purples and oranges, compliments of the legendary Athenian smog.

She walked up to the entrance and rang the bell. Moments later, Katarina opened the door. Leine had guessed right—the woman looked as though she hadn't slept.

"I thought you were coming later."

"I didn't want to waste any time. The first forty-eight hours are crucial."

Katarina stepped aside to allow Leine to pass and closed the door behind her. "I couldn't sleep, either. A loop of when Olga and her brother were children keeps playing in my mind."

"Look," Leine said. "I know what you're going through. Several years ago, my daughter was taken by a madman—a serial killer—"

Katarina's eyes grew wide. "No."

"She's fine," Leine assured her. "I was able to locate her before he did anything."

"I can imagine how frightening that must have been for you."

"Terrifying."

They moved into the main room. A large, ornately framed portrait of Katarina Sakharov above the fireplace and the gilt Rococo furniture looked out of place with the modern décor: dove gray walls and white trim with splashes of color, courtesy of an artfully placed throw rug or pillow. Floor-to-ceiling windows stood sentry over the backyard, consisting of a meandering, spot-lit garden path and a turquoise lap pool

"How were you able to find the killer?"

"It wasn't easy. A lot of factors contributed to his capture."

"How old is your daughter?"

"Twenty-three."

"Olga is eighteen," Katarina said. "Barely an adult." Tears welled in her eyes. She cleared her throat and looked away. "Can I offer you something to drink?"

"I'd love some coffee."

Katarina waved toward the main seating area. "Please, make yourself at home."

"Thank you." Leine walked over and chose one of the tufted silk couches.

Katarina joined her and pressed a button on a slim remote. A moment later, a young woman wearing a gray and white maid's uniform appeared.

"Amelia, please bring a pot of strong coffee and two cups."

"Of course," Amelia said and disappeared.

"My husband is due to arrive sometime this morning," Katarina said. "You're aware that Anatoly still does not trust you, yes? You're here because I want you here."

"I am aware, yes. With your permission, I would like to bring a colleague on board to help with the search. He has contacts in places I don't and could be very helpful."

"Of course. Whatever it takes to find my daughter."

"I don't have the particulars, but I assume any team he puts together will expect payment. These are not government types who would attempt to locate your daughter as a service."

Katarina nodded. "Understood. I'll deal with my husband." Her brown eyes were rimmed in red, and dark circles had formed underneath them. "He told me your real name, which is why he decided not to trust you. I defended you by saying that you must have had a good reason to travel under an assumed name. Was I correct?"

"Yes, you were," Leine said. "When I work for SHEN, I use Eve Mason in case someone objects to what I do to retrieve the victim. It's much safer than using my real name and risking my private life. In my line of work, I'm not interested in establishing a lasting relationship with most of the people I meet. Using a *nom de guerre* is automatic, which explains why I did it this time."

"I see." Her demeanor told Leine she was satisfied with her answer. "Tell me how you find someone."

"It depends on the case. I have access to several information systems through SHEN, which makes locating someone not exactly easier, but a good deal faster than if I were to start from scratch."

Amelia came back into the room, carrying an elegant coffee service on a silver tray, and set it on the table before them.

"Thank you, Amelia. That will be all."

Amelia smiled and left the same way. Katarina poured the coffee and slid a cup toward Leine.

"What is your success rate?"

"I've located all victims I've been sent to recover."

"What happens if you fail?"

"I don't fail." Leine matched Katarina's gaze.

Katarina nodded. "That's all I needed to hear." She rose from the couch and walked to a credenza sitting against a wall. Opening the front, she retrieved a photo album and returned, handing it to Leine. It was the kind where the photographs had been printed on the pages of the book.

"There are several in there of Olga." Her eyes misted over and she blinked several times. "Mikhail is in many of them, as well."

Leine opened the album and flipped through. Images of parties, friends, and various trips filled the pages. Through all of them Olga and Mikhail appeared to be the perfect brother and sister. "They got along well, didn't they?"

Katarina nodded and brought the cup to her mouth to cover trembling lips. Leine went back to the photographs. She flipped to the next page and stopped. It was a picture of a slightly overweight man about Anatoly Sakharov's age, with light brown hair, thick lips, and a clean-shaven face. He smiled indulgently as Olga blew out the candles on her birthday cake.

"General Tsarev?" She turned the album toward Katarina.

A look of distaste hardened her features and she visibly shuddered. "Yes." She practically spat the word. "The man responsible for the murder of my son."

Leine turned the album back around. "Is this recent?"

"Yes. It was taken this past summer on Olga's birthday."

"Would you mind if I took a picture of it with my phone? We'll need a recent photo of your daughter, and one with the general would be especially helpful."

"Be my guest. I'd print you a copy but I don't have that particular file on my laptop."

Leine retrieved her phone and brought the album over to the window for better light. She took three images using different angles and settings, and then returned to the couch with the album to look through the rest. Two more showed Olga in various poses, which Katarina said she would print for Leine.

She finished looking at the book and placed it on the table. "There's one more thing I'd like to ask of you."

"Anything."

"I need your phone. And your husband's. Art, the man who is going to help find your daughter, is due to arrive here in an hour or so. One of the things he wants to do is download an app that will record incoming texts and calls and be able to pinpoint their origins. It will also track where you are as long as you have the phone on your person. This way, we'll be able to monitor your location and your husband's, any communications, and be able to pinpoint where the kidnappers are calling from."

"And you need to be able to track us if one of us is required to leave here."

"Yes."

"I have no problem doing this, but my husband's consent is another matter."

"I know. That's why I wanted to tell you now, before Art or your husband gets here. There will be other aspects to the search, of course. Art will brief both you and your husband when everyone is here. Is there a way to convince your husband to do as Art asks?"

"I doubt it, but I can try." Katarina picked up her phone from the table and punched in a number. "I need to alert the guard. What is your friend's name again?"

"Art. He drives a black Mercedes SUV."

She gave the information to the guard and ended the call. When she returned her attention to Leine, they locked eyes. "I am putting my trust in you. This is my family. It means everything to me. If anything happens and I have reason not to trust you, there will be consequences. Do you understand?"

"Of course. We will get your daughter back. All I ask in return is that your husband keeps his part of the bargain when I go to my government with the information that is on your son's flash drive."

"I'll make certain of it."

At Leine's request, Katarina took her on a tour of the house. Leine committed the floorplan to memory, mentally cataloging door and window locations, where the security cameras and monitors were, and who was in charge of watching them, how many security guards were patrolling the property, and how often. Katarina instructed one of the guards to run through the video feed showing Farid and Olga leaving the villa and the grounds. Leine noted the SUV's plate numbers and direction of travel, then sent the information to Art to begin checking CCTV feeds.

Several guards had been positioned at various points along the perimeter of the property with one hundred percent visibility between them, and at least two covered the interior of the house, including one who monitored the video feeds. Leine recognized Yevgeny, one of Anatoly Sakharov's guards from the gala at the Archaeological Museum. She hadn't met the other, whose name was Beck. Tight-lipped and stoic, both gave satisfactory answers when she quizzed them on security protocol.

Katarina's phone rang, and she excused herself to answer it. Leine continued exploring the home, wondering where Farid had taken Olga. Many if not most kidnapping events could be traced back to someone who either wittingly or unwittingly passed along information that facilitated the abduction. Nannies, maids, relatives, and friends of the family were all fodder for leaking the habits or whereabouts of a wealthy family's offspring, making them vulnerable to manipulation by greed, misplaced trust, or blackmail. An inside job was far easier to pull off, although now that Farid was out of the picture the general no longer had an inside man.

Unless he'd installed two. She'd have to check Yevgeny's story, since Sakharov had replaced the rest of his security contingent.

"That was Anatoly," Katarina said, returning from taking the call. "He's just landed and will be here within the hour."

A short time later, after they'd finished their tour of the house, Katarina's phone rang again. This time it was the guard at the gate informing her of Art's arrival. She put her hand over the phone and said to Leine, "He says there are three other men with him."

"Those would be members of his team. I believe he mentioned doing a sweep of the property and adding some enhancements to your security."

Eyebrows raised, Katarina nodded and told the guard to let them through before she ended the call. "I'm giving you permission to do whatever you think is necessary, although my husband will not be pleased. He was intimately involved with setting up the current system. If Anatoly has a problem with your plans, I will do my best to persuade him to accept the changes."

The doorbell chimed and Leine followed Katarina down the stairs to the front door. Art and three other men walked into the entryway, filling the large space with their presence. Art stepped forward and offered his hand.

"Art Kowalski. And these are my colleagues—Daniel, Zarko, and Ben."

Each of them nodded at the mention of his name. All three could have come straight out of *Soldier of Fortune* magazine: Daniel and Zarko were well over six feet tall, with the third, Ben, a full head shorter but still formidable. All were in good shape with wide, meaty shoulders, narrow hips, and bulging biceps. Daniel and Ben had buzz cuts and no visible tattoos. Zarko was the exception. His arms were covered in colorful ink and a silver hoop earring peeked out from under his long, dark hair.

"Thank you for coming, Mr. Kowalski. Leine tells me that you are well versed in this type of work."

Art nodded. "Thank you, Mrs. Sakharov. But please, call me Art. I met your husband several years ago. Not that he'll remember."

"You'd be surprised. My husband has an excellent memory."

"Leine, can I talk to you for a minute?" Art jerked his head toward the living room.

"Sure."

They walked out of earshot and he turned to Leine.

"My guys found footage of the SUV and tracked it to a marina where they hustled Olga onto a boat. After that, nothing. I've got them looking at satellite feeds, but it'll take a while and I doubt we have that kind of time."

"I'll call Lou. See if he can lend a hand with that. Do you have a description of the boat?"

"I'll send you the photographs." Art took out his phone to forward the files, and Leine called Lou.

"How are things going? Are you getting along with Art?" Lou sounded chipper.

"Well, things have taken a bit of a turn, actually. And yes, I've met Art." She glanced at him as he spoke with Katarina, explaining something about her phone.

"What do you need? I got your message, by the way."

Leine explained everything that had happened up to that point and how the simple operation she'd expected had turned into a high-profile kidnapping.

"So I take it you need me to peruse satellite footage for the boat. See if I can find out where they took Sakharov's daughter."

"You did such a great job with his yacht—I figured it'd be a cakewalk."

"The *Black Swan* is a little bigger than a fishing boat. This could take a while."

"That's just it. We don't have a while."

"I'm happy to do it, Leine. But I'm not going to promise anything."

"I know, and thanks. Art's got his guys working on it too. In the meantime, we'll wait for the call. All evidence points to Roman Tsarev as the one responsible."

"General Tsarev?"

"One and the same."

"I may have some information for you regarding the general. I'll need to do a little digging, though."

"That would help. I checked the database. There was the usual bio, along with phone numbers and addresses."

"I know someone who's been tracking his finances."

"That could be interesting. Do you have some people you can hand off the satellite work to?"

"Sure. Let me get back to you. And Leine?"

"What?"

"Don't do anything rash."

Leine rolled her eyes. "And just when have I ever done anything rash?"

The silence that ensued answered the question.

"Okay, okay. Don't answer that. I'm a different woman than I was back then. Wouldn't you agree?"

Lou's deep chuckle made her smile.

"Oh, yes, I'd agree. But don't kid yourself. That woman is still lurking somewhere inside of you. Just be careful. These guys don't fuck around."

Leine assured him she would and ended the call. She forwarded the file with the photos of the fishing boat to him and then slipped her phone back into her pocket.

Sometimes circumstances required rash.

CHAPTER 26

Private airfield, Athens, Greece

Anatoly Sakharov glanced outside the window at the brightening sky of Athens as the jet taxied to the terminal. The news from his man in Moscow hadn't been good. The car bombing failed to achieve its objective, and Tsarev had retaliated. He checked his watch. Six thirty local time.

Six and a half hours had passed since his daughter's abduction.

The man works fast. Roman had always been efficient. And utterly ruthless. If Roman wanted him dead, then the sniper would not have missed him on the hotel balcony. No, the murder of Sergei and Nataly and the attempt on his life had been warnings. His daughter's abduction was in response to the car bombing, yes, but was also a bargaining chip, a way to force Sakharov to comply with Tsarev's demands.

There had to be a way to get Olga back without giving in.

His phone rang, breaking into his thoughts. He retrieved the device from his coat pocket and checked the number. Private party.

"Anatoly Sakharov," he answered.

"You received my message?"

Sakharov tensed at the familiar voice. He tapped the screen of his iPhone, launching an app to record the conversation.

"Roman," he said, trying to control his anger. "I didn't recognize that it was you. The ID said private caller. Let me guess. You're using a burner phone so you won't be tracked, yes?" Sakharov gripped his phone and stared out the window. "Tsk, tsk. How paranoid."

"You're the one who should be paranoid, old friend."

"Oh? And why is that? Because of your failed assassination attempt?"

"I'm sure whoever tried to kill you was instructed to miss. Think of it as a message."

"Like Sergei and Nataly?" Sakharov's cheeks flamed as hatred for his old friend burned in his chest.

"I know where you are every minute of every day. My spies are everywhere. There is no escaping me, Anatoly. You of all people should know this by now."

"I'm sure there is some truth to what you say. You are a powerful man. In Russia. But there are limits to your reach, Roman. You could have detained me in Moscow, but you didn't. Now we're on my playing field."

"I wanted you to experience the consequences of your actions. The car bomb was beneath you." General Tsarev sighed. "Go home, talk with your wife. I'm sure she'll be more than eager to inform you of recent events."

"You mean my daughter's abduction?" Sakharov sat forward in his chair, his fingers itching to close around Roman's throat. "Olga is an innocent. Your actions have changed everything. You will *not* use my daughter against me." His rage at a full boil, he rose from his chair, fist clenched. Lina, the flight attendant, peeked around the bulkhead, alarm evident on her face. Sakharov waved her away as he fought to control his anger.

"From what I understand, the Libyans are angry that you did not keep your end of the bargain, the contract to which you had agreed. I'm sorry that Olga has been caught in the middle, but the men who are holding her may very well do terrible things to her until you comply. You know of these terrible things, yes? I believe the Americans call it enhanced interrogation. Although, interrogation might not be the correct word to use in this instance."

Blood pulsed through Sakharov's ears, and black spots appeared around his periphery. He took a deep breath and let it go. *Calm down. What help will you be to Olga if you die of a stroke?*

"Well?" Roman Tsarev demanded. "What will it be? Your daughter's well-being and the conclusion of your promised shipments to Libya, or her pain and terror? They tell me that the men she is with now are experts in the dark art of torture. You may even be acquainted with one of them. A man named Drago Milosevic?" At Sakharov's silence, he went on. "I believe you had dealings with him in the old days. Is it true that he is a cousin of Slobodan?"

Sakharov knew Drago Milosevic well. A distant cousin of the now-deceased president of Serbia, Slobodan Milosevic, Drago was well versed in brutality. They'd crossed paths on one occasion many years before, when he'd been suggested as a possible member of Sakharov's security force. Sakharov had declined.

And now, if he was telling the truth, the ruthless Serb had his daughter.

"You use thugs to carry out your orders now, not soldiers? Your actions speak volumes, Roman. Your ambitions rule you."

"You're wrong. My ambitions guide me, not rule. And whoever did this was smart to use men unfettered by their humanity. Carrying out unpleasant orders is so much easier when one has no moral objections."

Sakharov took a deep breath and slowly let it go, attempting to control his anger. He needed to make Roman believe he was going along with him or they'd be trapped in a never-ending cycle of retribution with his family caught in the middle.

Gritting his teeth, he said, "What do you want?"

Roman chuckled. "That's the Anatoly I remember. I only want you to comply with our agreement. I believe you missed the last contracted shipment date. My friends in the Libyan army are not pleased."

"Stop the charade," Sakharov snapped. "You know as well as I do that the weapons are being diverted."

"Oh? And where do you think they're going? American forces?" He snorted at his joke.

"Just remember, Roman, this is a dangerous game you're playing. Do you actually believe that arming terrorists won't come back to bite you? History tells us it's not a good idea."

"I'm a great student of history, as you well know," Roman snapped back. "Nothing will 'bite me,' as you so elegantly phrase it. When I'm through, Izz Al-Din will no longer exist."

"I'm weary of this conversation." Sakharov had no choice but to tell him that he would comply. His daughter's life hung in the balance. *Let him think he has won.* "I will do what you ask, but you must promise to let Olga go free as soon as you receive word that it is done."

"As I recall, there are three more shipments to complete the contract. As soon as the third is delivered, I'm sure those animals will free your daughter."

"They must not harm her in any way, Roman. If they do, I will not rest until you have paid for what you've done."

"She'll be fine. As long as you cooperate."

CHAPTER 27

Sakharov villa, Athens, Greece

Anatoly Sakharov walked through the door of the villa flanked by three muscular men. Judging by the identical dark suits, short haircuts, and bulges near their armpits, they were part of his security team. Leine didn't recognize any of them.

Art handed Katarina's phone back to her. "We need to speak with your husband, let him know the plan and find out if he has anything he'd like to add."

"I will be part of that conversation," Katarina said.

Art nodded. "Of course."

"You must let me talk to him first."

Art moved to the side as she walked past them to join her husband. She took Sakharov's briefcase from him and set it on the hall table. They exchanged a quick kiss followed by a low conversation. A few minutes later she rejoined Leine and Art near the staircase.

"My husband would like to change his clothes before the briefing. Then we will meet in the library to discuss what needs to be done."

"Works for me," Art said.

"Has the library been swept for listening devices recently?" Leine asked.

"He has it done weekly, sometimes more often. The last time was three days ago."

Leine turned to Art. "Want me to take this, or would you like to?"

"Be my guest."

Leine picked up the case containing the compact bug detector Art had brought with him and climbed the stairs to the second floor. The library was located a third of the way down the hall, accessed by two oversized double doors. The ceiling-high bookshelves were filled with all manner of books, the majority history and politics. She wondered if they were supplied by the home's leasing agency or if they'd come off the *Black Swan*.

Two sleek leather couches flanked a low glass and chrome table next to a large fireplace. On the table a miniature version of the Venus de Milo rested on a large coffee table book with the title *Treasures of Ancient Greece*. The far end of the room had a distinctly modern glass-topped desk and three chairs. It didn't fit with Sakharov's personality. She expected something much more substantial. Potted palms punctuated the blank spaces between the oversized artwork and bookshelves.

Three big-screen televisions covered most of one wall, allowing a central view of all three from the desk. Leine turned on the detector and slowly walked the perimeter of the room, testing outlets and light switches, narrowing her arc with each sweep until she arrived at the center. Next, she ran the device along each piece of furniture, paying particular attention to lamps and other mundane objects. Lastly, she extended the telescoping wand and swept the ceiling and cove molding.

Satisfied the room was clean, she retracted the wand and turned off the device. A shadow darkened the doorway and Anatoly Sakharov walked into the room. He'd changed into a royal blue polo shirt and pressed khakis. His expression said he was anything but pleased.

"What are you doing in here?" he demanded.

Leine showed him the detector. "Sweeping for bugs."

Sakharov moved to the desk and scanned the surface, paying particular attention to the stack of papers lying on top.

"I didn't read those, if that's what you're wondering. And I certainly wasn't looking for anything."

Sakharov ignored her and jiggled the desk drawers. Leine set the detector on the desk and folded her arms.

"If they were locked when you left, they're still locked."

He didn't say anything as he tried the last drawer.

"We need to get past this animosity you seem to harbor toward me. Wouldn't it be better if we concentrated on finding your daughter?"

"You lied to me and used my wife." He watched her, his gaze cool and unflinching. "Why should I trust you?"

Leine didn't answer.

"You do not defend yourself?" Sakharov raised an eyebrow.

"Defending my use of a false name would only give you more ammunition, and I'm not in the mood to be your whipping girl. Surely, you deal with noms de guerre every day. In your business, I mean."

"That's not the point," he retorted. "How can I trust anything you say? You report that my son is dead, but you did not see him killed. You say the other files on your flash drive are his. Prove this to me."

"You're going to have to trust me on this." Leine put her palms flat on the desk and leaned forward, holding his gaze. "I'm here to help you. *We're* here to help you. It's what we do."

Sakharov mirrored her stance and leaned toward her, matching her gaze with a deadly stare. "I will work with you, but *only* because my wife requests your presence."

"Fine." Leine pushed off the desk. She turned as Katarina and Art entered the room. They both paused, apparently sensing the emotional charge still hanging in the room. Katarina narrowed her eyes, trying to gauge her husband's mood. Art had a neutral expression, but Leine could tell by the look in his eyes that he had correctly assessed the situation and found nothing to worry about.

"Since everyone's here, I think this would be a good time to brief you two about the operation." Art held out his hand, which Sakharov shook. "Mr. Sakharov. I'm Art Kowalski."

"You look familiar," Sakharov said. "Have we met?"

"We have—several years ago when you were shopping for security."

Sakharov lifted his chin in recognition. "Ah, yes. You declined my offer."

Art gave him a self-deprecating smile. "Afraid so. It was nothing personal."

"No offense taken. I secured several loyal employees from Global Secure."

"They're a good outfit," Art agreed.

Anatoly Sakharov took a seat on one of the couches and the rest joined him.

"Your wife mentioned that she told you about the program I'd like to download onto your phone so that we can track you as well as all incoming calls—" Art began.

"I have already received a call," Sakharov said.

Art glanced at Leine. She shook her head, indicating she didn't know what he was talking about.

"When?" he asked.

"On the jet."

"Who was it? What were their demands?"

"Roman Tsarev."

"I knew it," Katarina hissed. Sakharov gave her a sharp look. She pressed her lips together.

"He says he will torture her if I do not fulfill the contract I negotiated with him to supply weapons to the Libyan army."

"He's blackmailing you," Katarina said. "Those weapons aren't going to the Libyan army."

"This is correct. I spoke to the procurement officer in Benghazi. He told me everything had been accounted for, but he was lying. As for Roman"—he took out his phone and laid it on the table—"I recorded him. Not that it will do any good."

"Why not?" Katarina asked, nodding at the phone. "You have evidence of him implicating himself in this deception."

Sakharov shrugged. "He did not implicate himself on either count. He's too careful for that. He only mentioned the weapons were going to the Libyans, not the terrorists. As for the abduction, he blamed others. Even if we were able to prove he was involved, nothing would be done. Kidnapping is practically a national pastime in Russia and Roman is a high-ranking officer in the GRU. He would never be prosecuted."

"He will pay for taking Olga." Katarina's face had paled, but her voice was clear. Her eyes glistened with tears. "We *must* get her back, Anatoly. We must."

Sakharov put his arm around her and pulled her close. "We will, my *solnyshko*."

Leine took up the thread. "How long does it take for you to put a shipment together?"

"It depends."

"Let me rephrase that. How long *can* you take to put a shipment together?"

"How long do you need?"

"That will depend on how quickly we can locate your daughter," Art answered.

"We've got several people working with satellite imagery," Leine added. "My colleague, Lou Stokes, uses a computer program that searches for similar images quickly. Thanks to Art's contact we have a launch location and a positive ID on the boat used so it shouldn't take long to pinpoint where they took her. They are also checking into properties belonging to the general."

"And then?" Hope suffused Katarina's face.

"And then we launch a rescue operation, which is my guys' specialty," Art answered.

"And mine, as well," Leine said. "Hopefully we'll have her back within forty-eight hours."

Sakharov leaned forward. "At most I can delay completing the shipment for three days without Roman growing suspicious. Any longer, he'll realize I'm stalling and I risk my daughter's life. This is something I will not do."

Leine nodded. "Hopefully that will be enough time."

"It will have to be." Sakharov rose from the couch. Katarina joined him. The meeting was over. "If you'll excuse me. I have business to attend to."

After the Sakharovs left, Leine turned to Art. "So what do you think?"

"I think we're gonna need more guys."

CHAPTER 28

An island in the Aegean Sea

Olga woke the next morning with a splitting headache. At first she didn't know where she was, and an unspecified anxiety wound its way up her chest and into her throat. Soon, images from the previous night flooded the cottony recesses of her mind and the anxiety went into overdrive. She'd come to in the hold of a boat that smelled of diesel and rotting fish, with her hands and ankles bound. As soon as the vessel docked, she was heaved over the shoulder of one of her captors before being dumped on the desolate, rocky shore. Another man, one who looked like a bull with massive, sloping shoulders, then tossed her onto the back of a donkey like a bag of potatoes to make the arduous trek up a mountainous trail.

More images raced through her mind. She'd been in the backseat of Farid's SUV, heading to the club. Then...nothing. She closed her eyes and took a deep breath to clear her head.

What happened to Farid? She hoped he was all right.

What did they want? Money, obviously. Ransoming the daughter of one of the wealthiest men in Russia would be seen as lucrative. Except her father wasn't one to take this kind of coercion lying down. He had powerful friends. Surely that would count for something.

Why had she defied her parents? Despair at the folly of her choice to leave the villa clawed its way into her chest. *That's what you get for trying to have things your way.*

Her legs unsteady, she cracked open the door to her tiny, airless room and looked out into the main part of the cottage. Two men she didn't recognize were seated at the table, playing chess. One was smoking, while the other took a swig off a bottle of beer. Both had automatic weapons.

Heart beating in her ears, she eased the door closed and leaned her forehead against the wood. She didn't want to walk past the gunmen, but she couldn't breathe. Claustrophobic from the windowless room, she knew she'd lose it if she didn't get some fresh air.

She eased the door open again. Then, with a deep breath she pushed it wide and walked into the room. The man who was smoking glanced at her and then returned his attention to the chess pieces on the board in front of him. A slow smile curving his lips, the one with the beer looked her up and down and kicked the chess player in the leg.

"Well, well. Look who finally decided to grace us with her presence." He set his beer on the table and stood up, nonchalantly slipping his gun over his shoulder. Solidly built, he wore tan camouflage pants and a dark green T-shirt. Ring tattoos covered his fingers, with a skull and bloody knife on the back of one hand, an angel with a woman's name on the other. "Would you like a tour of the patio?" He held out his hand in an invitation.

Unsure if he was putting her on, she didn't move. "I-I would like to go outside." She glanced back at her bedroom. "It's so stuffy in there."

"But of course. Please, allow me. I'd be happy to show you your new home."

The other man smirked.

Olga reached out a tentative hand. He smiled and nodded.

"My name is Frederik. What's yours?"

"Olga," she said, feeling the corners of her mouth respond in a smile.

"Olga. That's a lovely name. Shall we?"

He led her through the small room and out the front door. The day was already warm, but the flagstones were still cool on her feet.

"So, Olga. What will you do for us?"

Olga frowned in confusion. "What do you mean?"

Frederik grinned, revealing yellow teeth. "What will you do for us so that your stay here is more comfortable?"

She let go of his arm and stepped back. "I don't understand."

"Oh, I'm sure you do," he said. He grabbed the back of her neck and forced her head down toward his crotch. Olga twisted out from under his grip and backed up until her knees hit the low stone wall.

Frederik's booming laugh echoed against the hillside. "Don't play the innocent with me, little princess." He advanced toward her, a lascivious grin on his face.

"Frederik." A man's deep baritone reverberated across the patio. It was one of the men from the previous night—the one who resembled a bull. He walked toward them from the steep trail they'd traveled the night before.

In his hand was a device the size and shape of a large mobile phone. "Don't touch the merchandise."

Frederik shrugged. "I was only teasing, Drago."

Drago waved him back into the tiny stucco cottage. "Keep it in your pants, or you won't have anything to keep inside them." The other gunman scowled but did as he was told.

Ignoring her, Drago walked to the end of the patio. Curious, she watched him as he fiddled with the device he carried. The screen flickered to life. Moments later, a buzzing sound echoed through the still, warm air and grew louder. A large white drone appeared over the crest of the hill above them. Drago worked the controls and the drone swooped left, then right, then straight up. Some kind of weapon was attached to the underside. Absorbed by the machine's acrobatics, at first she didn't notice Frederik standing in the doorway, watching her. She felt his stare and glanced at him. He grinned and made an obscene gesture, and she quickly looked away.

Without warning, the gun attached to the drone erupted in a rapid barrage of bullets that strafed the dun-colored hillside. Startled, Olga leaped to her feet, ready to run. Laughter erupted from the doorway as Frederik clapped at the show.

"Good job, Drago. You scared our little princess."

Drago smiled, obviously pleased with how the drone performed. "An added bonus, then." He fiddled with the controls and the drone flew up and over a small stand of olive trees, then disappeared over the hill. He slid the controller into the side pocket of his fatigues and walked back inside the cabin.

Left alone, Olga walked under the tarp, which had a mottled tan and green pattern woven throughout. A dazzling blue sky beckoned just past the edge, and she caught the distinct scent of the sea below. *Maybe they'd let me go for a short walk?* She wouldn't be able to escape—not without a boat. And it wasn't like she'd be able to swim back to Athens from an island in the middle of the Aegean.

A second man from the night before appeared near the crest of the hill, his rifle slung over his shoulder. He wore the same fatigues as Frederik. She stepped outside the covered section and raised her face to the warm sun but tensed when she heard a shrill whistle. Startled, she glanced up to see the other guard racing toward her.

Olga quickly stepped back under the tarp and braced herself. When he reached her, chest heaving from the sprint, his expression was dark.

"I-I'm sorry. I didn't know I wasn't supposed to—"

"You must never leave the shade cloth." He pointed to the tarp above them. "If you do, Drago won't be happy." He added, "You don't want to make Drago unhappy."

Olga looked at her feet. Dark splotches of oil from smashed olives dotted the flagstones. "I'm sorry. It won't happen again."

She glanced at him through her lashes. A chunk of hair the color of sand fell across his forehead, and he pushed it back. Flirting was the last thing she felt like doing, especially with a man who had her under armed guard, but she kept replaying what her father's chief of security, Yevgeny, told her about humanizing herself if she was ever kidnapped. She hoped it would work. Besides, he wasn't all that bad looking.

"Make sure that it doesn't." His words were a warning, but his demeanor told her otherwise. The corner of his full mouth twitched as he tried to suppress a smile. He was a few years younger than the other men, making him seem much less hardened, and more like someone from her generation. Olga thought she saw a spark of humanity in his brown eyes. In contrast, Frederik's expression showed nothing but cold calculation.

A loud cough came from inside the house, and the man nodded toward the open doorway. "You should go inside. Drago will have food."

"Thank you." Olga turned to go, but then stopped. "What is your name?"

"Call me Luka." With that, he turned and began the climb back to the crest of the hill.

Olga walked inside the house, blinking to help her eyes adjust to the dark interior. Drago sat at the table with Frederik and the other gunman. His rifle was nearby, leaning against a chair. A plate of olives and cheese was on the table next to him. Olga's stomach growled, reminding her how long it had been since she'd last eaten. Drago looked up from what he was doing and eyed her coldly. A chill swept through her at his examination, and she averted her eyes.

He pushed the plate of food toward her and grunted. Hesitantly, she stepped forward and reached for a slice of cheese. When all three men ignored her, she selected a few olives and another slice of cheese and walked over to the makeshift kitchen.

"May I have some water?" she asked. By the feel of her parched tongue, it had been hours since she'd had anything to drink.

"In there." Drago's voice echoed in the small room. She bent down and lifted the lid on the cooler. Inside were several large bottles of water, some still and some carbonated. Olga chose a bottle of still and looked around for a glass. Not finding anything to use and wary of engaging any of the men in a conversation, she unscrewed the lid and tipped her head back as she drank directly from the bottle.

Frederik leaped out of his chair and ripped the bottle from her hand. Olga cowered in the corner, expecting him to hit her. He slammed the plastic bottle on the counter and glared at her.

"Use a glass. Or don't they do that where you come from?" he asked, his voice dripping with sarcasm. With exaggerated deliberation, he pulled aside a curtain beneath the counter, revealing two shelves. On the top shelf were four mismatched glasses. The bottom shelf had a well-used frying pan, four chipped plates, and a bowl. His expression told her he was waiting for her to make another misstep. Violence rolled off him in waves and she dared not look in his eyes for fear of what she might find there.

"Thank you," she murmured, and bent to choose a glass. Half expecting him to wrench her arm, she was relieved when he strode to the table and resumed his game. She would have to be careful to watch everything she did. She quickly filled her glass with water, screwed the cap back on, and returned the bottle to the cooler. Then she walked outside and sat on the low wall to sip her drink.

Her view was limited. She caught glimpses of blue through dips in the rocky surroundings, but she couldn't get a good look from her position under the tarp. If she could edge out to the perimeter of the patio she might be able to see more, but her encounter with Drago, Luka, and Frederik had shaken her confidence, and she wanted nothing more than to stay out of their way.

Luka was no longer in view, but she got the feeling that he wasn't far. She took another drink and sighed. She wished Mikhail was there. He'd have already thought of a plan of escape and be halfway home. If only she had paid more attention to the action adventure movies her brother and father loved so much. Maybe she'd be braver, or at least have some idea how to get away.

She looked down at her manicured toenails, at the scratches on her legs from the midnight transfer on the boat, and at the stains and ripped material of her once-beautiful dress. Her rush to escape the villa and go to the club seemed so stupid now. She found it hard to believe it had only been the night before. Bile crept up her throat and her stomach roiled. She clapped her hand over her mouth but couldn't hold back, and vomited in the dirt.

She stood up and wiped her hand across her mouth. The water must have made her sick. She scraped dirt into a small pile and spread it over the mess to conceal the evidence. It still smelled rank, but maybe it would soak into the soil before Drago or one of the others came outside.

She held the glass up and peered at the water. It looked clear. Maybe it was an aftereffect of whatever drug she'd been given. She moved to another section of the patio and set the glass of water down. The sun was directly overhead. It must have been close to noon. The air was stagnant under the tarp, and Olga's stomach made ominous gurgling noises. She stood up and moved to the edge of the patio, hoping to catch a slight breeze.

As soon as she did, Luka appeared. He gave her a warning glance and shook his head, his hand on the butt of his rifle. Drago appeared at the door, a gun in his hand.

Without a word, Olga stepped back under the stifling shade.

CHAPTER 29

"We found it." Lou's voice held a note of triumph. "On the night of the abduction, the boat was spotted in the Cyclades at a rocky outcropping that could barely be considered an island. Population one burro, but there's an old jetty that's been used for decades by fishermen to tie up their boats when bad weather hits."

"That's great, Lou. Are there any structures? Somewhere they might be holding her?" Leine asked. The kidnappers could be using a cave. If that was the case, it would take more manpower to root them out.

"There's an interesting anomaly at the crest of the island so I had the pictures enhanced. Looks like there might be something. I just sent you the coordinates with the enhanced images along with a bird's-eye view. Check out the southwest quadrant. Looks like a good landing area."

"You're amazing. Thanks."

"Thank the genius who developed the program. It would have taken a hell of a lot longer without it."

"Remind me to take you and your lovely wife out to dinner when I get back."

"You can count on it. Be safe."

Leine ended the call and opened the file he'd sent. The bird's-eye view showed an island shaped like a pie with a bite taken out of it where the jetty was located. She enlarged the photograph to look at the southwest section. Lou was right—there was ample space to land at least two, maybe three inflatable boats next to a small cove. The highest point of the island wasn't terribly steep, so the climb wouldn't be too arduous. They'd have to be prepared for snipers, of course. Coming in low was never good. They could fast rope down to the island from a helicopter, but the rotor noise would alert the men holding Olga hostage, and there was no telling what they'd do if they realized they were under attack.

Leine forwarded the information to Art and went in search of him and his men. Art had managed to find a total of eight guys he'd worked with before. Counting Art and Leine there were ten. All were seasoned soldiers hailing from four different countries. She'd wondered about the language barrier but was happy to find out they all had a varying command of the English language, so communication wouldn't be a problem. Obviously feeling the weight of his failure for not being at the villa to stop the abduction, Yevgeny had expressed a fervent desire to join them. Art told him no, that he was too close to the situation and his emotions would be a detriment to the operation.

He was right, of course. With this kind of exercise cold, objective, and calculating was the only way to go.

She found Art and two of his guys watching soccer on the three televisions in the library. Art looked up when she entered.

"I got the text," he said, holding up his phone. One of the teams scored a goal and the guys cheered. He led her into the hallway and closed the doors behind them.

"I thought we could discuss the operation," she said. "Lou mentioned a possible structure at the crest of the hill. I sent you the enhanced photos."

"Good. Let's go somewhere we won't be disturbed."

They ended up in the backyard under a gazebo covered in magenta bougainvillea. The late afternoon sun bathed the well-maintained yard in deep gold. Leine took a seat on one of the wicker chairs next to a low table. Art sat across from her.

"I assume we'll stage the operation from the *Cyclops*," she said.

Art nodded. "We've got the use of two Zodiacs, mine and Daniel's, which gives us plenty of room to carry men and equipment."

"Perfect. I suggest we approach at oh-three-thirty and stash the Zodiacs in that cove on the southwest side. It looks like there's an outcropping that should give us good cover from above. We'll need someone to do recon to find out how many gunmen are guarding Sakharov's daughter."

"I've got a drone."

"That could work, but I'd still like to have verification on the ground." She took out her phone and brought up the enhanced photos Lou sent. "Take a look." She slid the phone across the table. "He was right. There's some kind of structure at the crest of the hill. Looks like they're using a camo tarp."

"What about the video? Any movement?"

"I haven't looked at it yet." She tapped the screen and brought up the enhanced satellite footage. Several seconds into the video a figure seemed to appear out of nowhere and continue over the rise to the south. Leine backed it up, zoomed in, and they watched it again.

"Yeah, that's definitely camo. See the shadow?" Art tapped the screen to freeze the video and pointed to a dark square to the right of the frame. "There's something underneath. Nothing nearby is the right shape to cast that kind of shadow."

They watched to the end, but there wasn't anything else to see.

Leine checked the other video Lou sent. A burro stood in the shade of a large olive tree near the jetty. He didn't move other than to nibble at the sparse grass below him. Not another soul could be seen.

"There has to be more than one guard."

Leine stopped the video. "Probably inside the structure with the girl. Lou's guy traced the island to a shell company owned by a friend of Tsarev's, so I think we can be reasonably sure it's a good choice. All the same, I'd like to get confirmation that she's physically there."

"Are you worried we've got it wrong?"

Leine frowned. "I'm concerned that it's a trap. Why didn't Farid erase the video?"

"Obviously, Tsarev wanted Sakharov to know who took her. The general probably didn't think he'd talk to anyone with access. His first thought wasn't going to the police."

"Maybe."

"We'll get confirmation or we won't execute."

"I'd like to be the one to confirm."

"No problem." Art pulled something out of his jacket pocket and set it on the table. It was a one-inch by one-inch white disc with two tiny wires and a battery.

"Geotracker?"

"Everyone on my team wears one. That way no one gets left behind. Fits real nice in the sole of your shoe."

Leine picked it up. "Good idea." She slid her knife from the sheath attached to her calf and took off her shoe to make a slit on the inside big enough to hold the device. Then she put the knife back and slipped on the shoe to test it out. She couldn't tell it was there.

"I need a few more things," Art said. "It's three and a half hours to the island, give or take, and at least another ninety minutes to infiltrate, do recon, and decide when or if to execute." He checked his watch. "Let's meet at the boat at twenty-three hundred. That should give us plenty of time to load, brief everybody, and make the island. Once we're there, you and Ben do recon, find out what we're up against and whether she's there. After that, we'll make the decision to go or not." Art had introduced Ben as his main guy, someone he'd worked with often. Leine had grudgingly come to trust Art, especially after she'd had a long talk with Lou about him, so she was comfortable with whatever recommendation he might have.

Within reason.

Leine nodded. "Sounds good." She grabbed her phone and stood to leave. "See you tonight."

CHAPTER 30

Aegean Sea

The surface of the water shimmered, reflecting a mass of brilliant stars as the rescue team raced toward the island. Both Zodiacs had been fitted with ultra-quiet motors so that the sound of their approach wouldn't carry. Visibility was good, with only an occasional thin cloud scudding across the moon.

Leine checked her H harness to make sure everything was secure. In addition to wearing a tactical vest, she carried a radio, night vision goggles and binoculars, and a sniper rifle fitted with a suppressor and a thermal vision scope. She also carried a suppressed 9mm semiautomatic, flashbangs, frag grenades, and a knife strapped to her thigh. Everything shiny or loose and loud had been taped. Ben, Art's right-hand guy, was similarly endowed, but instead of a long-range rifle he carried a suppressed MP-5 with extra magazines. The rest of the team carried thermal vision gear, NVGs, HK-416 assault rifles, grenades, and knives, and would wait in the cove while she and Ben did recon.

Three men were seated next to Leine in the boat while Art steered toward the island. The other five rode in the second Zodiac. The team was divided into three elements: Alpha and Bravo with two men each, and Delta with three. Art would stay with the boats. On board the *Cyclops,* everyone had been thoroughly briefed about the operation and all were eager to get on with it. First, though, Leine and Ben would climb to the upper ridge of the island to get a better look at what they were up against.

Art slowed the craft before cutting the motor to drift into the tiny cove on the southwest side of the island. Daniel, piloting the second Zodiac, followed him in. Once aground, they secured the boats and unloaded the equipment. Jorge was in charge of medical supplies. A trained medic, his shaved head emphasized the tattoo of the Rod of Asclepius that ran up his neck. Hopefully, his expertise wouldn't be needed that night. Zarko had braided his hair and exchanged his silver hoop for a matte black stud. Without a word, Leine and Ben donned their NVGs and set out for the apex of the island.

At first it was steep going, but the rocky terrain flattened out and became easier to navigate the farther they climbed. Once they reached the ridge Ben split off to the east. Leine worked her way west to come up behind the area in the satellite photos with the anomaly.

The NVGs altered the terrain to an eerie green and black. Her measured breathing joined the buzz of insects and the quiet crunch of gravel underfoot. Pausing at intervals, she listened and scanned her surroundings.

She came upon a small outcropping and slowed. A light breeze blew toward her from the north, bringing with it the faint scent of tobacco. She slid the suppressed 9mm free and soundlessly skirted the ledge.

Several yards away, a man smoking a cigarette stood with his back to her, an AK-47 at his side. He appeared to be alone. Without a word, she raised the gun and fired, hitting him twice in the back of the head.

He dropped to the ground with a thud. It wouldn't be long before someone discovered him, compressing the length of time she and Ben had to do recon. Ignoring the stench from his voided bowels, she put out the burning cigarette with her heel, removed the magazine from the Kalashnikov, and hid them both. She unclipped his radio, turned down the volume, and secured it to her belt.

"One down," she murmured into her mic.

"Copy that," Art replied.

With a quick check of her Lensatic compass, Leine moved silently along the ridge, adjusting her path to a more northerly direction. Near where the structure was supposed to be located, she dropped to a crouch and crept forward, coming to rest next to a large boulder. According to the satellite photo, the tarp should have been visible from her position. She peered through the binoculars.

There.

Straight lines to her left and down revealed the camouflage tarp below her. She squinted to clear her vision. The top of what appeared to be a low rock wall came into focus.

She checked for perimeter patrols before moving toward the structure. Taking her time, she made her way down the steep slope, careful not to dislodge any rocks and to keep cover between her and the wall.

A stone patio came into view beneath the camo tarp and she stopped. A stucco building the size of a small cottage stood at the far end. A narrow strip of light glowed through the gap in a window shade on the east side of the structure. The door opened and a muscular man with sloping shoulders and no neck walked outside onto the patio, an AK-47 hanging from his shoulder. Concealed from his line of sight, Leine remained where she was.

He made his way to the end of the patio, unzipped his trousers, and took a leak. The man finished and zipped up, then stood quietly as though listening. A moment later he reached for the radio clipped to his belt.

"Kolek. Check in," he said in Russian. There was no reply. He tried again. "Kolek. This is Drago. What's your position?"

Nothing.

Leine discarded the idea of shooting him. Not without knowing how many more gunmen there were. She'd have a difficult time hiding the body.

Frowning, the man keyed the radio. "Pavel. Vasily. Check in."

The radio crackled and a voice replied, "Pavel here."

"Have you heard from Kolek?"

"Not recently."

"What's your position?"

"Northeast quadrant."

"Vasily?" Drago asked.

"Yes, I'm here," answered another voice. "Southeast quadrant. I have not seen him."

"He is supposed to be patrolling the ridge. Pavel, find him, now. Vasily, stay where you are. We will remain with the girl." Drago pivoted and strode across the patio into the cabin. Muffled voices could be heard inside. Moments later, a man wearing NVGs and carrying a Kalashnikov exited the structure and climbed the hill, headed west. She watched him through the rifle scope until he'd disappeared over the ridge.

"Affirmative on the structure and the camo," she murmured into her mic. "A guard wearing night vision gear and carrying an AK is headed west over the ridge to look for the downed man. One of the guards has been redirected from the northeast to search for him, too. There's an additional guy patrolling southeast of here. The man who appears to be the leader said something about staying with the girl. I'll see if I can get eyes on the occupants in the structure."

Someone keyed the mic, signaling the message had been received. She skirted the patio and quietly positioned herself behind an overgrown mastic tree next to the open window. Inside, a man was speaking Russian.

"Don't worry. Kolek's probably turned off his radio and is beating off in the bushes somewhere," one said, laughing.

"I don't like idiots," grumbled another. Drago's voice. "Especially unpredictable ones."

Careful to remain hidden from view, Leine stepped closer to the window and peered through the gap at the bottom of the shade.

Two men dressed in fatigues sat at a table inside the cramped living area. The same number of assault rifles rested against the wall nearby. The harsh light of an electric lantern illuminated the table, spilling into the main room. An overflowing ashtray and several beer bottles crowded the table. Drago stood next to the door, radio in hand.

"Everything's fine, Frederik. Look where we are." The gunman closest to the window swept his arm in an arc. "No one knows of this place. We're one tiny island in the middle of hundreds of tiny islands. That's why I took this job. Easy money."

"A taste of the princess would make things even easier," muttered the one called Frederik.

"I told you before." Drago's menacing tone brooked no argument. "You are to keep your hands—and everything else—to yourself."

Frederik scowled but held his tongue.

Leine scanned the room, noting three doors to her right, two of them closed. The open door led to what appeared to be a small bathroom. One room was probably being used by the guards as sleeping quarters, the other to hold the girl. She glanced along the outside wall, noting the absence of additional windows. She needed to see the rest of the structure to determine if there were other exits.

A rock skittered behind her and she pivoted, automatically reaching for her 9mm. Ben appeared near the edge of the patio and indicated his intention to check the rear and west side of the cabin. She gestured that she understood and would meet him further up the hill. He nodded and disappeared around the end of the building.

Leine moved back up the hill to the boulder and leaned against the cool stone, scanning the hillside to make sure no gunmen were nearby.

"There's a wall about a meter high surrounding the patio," she said into her mic. "Looks like there's one door in or out, and a small single window on the east side. I count three gunmen in the structure, although two rooms have closed doors, so there could be more. I didn't see any sign of Olga, but she's likely inside one of the rooms." Leine did another quick scan of the area. It was still clear. "That makes a minimum of six gunmen armed with AKs, not including the one I neutralized. Ben's covering the back and west side of the cabin and will join me shortly."

"Copy that," Art answered. "Alpha's coming from the south, Bravo from the east, and Delta's headed north using your route. Leine, once you're in position, let me know. No one moves on the cabin until I say go. We don't want to alert the others, however many there are."

Leine and the rest of the team keyed their mics to acknowledge transmission. She shrugged her shoulders and cracked her neck to release the built-up tension.

Ben materialized from behind the cabin and climbed the hill to join Leine.

"Other exits?" Leine asked.

Ben shook his head. "No. Only the front door and window. I didn't see any other guards. Looks like the place has been there a long time. Part of it's built over a deep ravine."

"Everyone get into position," Art interjected. "It won't be long before they discover their dead compadre."

"Copy that." Leine moved higher on the hill to a spot she'd chosen earlier and set up her rifle. The area had a slight depression in the earth, some vegetation for cover, and a good view of the patio and front door. A large outcropping rose behind her, giving her cover from the west.

Ben moved closer to the cabin. "We're in position."

"Bravo, SITREP," Art said, requesting a situation report.

"Bravo in position near the main trail."

"Alpha?"

"We've got eyes on the entrance."

"Delta's in position on the ridge," Zarko reported.

"Delta, did you spot the men looking for the dead guy?" Art asked.

"Negative. You want me to find them?" Since Delta had three men, Zarko could act as a floater if needed.

"That's a go, Z."

"Roger that."

Leine studied the front door and patio through the rifle scope. A slight breeze ruffled her hair, bringing with it the scent of the sea. The chorus of insects from earlier had diminished, making it easier to hear if someone decided to pay her a visit.

A few minutes had elapsed when she detected a hum in the air behind her. It didn't sound like an insect. At first barely audible, it began as a low buzz from the west and continued to grow louder. She keyed the mic.

"Art, did you deploy the drone?"

"Not yet, why?"

A staccato burst of automatic gunfire erupted on the ridge behind her.

"Shit!" Leine swiveled her head, searching the ridge. "Delta! What's happening?" She looked up, scanning the sky. Seconds later, something flew overhead, temporarily blotting out the stars.

CHAPTER 31

Rounds thudded into the earth next to Leine, spraying rocks and dirt. The microphone erupted with concerned chatter.

"What the hell is happening up there?" Art bellowed into the mic.

"Drone," Leine managed as she dove for the outcropping. She rolled to her feet and spotted the weaponized UAV. Like a deranged wasp, it weaved back and forth above her, searching for its prey.

"Hold on, Leine. I'm coming to you," Ben said, and broke cover. Just then, the door to the cottage slammed open and the gunmen opened fire, strafing the hill. Alpha Team drilled the patio, and the two gunmen dove back inside the cabin.

Leine raised her rifle and sighted the drone through the scope. The gun barrel's heat signature was enough for her to find the target, but the crazy gyrations made it difficult to lock on.

"Come on," she breathed, willing it to pause long enough to get a clear shot.

"Heads up."

Ben's voice. Leine squeezed her eyes shut as a flashbang grenade exploded forward of her position. Ears ringing, she opened her eyes and tracked the drone as it paused in midair and swiveled toward Ben. The smoke from the grenade obscured the machine's visibility and the next volley of rounds went wide. She locked on the drone and fired.

The round ripped through one of the UAV's propellers and it stuttered, dipped, and stuttered again. Leine kept firing. The next shots tore up the frame and two additional propellers. The drone wobbled, tipped, then dropped like a stone. Leine flipped over and low-crawled to a nearby olive tree, taking her rifle with her. Rounds coming from the cottage door pummeled the dirt just short of her position. Heart pounding, she unclipped the radio she'd taken from the man she killed and turned up the volume.

"Everyone, back to base, now," Drago snapped, his voice crackling over the airwaves. "There are two gunmen on the ridge. Make sure they're dead. Two more are trapped on the rise behind the house, but we're taking fire from the south and are unable to neutralize. Take them out." He gave them Ben and Leine's positions.

"Goddammit," Art growled in her earpiece. "Check in! What's happening up there?"

Leine leaned against the base of the tree. "Leine here," she said in a low voice. "Ben?"

"I'm good," Ben answered.

"Delta took the bulk of the attack," she added.

"Delta?" Art said.

There was an excruciatingly long pause, then, "Delta, Roger."

Leine exhaled with relief. "The leader just ordered the other three gunmen back from their search. I took out the drone before the thing did any damage, but we're taking fire from the cottage." She paused. Several bursts of gunfire from below punctuated her words.

"Okay. Change of plans. How are you two doing on ammunition?" Art asked.

Leine checked her harness. She counted three full magazines for the 9mm and several rifle rounds, along with two grenades and a flashbang. "I'm good."

Ben reported the same.

"You two stay put, do what you can to keep 'em in the cabin. Bravo, hold and watch for squitters. Alpha, hold and cover the patio. Delta, I want Jorge on the ridge, ready to lay down fire. Daniel, get with Zarko and find the other three."

"What if they have another drone?" Ben asked.

"I've got it covered, amigo."

Leine peered around the olive tree to get a look at the stucco cottage. Rounds thudded half way up the hill toward her and she ducked back behind the trunk. Ben and Alpha Team returned fire. Her position wasn't perfect, but she had a partial view of the front door. First, she'd need to take care of whoever was shooting at her.

Dropping back, she positioned herself in a shallow depression made by the tree's roots and sited the rifle. Ben and the others continued to return fire, keeping the gunmen in the cottage busy. Leine peered through the thermal scope and took a bead on the front door. She could just make out the partial glow of one of the gunmen near the entrance. Ben fired again, and the gunman darted from behind the door to take a shot. Leine exhaled and fired. The body dropped, sprawling headfirst onto the patio.

Two down, five to go.

Hopefully, Zarko and Daniel would locate the gunmen Drago deployed and neutralize them. That would leave two—Drago and one other—unless there were more inside.

Leine sighted on the door and waited.

"Pavel, what's your position?" Drago's voice crackled over the radio.

"We're five min—" There was a sharp cry, followed by abrupt silence.

"Pavel? Pavel! Answer me." No response. "Vasily. Manuel. What's going on?" The alarm in Drago's voice told Leine that Zarko and Daniel had found their quarry.

"Mission accomplished," Zarko's voice came over the mic moments later. "Three down."

"Good work," Art said. "Now get your asses back to the cottage and let's smoke these motherfuckers."

Ben and the three teams closed the loop, surrounding the building. Jorge joined Zarko and Daniel as they moved toward the patio. Leine relocated to a position farther up the hill with a full view of the front door and side window. Releasing the bipod, she set up the rifle and dialed in the scope.

"Bring out the girl, Drago," Ben yelled, his voice echoing off the hillside. "You're not getting out of here. There's too many of us."

At first there was no reaction. Moments later, the front door opened and a woman with long black hair stumbled out. A man stood behind her holding a pistol to her head. Leine peered through the binoculars and confirmed that it was Olga. But the man with the gun wasn't Drago. It was Frederik.

"Let me go, or the princess is dead," he yelled. Frederik's gaze skated left and right, unsure where his biggest threat was.

"Easy, everybody. This guy's squirrely," Leine warned. "I'll see if I can take him."

Frederik kept moving, using Olga as a shield. Tears streamed down her face. His back to the wall, he dragged her to the corner of the cottage and stopped.

"Alpha, he's at the southeast corner of the cottage," Leine said in a low voice. "It looks like he's going to run."

"Copy that."

Eyes wild, Frederik started to look around the side of the cabin but stopped, apparently thinking better of it. Leine exhaled and blinked to maintain focus. Olga closed her eyes and gave a slight shake of her head.

Olga, what are you thinking? Alarmed that the young woman might try something foolish, Leine took a deep breath and refocused.

With a cry, Olga gripped Frederik's arm and dropped, leaving him open for a split second. Leine took the shot. Half of Frederik's head exploded in a red mist. Olga screamed and staggered away as he slid to the ground, the gun at his side.

"He's down."

"Good work, Leine. Alpha, grab the girl. Everybody else, stay focused. There's one more gunman that we know of."

One of the members from Alpha Team showed himself and gestured for Olga to meet him halfway. Half crying, she stumbled toward him and collapsed in his arms. They disappeared into the shadows.

"Bingo," Ben said.

"Excellent," Art replied. "Where's Drago?"

"He hasn't come out." Leine kept her rifle aimed at the front door.

"Give him a chance to surrender and then blow the bitch," Art said.

"Copy that," Ben replied.

Leine stayed put to provide sniper support in case things went sideways. The rest of the unit spread out along the hillside. Ben and Zarko slid down the hill toward the cottage.

When they were within range, Ben cupped his hands to his mouth and yelled, "Drago! This is your last warning. Give yourself up now, or we'll blow the cabin."

They waited thirty seconds, but there was no response. Ben pulled the trigger on his MP-5 and fired, chewing up the door until there was nothing left. Then Zarko unclipped a grenade, pulled the pin, and was about to lob it through the front door when someone yelled from inside.

"Wait! I am coming out."

The voice wasn't Drago's.

Moments later, a tall man with sand-colored hair emerged from the open doorway with his hands behind his head. Younger than the others, he seemed almost cherubic.

"Who the hell are you? And where's Drago?" Zarko demanded.

"My name is Luka." He looked behind him, into the cottage. "Drago...is gone."

"What the fuck?" Ben got to Luka first and zip-tied his wrists. Then he frisked him for weapons. "He's clean. What do you want me to do with him?"

"Interrogate him. He might have information on the asswipe who ordered the kidnapping," Art replied. "Search the place. Drago's got to be in there."

Zarko replaced the pin in the grenade and followed Daniel and Jorge into the cottage. Moments later Zarko came back through the door. Jorge and Daniel followed a short while later.

"The house is empty. Looks like he escaped through the shitter."

"Find him," Art growled.

Zarko, Jorge, Daniel, and Ben took off at a fast clip down the main trail. With the all clear, Alpha ushered Olga out of the shadows, steering her away from the cottage and Frederik's body. Leine joined them. Olga glanced at the rifle in her hand and then at Leine.

"It was you who killed him?"

Leine nodded. "With your help."

Olga raised her chin. "Thank you." Tears welled in her eyes, glistening in the moonlight.

"You're welcome," Leine answered. "Let's get you back home."

CHAPTER 32

Moscow, Russia

S ir, you have a phone call."

Roman Tsarev waved his assistant away. "Not now. Can't you see I'm busy?" He glared at the man and cocked his head toward the assembled dinner guests.

The elegant, linen-draped table shimmered in the candlelight. A warm glow reflected off the extravagant crystal centerpiece and bathed everyone in its golden radiance. Prime Minister Fedorov laughed uproariously at something Pearl said as she coquettishly touched his arm. Tsarev had originally intended the buxom blond to be his own companion for the evening, although it looked like she had her sights set on a bigger score. He'd have to remind her who paid the bills.

Still, chatting up the prime minister wasn't exactly a bad idea. There was much he wanted to discuss with him. Their past friendship would only get him so far. First and foremost, he needed to plant the seeds of doubt in his mind regarding Anatoly Sakharov. If worse came to worse and it was his word against Sakharov's, having the prime minister on his side could only help.

And then Tsarev would show him the photographs he'd had taken of the prime minister at an exclusive club based in the Minskoye Shosse area, one that catered solely to men with uncommon tastes in their private activities.

"The man is adamant that he speak with you. Something about an island in the Cyclades?" the assistant urged.

With a grunt, Roman Tsarev excused himself and walked down the hallway and into his office next to the ornate entryway. Closing the door behind him, he went to his desk and took a seat before picking up the gold-plated handset. He jabbed at the blinking light to access the correct line and growled, "General Tsarev."

"General. I have bad news." The voice belonged to Farid, his mole in Sakharov's security detail.

"Why have you called me at home?" Tsarev snapped. "This phone is not for business."

"I'm sorry, sir. I tried the other line, but you didn't answer."

"Of course I didn't answer, you fool. I'm in the middle of a dinner party with the prime minister." The general drummed his fingers on the desk in irritation. "What is this important news that cannot wait?"

"I'd rather not—"

"Farid. Tell me. Now."

"The girl is back."

"What exactly do you mean by 'back'?"

"She's home. In Athens." Farid stopped speaking as a vehicle roared past in the background, drowning his words.

"Wait for my call." Tsarev slammed the receiver down. He wiped his clammy palms on his tailored slacks and drew in a long breath. The blood beat heavy in his ears as he opened the top drawer of his desk. Lying beside a suite of burner phones was a vial filled with emergency heart medication. He took out one of the phones and slid the drawer closed. He didn't need the vial now but was comforted to know it was there. After wiping the perspiration from his face with a handkerchief he called Farid back.

"Who rescued her?"

"I don't know. I did as you instructed and haven't been back to the Sakharov house. None of the other guards knew what they were planning."

"Where is our team now?" Tsarev would call Drago to get his take on the rescue, and hopefully piece together who ordered the operation.

"I haven't heard from any of them. I had hoped someone called you with news."

"Did you try contacting Frederik or any of the others?"

"No one responded."

Tsarev covered his eyes, trying to think of some way to explain the lack of contact from the men guarding Sakharov's daughter, but the only thing that made any sense was that they were now either dead or being held somewhere for the purposes of extracting information. Except for Drago Milosevic. The general couldn't imagine that bull of a man going down without a fight.

"Where are you now?" he asked.

"Downtown Athens. I called you as soon as I realized she'd been rescued." Farid paused. "Now that my cover is blown, what are my instructions?"

"Disappear until Dmitry contacts you," he ordered. Shaking with anger, General Tsarev set down the phone. The shock of the reversal along with the two glasses of wine the general had consumed at dinner was a bad combination for thinking clearly. He should never have allowed himself more than one.

How could this be? No one knew of the island. Nothing could be traced back to him. He would have to find out from Milosevic what happened. And then, for his failure, he would have him killed.

But what of Farid?

He thought back to the last time the bodyguard had checked in, informing him that everything had gone as planned and that Olga was on her way to the island. He hadn't called back with an update, which had seemed odd. Now he knew why.

The rescue operation had to have been instigated by the Basso woman. There was no other explanation. She was almost certainly the reason Anatoly Sakharov had been able to pull off his daughter's rescue without tipping his hand to the general. Even if Farid had gone back to the villa and erased the security footage, he wouldn't have been privy to the details of the rescue operation. If Basso was American intelligence as he suspected, then she would certainly have shut out Sakharov's bodyguards, suspecting a plant. There were too many opportunities for leaks.

And what of Drago Milosevic? The general pulled out another phone he used for communication between himself and the Serb and tapped in his number. After the sixth ring, Tsarev hung up. Drago always answered on the first or second ring. Always.

What of the other guards? He'd assigned a contingent of eight, relatively small by modern warfare standards. But that amount of men under the command of someone like Drago Milosevic should have been sufficient to counter an attack on the small island.

Especially from below, where a rescue force would have had to originate.

He closed his eyes, envisioning his plan and how it could work now with the new development. *You must be nimble, Roman. Always work with what is, not with what you wish.*

His mother's words rang as true today as they did when she spoke them so many years ago. They'd stood him in good stead throughout his career. A pang of yearning for her presence surged through him, and he got to his feet, a renewed sense of purpose burning in his chest. He could handle this small reversal. He was General Roman Tsarev, the man who would single-handedly bring Russia back to its former greatness. His mother would be proud.

Encrypting his communication, he sent word of the latest development to Dmitry and ordered him to double his efforts to detain the Basso woman. There was no time to waste. He added a bonus to the money he'd already paid him. Dmitry was an assassin motivated entirely by finances, which made him easy to work with. And trust.

His next communique was to the operative called Salome.

It is time, was all he wrote.

CHAPTER 33

Sakharov villa, Athens, Greece

Leine waited until Sakharov returned to the living room. His expression was a mixture of triumph and weariness. She was happy for him, but Olga's rescue wasn't the main play—not by a long shot. The abduction set back their timeline by a couple of days, but there was still time to get the information to the right folks before the US moved to commit troops to the Libyan conflict.

She couldn't help but wonder if the general would be satisfied when and if events played out the way he wanted them to. Yes, US troops were spread thin, involved in multiple engagements around the world, but what would one more conflict accomplish? There was something larger at stake here, and Leine needed to find out what it was.

Why not set herself up as bait? Surely Tsarev knew of the rescue by now, and possibly of her role in the operation. He knew she'd given Sakharov the information on the flash drive, casting doubt on the general's motives. He'd be eager to find out what else she knew. Then she'd see if she could smoke him out by floating a little *maskirovka* of her own.

Sakharov crossed the room to where Olga and his wife were sitting and kissed the top of his daughter's head. Katarina hadn't stopped crying, and Olga wasn't far behind. The relief in the air was palpable, an emotion Leine knew only too well.

She let them enjoy their moment but checked her watch, itching to move forward with their plan. They needed to establish where, when, and how Sakharov would help bolster the evidence she was going to take to her old boss, Scott Henderson. She'd made the call to his assistant to set up a meeting and had been surprised when he'd given her a date and time. Maybe she wasn't as much of a pariah at her old agency as she'd thought.

Leine leaned against a wall, waiting for the Sakharovs to finish their impromptu lovefest. Art and four of his guys were standing watch outside while Leine debriefed Sakharov and planned the trip to DC for their meeting with Henderson. The other five operatives had been paid and were in the wind.

Sakharov extricated himself from his family's embrace and joined Leine.

"Shall we?" he asked.

Leine nodded and they climbed the stairs to the second floor.

Sakharov closed the doors to the library behind them. She took a seat on one of the couches, while he walked over to a table with several bottles of booze and some highball glasses on it. He chose a fifth of vodka and grabbed two glasses, before returning to sit on the opposite couch.

"You must drink with me to celebrate the return of my daughter." He took the cap off the bottle and poured them both a healthy shot, then slid one toward her. He raised his glass. "To your health."

"To yours." Leine raised her glass and threw back the drink. The smooth burn of the alcohol warmed her throat and she felt herself relax. Sakharov poured another and motioned for hers. Leine slid her glass toward him and he poured her a second shot.

"To my daughter," he intoned and downed the drink.

"To Olga," Leine said, and did the same.

He poured them both another but Leine left hers. "To the health of my wife." He threw the third drink back and pounded the empty glass on the table with a satisfied smile. "You brought my daughter back to me. For this, I am grateful," he said with a nod. "You and Art will always be welcome in my home." He poured another drink, toasted his mother, and threw that one back.

"Thank you for your generosity, Mr. Sakharov."

"Please, call me Anatoly."

"Anatoly. I'm glad we were able to do this favor for you."

When he realized she'd stopped drinking, he gestured toward her glass. "Please. Drink with me." He filled his again and waited for her to comply.

Leine lifted the vodka to her lips, but when he downed his, she quickly poured hers into a potted plant next to the couch. She waited for him to set the bottle down, signaling that business would be next on the agenda. He poured himself another, but then set the bottle on the table.

She caught and held his gaze. "Now it is time for a favor from you."

"Yes, yes." He waved at the air, dismissing her words. "I promised I would help you with your government, and I will. But first, you must tell me what other information you have."

Leine nodded. "We questioned Luka, the surviving gunman. He said Milosevic took his orders from someone called The General."

Sakharov nodded, his face a mask. "And Drago Milosevic is still alive?"

"As far as we know, yes. He escaped through a hole in the bathroom. The toilet was essentially an outhouse incorporated into the cottage. The hole had been enlarged and he shimmied down a rope. We were unable to find him after that."

"So he's crawled back into the rat hole from which he came."

"That's what we believe, yes." Leine leaned forward. "It's good that you've increased your security detail, but if Tsarev was able to insert a mole once, he may do so again."

"I'm well aware."

"Your wife mentioned a double assassination prior to Olga's abduction. I believe she said they were friends of yours?"

"And?" Sakharov's gaze intensified.

"Not long afterward there were reports of a car bomb in an upscale neighborhood in Moscow. No bodies were found, but the timing does seem interesting. Is there anything you'd like to tell me?"

"What are you implying?" Sakharov narrowed his eyes.

Leine chose her next words carefully. "I don't want to waste my time, or yours. If you're at war with your old school chum, that changes things and I need to be aware of it."

"I am not 'at war' with Roman Tsarev. This does not mean, however, that if I'm presented an opportunity I will not hesitate to take advantage and rid the world of that stinking pile of shit."

"Good to know."

"When is the meeting in Washington?" He pulled out his phone and tapped the screen, opening a calendar app.

"Tomorrow evening."

He checked the screen and nodded. "That shouldn't be a problem." He looked over the top of his reading glasses at her. "Didn't you say this Henderson would be difficult?"

"I said he *might* be difficult. He's taking the meeting. That's a good sign. It's possible enough time has passed since my...transgression. Maybe he's ready to forgive and forget." Not likely, Leine thought, but one could always hope.

"My assistant will need to make arrangements. When and where will this meeting take place?"

"Actually I'd prefer we leave together. It's a long way between Athens and DC. Much can happen."

Sakharov nodded. "As you wish. I'll have the jet ready in the morning. I'd like to spend some time with my wife and daughter before I leave the country again. We can discuss the meeting on the plane." He looked at his watch. "If we leave at eight we should arrive in Washington in plenty of time for lunch."

"Perfect. I'll get my things and meet you at the plane."

"My offer still stands. You and Art are welcome to sleep here. You will be safe."

"Again, thank you for your generosity. I can't speak for Art, but I must attend to some things before we leave."

She made note of the private airfield where Sakharov housed his corporate jet, and left the library. She'd need a good night's sleep before dealing with Henderson, especially when factoring in jet lag, but didn't know if that would be possible with what she planned for that evening.

Leine headed back downstairs to the living room to say her goodbyes. Katarina and Olga walked her out.

"I don't know how we can ever repay you," Katarina said, her arm around her daughter's shoulders. The two had been inseparable since Olga came home.

"Yes. Thank you for bringing me back to my family." Fresh tears welled in Olga's eyes, and she wiped them away.

Leine smiled. "I'm glad it worked out. And I'm glad your husband has agreed to hold up his end of the bargain."

"I'll make sure that he does," Katarina said.

The three women embraced, and Katarina and Olga walked back inside the house. Leine headed for her rental. Art waved at her from across the driveway, and she walked over to join him.

"What's the plan?" he asked.

"We're headed to DC in the morning."

"I'd suggest having backup tonight. My guys and I are available, if you need us. That asswipe from the boat's still in play, and Tsarev's gotta be shitting bricks. He's sure to know you were involved by now. I wouldn't be surprised if he made a play to nab you."

"Now that you mention it," Leine said. "I do have a little something you could do for me."

CHAPTER 34

The villa's guard waved Leine through the gate. She turned right and then left and continued toward downtown Athens, keeping an eye on the rearview mirror.

It wasn't long before she picked up a tail. A dark Lincoln Navigator pulled in two cars behind her and remained roughly the same distance back each time she turned. Leine hooked a right off the main boulevard, driving at a normal speed. The Navigator followed.

Good. Time for the show.

Leine performed several elementary maneuvers designed to identify the tail, knowing that the driver would likely fall back while still maintaining visual contact. It was possible the SUV was part of a tag team, but she hadn't noticed a second vehicle yet.

The tail dropped back and she lost them for a moment. She took a quick left onto a tree-lined residential street, drove to the end, and turned left again, all the while scanning her mirrors for the dark SUV.

Satisfied she'd temporarily lost them, she continued toward Kolonaki Square and pulled to the curb a few blocks away from the busy tourist area, next to a small shop that sold cellular phones. She got out of her vehicle and walked into the store. Greeting the shopkeeper behind the counter, she perused the merchandise for a few minutes while keeping the street in sight. Five minutes later, the Navigator rolled by. Leine waited a while longer before an identical Navigator drove by. She thanked the shopkeeper and left the store.

She took out the keys to her rental, tucking the ignition key between two fingers, and walked to the driver's side door. Seconds later, one of the Navigators pulled up alongside her and the back door swung open. Two men jumped out and grabbed her by the arms in an attempt to drag her inside the SUV. Leine pivoted and wrenched an arm free, then jabbed the other man in the eye with the key. His hand flew to his face as blood flowed through his fingers. The first guy wrapped her in a bear hug, pinning her arms while the other man squeezed his injured eye shut and yanked the gun in his shoulder holster free. Leine threw her head back and slammed the guy behind her in the face. There was a sickening *crack* as her skull connected with his nose, but his grip didn't loosen. The thug with one good eye stepped back and raised his .45.

"Enough," a man's voice commanded behind them.

Leine continued to struggle, but the sight of the semiautomatic pistol dampened her enthusiasm. The guy behind her wheeled her around to come face-to-face with the driver. He matched the security footage from the villa.

"Farid, right?" she asked. She hoped her little act had been convincing. Although if not, she was still pretty happy with what she'd done to his two henchmen.

"Get rid of her purse," Farid said, ignoring her comment.

One Eye wrenched the keys out of her hand and picked up her bag where it had fallen to the street. He rummaged through the purse and pulled out her cell phone, which he dropped and ground into pulp with the heel of his shoe. Then he pressed the key fob, opened the door, and tossed the bag inside her car.

Under the watchful gazes of the other two, Farid zip-tied Leine's wrists behind her back and patted her down. He found the knife strapped to her calf, slid it free, and handed it to one of the thugs. The guy with the broken nose looked like he was in a world of hurt. Blood streamed down his face and neck onto his shirt. Now holding a pistol in one hand, he gripped the bridge of his nose with the other, trying to stem the flow.

Farid opened the back door to the dark gray SUV and One Eye shoved her inside. She caught a glimpse of the second SUV idling just down the block. Farid climbed into the driver's seat, while One Eye took the passenger side and The Nose slid in beside Leine.

"Here." Farid tossed a hood to The Nose. "Put this on her."

The man complied, jerking the balaclava over Leine's head.

"Where are you taking me?" Leine asked, wondering who had ordered the abduction. Tsarev? The man who had attacked her on the *Cyclops*? She didn't really expect an answer.

She didn't get one.

The vehicle pulled out and started to move. They stopped and turned left before picking up speed. Leine counted the turns, drawing a map in her mind of where they were taking her. Someone tuned the radio to a talk show. No one spoke for the duration of the drive.

Leine estimated that approximately forty minutes had lapsed before the SUV rolled to a stop. The front doors opened and closed. The man beside her leaned across to open her door and then pushed her out. He exited behind her and pressed the barrel of his gun into her back.

"Walk."

Unable to see through the dark material of the hood, Leine took a couple of tentative steps before one of the men grabbed her by the elbow and yanked her forward.

The briny smell told her she was near the sea, and the echo of their footsteps on a hard surface suggested a large structure. A warehouse? At one point a bird took flight. Flapping wings and the coo of a pigeon receded in the distance.

The sound shifted, and the echoes of their footsteps grew louder. She assumed they'd walked into a smaller room or a corridor. Still large, but not as open as what they'd been through. Several steps later the sound shifted again. This time the echoes weren't as close. A larger space. They covered a few more feet before whoever clutched her arm pulled her up short. The hood came off and she blinked against the sudden light, dim though it was.

She'd guessed right—they were inside a warehouse, empty except for a wooden chair in the middle of the cavernous space, its legs and arms covered in peeling yellow paint. A table and light stand stood off to the side, with a green duffel bag on the floor nearby. The room had large, yellowed windows reinforced with grid wire around the perimeter, near the ceiling. Most of the glass had either been broken out or removed, evidenced by shards scattered across the concrete floor. A pair of steel doors took up part of the wall near the back.

A man wearing wraparound sunglasses stood next to the chair. His dark hair spiked straight up with the sides buzzed short, emphasizing a ragged scar along his jawline. A pair of gold crosses dangled from his ears, and his right arm hung limp in a sling. He reminded her of someone, but she couldn't quite put her finger on it. Good looking in a feral sort of way, his broad shoulders tapered to a narrow waist and long, lean legs, giving the impression that he took pride in his appearance. He was also dressed like Johnny Cash: black jeans, black shirt, and a black leather jacket. Even his pointed, embossed boots were black. All that was missing was a guitar and a bolo tie and he'd have the deceased singer's wardrobe down.

"Bring her here," Johnny said in Russian. Farid and the two gunmen walked her over. Behind him was the table with a bottle of water and a cell phone propped up on a stand showing a split-screen of a hallway and the front of a warehouse. A pair of pliers, a curved knife, and a screwdriver had been laid out on a rectangular piece of cloth.

Apparently he was going old school.

"Please, sit." Johnny held her gaze as Farid led her to the chair and pushed her into the seat. Johnny handed him a roll of duct tape, and he proceeded to bind her to the chair. The security guard paid particular attention to her forearms and wound an extra measure of tape around them and the arm rests. There wasn't any point in struggling. Not yet. They'd just shoot something that would hurt and bleed, and she needed to stay in one piece. Leine had been in similar situations a handful of times in her life, and she'd developed a way of compartmentalizing to keep her from getting nervous and lessening her chances of survival. Besides, it fucked with their heads when they couldn't get her to respond in the way they expected, and that was always good.

Johnny circled her, testing the strength of the tape and drawing out the pre-torture foreplay. "You." He pointed at Farid. "Cover the perimeter with the other team. And you two," he said to the remaining gunmen, "I want one of you at the end of the hallway, and the other on the door." They scrambled to comply.

He watched the phone screen until his men were in place. Then he turned back to Leine, frowning as he studied her. "Leine Basso? Or Eve Mason? Those names did not give me much to go on." He shook his head, a grave look on his face. "Eve is like the perfect ghost: no online presence, not much of a life. On the other hand, Leine turned out to have a bit more meat on the bones. At least with her I had something to work with."

His black shirt was open to the third button, revealing a delicate gold necklace, the cross at the end so small as to be almost unnoticeable. A present from a girlfriend? His mother? The local priest? He was younger than she was by a few years, but he had an air about him that said he'd been around. Was it arrogance? She hoped so. He'd be much easier to mess with.

He frowned at her. "You're not curious about what I have discovered for our little session together?" He leaned in close, the tiny gold cross swinging from his neck like a metronome.

"Not really, no."

"Well, let's see." He stepped away and stared at the ceiling. "You're divorced, have one child, a girl named April, and worked as a security consultant on a popular television show. I always wondered if Hollywood was how they depicted in movies. Are the parties really that insane?"

She didn't respond.

He gave her a disappointed moue and continued. "After that you were hired on as a bodyguard for mega movie star Miles Fournier." He clicked his tongue in mock sympathy. "He fired you. You then went to work for an organization that rescues victims of human trafficking."

"Yep. You nailed it. My life in a nutshell."

"No, not really. Prior to your marriage to businessman Frank Basso, there isn't really much to go on. In fact, there's nothing at all. It's like you never existed. You know what I think?" He waggled his finger at her and smiled. "I think you don't really work for an anti-trafficking organization. I think that's a cover for either the CIA or the NSA. What do you think?"

Leine rolled her eyes. Did everyone think she was a goddam spy? "I work for SHEN, which is an anti-trafficking agency. It is not a front for American intelligence."

"Well, see, that's not what I wanted to hear. My employer believes that you are a member of an intelligence organization, and he would like you to agree with his assessment."

"I can't agree with what isn't true. Why don't you let me talk to your employer and see if I can straighten things out?"

"No, that isn't possible. But I believe I may be able to induce you to see things his way."

He walked over to the table and picked up the phone, then tapped the screen a couple of times with his thumb before turning it around for her to see.

The video showed April walking with two of her friends along a shady, tree-lined street.

Leine stiffened and narrowed her eyes. He was bluffing. Santa would have called her if this asshole had taken her daughter. Last she'd spoken with the LAPD detective, he'd assured her that April was well protected.

"I thought that might get a response from you." He nodded toward the video, which was now showing her walking in the door of her apartment building.

"I know where your daughter lives, where she eats breakfast, what time she goes to her classes, even which professors she likes best. And yes, I know she has a contingent of security guards. I don't think she is very happy about it."

"Stay away from her." The words formed like a growl deep in Leine's throat.

Johnny shrugged. "That's up to you. If you give me the information my employer wants." He turned the phone back around and watched, a smile pulling at the corners of his mouth. "She's quite attractive," he said, before he tapped the screen to turn it off. He propped the phone against the water bottle so the split-screen was again visible. He turned back to Leine and removed his sunglasses.

That's when it hit her. "You're the guy who jumped me on the *Cyclops*."

His smile would have frozen the tropics. "You remembered."

So Art did shoot him, she thought, eyeing the sling. Good to know. "Tell me one thing," Leine said, pushing thoughts of April to the back of her mind. "How did you find me? I made sure I wasn't seen boarding the boat."

"The wonders of cyberspace, eh?"

For a moment she didn't understand. Then it dawned on her.

"A geolocator?" Digital geolocators were often used to trace the route of web traffic to a particular site. She must have accessed a monitored page. But Art had assured her he used a secure network. A simple traceroute command wouldn't have been able to locate their physical position.

"You have heard of bots, yes?" he asked.

"You mean like the ones hackers use to overwhelm social media sites?"

"Yes, of course."

Recently, a group of hackers had been caught deploying countless virtual robots across social media networks. These "bots" made it look like the messages generated were from actual account holders when in fact they were automated by a few select addresses located in Ukraine and Albania. The hackers were able to influence popular opinion in several different countries by making it appear that millions of people supported or opposed specific measures or candidates of targeted governments. Once the ruse was discovered, public outcry resulted in the majority of internet users becoming aware of the ploy, lessening its effectiveness.

"There is a new generation of bot. One that can insert a virus into any website without detection." He cocked his head and smiled. "It's amazing the amount of information that is available from an unsuspecting user."

She thought back to the night before he'd ambushed her on the *Cyclops*. She'd only accessed one site that could be linked to her online activity: the database of operatives. She had to warn Lou. Anyone using the list could be tracked, which was certainly damaging. But the list itself could be compromised, putting hundreds of people at risk.

Johnny grinned. "I see you've made the connection. Science is amazing, right?" He folded his arms across his chest. "So tell me how you and the old man were able to track Sakharov's daughter? An organization like SHEN wouldn't have access to the sophisticated technology that kind of operation requires unless it's a front for one of your American spy agencies. Which brings me back to my original question. Who do you work for?"

She needed to set the hook for the general before Art and his guys showed up. *If* they ever showed up.

Leine took a deep breath and closed her eyes to give him the impression she was reluctant to speak. "Okay. You got me." She opened her eyes and gave him a resigned look. "I work for an organization that tracks arms dealers under the auspices of the CIA. I've been surveilling Anatoly Sakharov for months."

Johnny's eyes widened with interest, and he pushed off the table. "I knew it. How did you come by the information of his son's death?"

"Intercepted from one of dozens of wiretaps we set up to monitor Sakharov's known associates."

Johnny lifted his chin in acknowledgement. "So General Tsarev is part of this surveillance?"

"He has been, yes. But not specifically." Leine paused for emphasis. "Don't get me wrong. Tsarev isn't the subject here. Sakharov is the one we're interested in. The general is only a byproduct of the original investigation."

"I'm sure he will be very interested to hear that." He narrowed his eyes. "He would also like to know how you came by the information on the son's flash drive."

"What flash drive?" Leine asked, feigning surprise.

Johnny gave her a hard stare. "Don't play coy. You know what I'm talking about."

She sighed. "He gave the drive to someone that was with him before he died. She gave it to me."

"How much did you share with the Sakharovs?"

"Enough that he made it worth my while. There's more on the drive that he's not aware of. Much more."

A knowing smile curved his lips. "Ah, so you aren't above a little blackmail, eh?"

"I like to think of it as a sales opportunity. I have a product for which certain people will pay money. I prefer to give the right of first refusal to the person who would be the most adversely affected. Seems fairer that way."

"And you'd be willing to part with this information if there was some kind of... incentive involved?"

"That's always a possibility."

"I'm sure the general would be quite interested."

"I also have information regarding US covert ops that may be of interest to the general. He can have it all, for a price. Tell him the future of his little plan depends on it. He'll understand."

Johnny scoffed. "You call this war of his a 'little plan'?"

Leine shrugged. "In a manner of speaking, yes. You can also tell the general I won't speak to anyone but him."

"That's not possible." He picked up the screwdriver and held it so the blade caught the light. "It is my job to find out if this information is worth paying for. I'm afraid you must tell me exactly what you know."

CHAPTER 35

She had to hand it to him. The man had focus. Leine braced herself for what would come next. Art and his guys should have been there by now. What the hell was holding them up? She'd have to stall for time or things would start to get unpleasant.

"Before we go any further, do you have a name? I've been calling you Johnny in my head, but I'm sure that's not right."

"It's Dmitry. A much better name than Johnny, don't you think?"

"Your accent. Have you spent time in Chechnya?"

A cloud passed over Dmitry's face. "Enough of this distraction. Tell me the information." When she didn't respond, he held up the screwdriver like it was a sacred relic. "I know what you're thinking. Where's the dremel? The pipe cutters? The bone saw?" A look of distaste crossed his features. "The simple screwdriver makes a much bolder statement, don't you think?" He walked behind her and ran the blade down her arm, hesitating above her right hand.

"Such fine bones. Did you know there are twenty-seven in the hand alone?"

Leine took a deep breath to prepare for the pain that would come when he thrust the tip of the screwdriver through her hand. She'd have to learn how to write again.

Good thing she could shoot with her left.

He moved to the front and held the screwdriver below her left nostril. "You know I must make you pay for this." He nodded at the sling he wore.

"Consider it a gift."

"It doesn't take much to kill a person," he said, ignoring her comment. "All I need to do is push the blade up your nose and into your brain." He jerked his hand toward her as though he was going to do what he'd just described, but stopped at the last moment. Leine continued to stare at him, unblinking. A slow smile creased Dmitry's face, and he took a step back.

"Your training is quite effective."

"I'm not sure what training you're talking about. I'm not a field agent." She caught movement on the phone in her periphery but kept her gaze level with his. "I will only speak with General Tsarev."

He sighed. "You do know, don't you, that if you don't tell me what I want to hear I will kill your daughter?" He shrugged as he walked back to the table and picked up the curved knife. "An added inducement to give me the information."

Returning to the chair, he brought the rounded section of the blade to her throat and guided it gently under her chin. The blade was so sharp, she hadn't realized he cut her until warm blood trickled down her throat.

He looked at her, mock concern in his eyes. "Pity about your shirt."

"Look. If I'm dead, damaged, or disappear, the information I have will go straight to the CIA."

"I'm not going to kill you, just make some modifications. Besides, by the time they find you, I doubt it will matter. The general has already put his grand plan into motion. There's no way to stop it now."

At that moment, a muted *pop-pop-pop!* erupted from the phone with an answering echo somewhere in the warehouse. Dmitry spun, eyes riveted to the screen. The hallway was empty.

Seconds later, one of Dmitry's men ran past, headed toward the gunfire. There was another *pop!* and three men appeared on screen, moving single file along the hallway, weapons raised to eye level.

Dmitry raced to the duffel bag behind the table and dug out a semiauto. He checked the magazine and sprang to his feet. Had he been ordered to kill her no matter what she told him? Anticipating the possibility, Leine threw herself to the right, expecting to feel the hot bite of a round as it entered her body. The chair tipped up on two legs, hesitated for an excruciating split second, and fell sideways onto the floor, taking Leine with it.

She landed hard, heard a crack. The chair? Or her ribs? The wind knocked out of her, she strained for breath. She hadn't been shot. Did he intentionally miss?

The sound of boots slapping hard against the concrete told her he'd decided to cut his losses. The metal doors at the far end of the warehouse screeched open and closed.

Dmitry was gone.

Her lungs finally cooperated and she sucked in a shallow breath. At the sound of approaching footsteps, Leine stopped struggling and closed her eyes. If the assault team turned out to be someone other than Art and his men, she hoped the blood on her neck and shirt would be enough to fool them into thinking she was dead and they'd move on.

"Oh, shit. We're too late," someone hissed. Footsteps pounded the concrete toward her.

"Leine?" It was Art.

At the sound of his voice she opened her eyes. "About time you got here."

"Fucking traffic." Art unsheathed his knife and bent to cut her hands and legs free. Leine climbed to her feet, pulling the vestiges of the tape from her arms. Zarko and Ben stood nearby.

"Well?" Art asked.

"It's the guy from the *Cyclops*. Name's Dmitry. Works for the general. He had his right arm in a sling." She nodded at the back of the warehouse. "He escaped through those doors."

"So I did hit him," Art said. The echo of gunfire could be heard from the other end of the warehouse. "Jorge. Daniel. Report," he said over his radio.

"He just left," Jorge replied. "We fired a couple of shots to make things real."

"Copy that." Art turned to Leine. "Did he take the bait?"

"Yeah, I think so. Time will tell." Leine checked her watch. "I've got some loose ends to tie up before I meet Sakharov in the morning." She gave Art a tired smile. "Thanks for your help. Let's hope things go the way we planned."

"Any time, Leine. Keep me posted." He stuck out his hand and they shook. "If you ever find yourself in Athens again, let me know. You've always got a place to stay."

"Thanks, Art. I'll do that." She let go of his hand and asked, "Feel like heading for New York tonight?"

He cocked his head. "Maybe. What have you got in mind?"

"I'd like to hire you and your guys for a few days. Dmitry just threatened to kill my daughter. Although she's already got twenty-four-seven security, I'd feel better knowing that you and your men were there. You know the threat Tsarev and his henchmen pose. You'd be able to anticipate what the other bodyguards might not. And, you can ID Dmitry."

"Which flight do you want us on?"

CHAPTER 36

Las Vegas, Nevada

Salome checked the sprayer mechanism attached to the underside of the drone and stepped back to gauge its effectiveness. The nozzles broadcast a wide, even spray across the concrete floor of the empty room. Perfect. She glanced through the open floor-to-ceiling rectangle meant to one day be a plate glass window with an expansive seventeenth-floor view of the city. Less than a quarter mile away, thousands of tiny tourists marched like ants along the Las Vegas Strip.

Donning heavy rubber gloves and a gas mask over a hazmat suit, she lifted the small metal canister sitting on the table before her and attached it to the drone's undercarriage. She then connected the plastic tube running from the sprayer to the canister and secured the end with a small clamp.

One drop of the canister's contents on her exposed skin would cause sweating and muscle spasms as the central nervous system went into overdrive. A small trickle and she'd need the slender cylinder lying on the table next to her. The prefilled syringe contained atropine—an antidote to the deadly chemical inside the metal canister.

Initially in liquid form, once released the lethal substance would vaporize, allowing for easy inhalation. Even low doses could cripple the respiratory system and paralyze the lungs.

Not an easy way to die.

But Salome wasn't interested in easy. She was interested in agony.

Not that the antidote would render the colorless, tasteless nerve agent completely harmless; even with atropine the victim's central nervous system would be tricked into causing involuntary drooling, respiratory distress, and muscle convulsions. The people who experienced a full-on sarin gas attack like the one she planned would have those symptoms ratcheted up to unbelievable extremes—excessive foaming at the mouth, uncontrollable convulsions, vomiting, release of the bladder and bowels—all leading to death by asphyxiation.

Sarin gas was eighty times stronger than cyanide— very little was required to carry out her assignment. The amount in the canister was a thousandfold more than she needed but she was curious to see what would happen when she used that much in such a confined space.

She tightened the last screw on the drone and checked the instructions. Much more robust than an average civilian drone, the machine's carrying capacity was several times that of one purchased in a hobby shop. The general had ordered several made to his specifications. All were capable of carrying an impressive payload.

Finished, Salome removed the gloves and mask and set them aside before opening an app on her mobile phone. The screen blipped to life, showing an infinite number of commands. She tapped an icon, and the motor whirred to life. She tapped another and all four propellers began to spin. The drone rose off its stand and hovered above the table, awaiting its next command. Salome tested the controls, flying it from one side of the empty space to another and back again.

Satisfied the drone was performing properly, she landed the UAV near the rectangular opening and programmed the integrated GPS. She could remain in the unfinished Russian-funded hotel until the drone had accomplished its objective—the app would show her exactly where the machine was in real-time—but Salome preferred to be on the ground to determine firsthand the effectiveness of the delivery mechanism. In her line of work, one could never have enough data; the general's mission was a sterling opportunity to gain experience using a drone as a weapon of mass destruction.

She took off the hazmat suit and booties and stuffed them into a garbage bag before sliding the syringe filled with atropine in her front pocket. She checked the area to make sure she hadn't left anything, and dropped the garbage bag into a large waste bin on her way to the elevator.

As soon as she made her way to the popular casino, she would text the prearranged signal to her accomplice at the entrance to open the doors. If all went as planned, the mission would be seen as a brazen attack by Izz Al-Din, whipping up even more support for the Islamic State from jihadis the world over. What better place than the City of Sin for Islamic terrorists to make their stand against the infidels? Once the Americans received intelligence regarding who had supported the attack, then everything would change.

There could be only one superpower. Salome's part in the general's plan would help bring America to its knees.

CHAPTER 37

Washington, DC

The jet touched down at a private airfield near Washington, DC, three hours before Leine and Sakharov's meeting with Henderson. Due to the prior evening's events, Sakharov had delayed takeoff to allow Leine time to tie up loose ends. During the flight, she briefed the Russian billionaire on the incident at the warehouse and Dmitry's ominous threat that the general's plan had already been set in motion. Then they discussed their strategy for the meeting with the director of Leine's former agency. Leine was surprised that Tsarev hadn't attempted to impede Sakharov's flight to DC, and mentioned as much.

Sakharov had shrugged. "As far as anyone knows, I am still at the villa with my family."

"Which explains why we're on a chartered flight and not the corporate jet." She assumed that Sakharov had chartered the flight under another name, and had either bribed customs officials or used a fake passport to leave the country undetected. Old habits died hard—Leine used a second passport with a different identity that she'd brought along as backup in case Eve Mason was compromised. She also carried one identifying her as Madeleine Basso but couldn't use it, since the general had identified her.

Art had made contact with April earlier that morning, and he and his men had taken her and her security contingent to an out-of-the-way, well-fortified cabin by a lake in Upstate New York. They would remain there until Leine contacted them that it was safe to return. Part of her was relieved that her daughter was safe, and part of her yearned to be with her in case anything happened.

An hour before the meeting with Henderson, Leine, Sakharov, and three members of Sakharov's security detail left from the airfield in a rented SUV. It was the height of the evening rush hour. Gridlocked drivers honked with futility, urging the massive backup to flow freely for once so they might actually make it home for pre-dinner drinks.

She checked the time. 6:10. Twenty minutes until the meeting. Henderson had given her an address belonging to an office building on the outskirts of Georgetown. Sakharov sat across from her, scanning documents in a file folder marked with the Sakharov Industries logo. She stared out the window at the light drizzle that had begun to fall. Neither spoke.

They arrived at the office building at 6:32. Highly reflective glass panels mirrored the shaded windows of the GMC Yukon as they pulled to the curb. The cold drizzle had turned to a cool mist, shrouding the upper floors of the building in a vaporous haze. With Sakharov's security hovering nearby, they exited the vehicle and walked to the front door. Two CCTV cameras noted their approach.

The lock made a snicking sound and the door opened, revealing a tall, heavyset man dressed in the dark-suited uniform of Henderson's security detail. He stepped aside as Leine and Sakharov walked past him into the foyer but raised his arm, barring Sakharov's men from entering. "Just you and Mr. Sakharov," he added, nodding at the bodyguards. "They stay outside."

"Go," Sakharov said, waving off his security. After a brief pause, the two men stepped back and the door closed.

Gleaming marble floors and glossy stone walls with no identifying characteristics marked the unexceptional entrance. A bank of elevators could be seen down a hallway to the right. Two more identically dressed, expressionless security agents—a woman with her hair swept back in a bun, the other a wiry, dark-haired man—stood to one side, hands clasped in front of them.

"Identification," said the first agent, his voice a monotone.

They both handed over their authentic passports. Henderson's man glanced at them and said something into his wrist mic before handing Leine's back.

"May I have my passport?" Sakharov asked.

"In a moment," the man replied. He motioned to the other agents, who stepped forward and verified that Leine and Sakharov weren't armed. Leine allowed the female agent to search her bag. Finding nothing but her phone, wallet, and a few other items, she returned it to her and then stepped back. The first agent muttered into his mic.

Moments later, Scott Henderson walked out to greet them. A tall, athletic man in his early fifties, Henderson's once sandy blond hair was now streaked with gray, and crow's feet etched the skin around his piercing blue eyes.

A deep crease between his brows gave him a perpetually fierce expression. The longtime director of the secretive agency looked as though life had dealt him a winning hand, but that it was a hell of a lot of work to keep on winning.

He lifted his chin in acknowledgement. "Leine."

"Scott," Leine replied.

Henderson glanced at the Russian billionaire's passport and nodded at the two agents, who walked over and seized him by the arms. Disbelief obvious on his face, Sakharov struggled against them.

"Anatoly Sakharov," Henderson said. "You are under arrest for colluding with the Russian Federation in an act of war against the United States."

Sakharov continued to resist the agents, disbelief obvious on his face. "You have no right to arrest me. What proof do you have?"

Alarmed, Leine looked from Henderson to Sakharov back to Henderson.

"What are you doing?" she demanded, taking a step toward Sakharov. "We came here in good faith with information vital to national security."

Henderson eyed her coolly. "National security is the reason he's being detained. Now step away and let my people do their job." He then addressed Sakharov, now in handcuffs. "I've received verifiable information that you knowingly diverted weapons to Izz Al-Din in an attempt to subvert our allies in Libya, and that you also supplied the materials used in the attack in Las Vegas."

"Wait." Leine stared at Henderson. "What attack?"

"Someone released a drone carrying sarin gas in a busy casino on the Strip. Dozens are dead, with hundreds more injured. The CIA received credible intel linking your friend and Izz Al-Din to the attack, and passed it along to me."

"Why have we not heard of this so-called attack?" Sakharov asked, ceasing his struggle against the agents' grip.

Henderson replied, "It happened at six twenty-five, EST. Look on your phone." He nodded at Leine. She pulled out her mobile and checked. He was right—the story was breaking everywhere.

He continued. "We hoped to avoid mass hysteria by attempting to keep the attack off the major news channels until we had more information. Unfortunately, live video and eye-witness accounts have blown up on social media, making the idea a non-starter. The news agencies that agreed to hold their stories are scrambling to put out the information."

"Your information is wrong," Sakharov declared. "I have no dealings with Izz Al-Din. This is the reason I have come to this meeting, so that this deception will be put to rest. If I initiated a terrorist act against the United States, why would I be here?"

"Why indeed?" Henderson answered. "Unless it's to prove that you're innocent when you're not. You're traveling under an assumed name. That in itself is suspicious."

Sakharov nodded at the passport in Henderson's hands. "That is my actual identification. Does it not say Anatoly Sakharov?"

"You've got it all wrong, Scott," Leine interjected, her alarm increasing. "Where did the CIA get the information?"

"That's classified."

"Bullshit. He has a right to know who's making the accusation."

Henderson shook his head. "You know as well as I do what rights are afforded an enemy of the State."

"An enemy of the State?" Sakharov's face flushed red with anger. "You don't know what you're talking about. I am a Russian citizen who has traveled here to provide information that directly affects your national security."

Henderson ignored his protests and nodded to the two agents holding him. "Get him out of here."

The security agents walked him toward the emergency exit. Before they reached the door, Sakharov twisted around to look at Leine. "*Call my wife.*"

The agents marched him through the exit into the stairwell, his declarations of innocence fading as the door swung closed. Leine turned on Henderson, her face inches from his. "You have to stop this, Scott. Sakharov is innocent—"

The first agent drew his weapon and yelled, "Hands on your head, now! Step away from the director."

Leine closed her eyes in frustration as she raised her hands, clasped them behind her neck, and took two steps back.

"It's all right, Danny," Henderson assured the security agent. "Leine and I go way back. She wouldn't do anything stupid," he added, giving her a meaningful look.

After a moment's hesitation, Danny stood down and holstered his weapon.

"Where are you taking him?" Leine demanded.

Henderson ignored her and turned to the security agent. "Show Ms. Basso out, will you?"

"Scott. Listen to me. Your intel is flawed."

"I need proof, Leine."

She held her purse out toward Danny. "There are photographs on my phone related to the diverted shipment."

Danny glanced at Henderson, who shook his head. "Who's the source?"

"Sakharov's son, Mikhail."

Henderson crossed his arms. "And you expect me to believe information from an arms dealer's son over intel from the Central Intelligence Agency?"

She pushed the bag toward him. "Look at the images, then hear me out. His son was embedded with Izz Al-Din and was going to warn his father about what happened to the shipment. It's why I went to such lengths to bring Sakharov to the meeting."

"There's more to the story than the diverted shipment."

"I realize that. But I'm confident Sakharov isn't behind the sarin attack."

"It's not just him, Leine."

"What do you mean?"

"We've picked up chatter implicating the Kremlin."

The Kremlin?

If what Henderson said was true, then that changed everything. Leine's mind whirled with the implications. What if General Tsarev wasn't the main architect of the deception? Were the Russian president and prime minister aware of the diverted shipment? Had they planned the sarin attack in a bid to support Izz Al-Din's fatwa against the US?

To what end?

The answer was obvious. The general's every move had been designed to weaken the United States and ultimately lure her into an unwinnable war against a country she'd finally begun to treat as an ally: Russia.

Had Sakharov played her? A chill spiraled down her back.

Henderson checked his watch. "Time's up. I have to attend a briefing with the vice president in two hours and I need time to prepare." He gestured to Danny. "Show Ms. Basso out."

"Scott. Listen to me," Leine pleaded, but Henderson had already turned his back and walked away.

Instead of letting her leave by the front door, Danny took her through the emergency exit and down a flight of stairs, where she found herself in an underground parking garage. A black sedan idled nearby.

"Tanya will take you back to your hotel." Danny nodded at the driver of the sedan.

"What about Sakharov's men?" Leine asked.

"We've already taken care of that."

CHAPTER 38

Leine checked the "tell" she'd attached to her door to make sure it was still intact. The almost invisible strand of hair was where she'd left it, indicating the door hadn't been opened since she'd left that afternoon for the meeting with Henderson. Satisfied that no one had been inside, she swiped her key card and entered her room.

She set her bag down on the bed and turned on the television for updates on the Vegas attack. Over one hundred hotel guests inside the casino at the time had died or were dying. One camera panned the elegantly carpeted floor of a hotel conference room, displaying a makeshift morgue with dozens of bodies covered in white sheets. Another camera showed the gruesome effects of the nerve agent in people who had been exposed but were still alive—massive secretions from the mouth and eyes, vomiting, paralysis, convulsions. Muting the volume, she rummaged in her bag for her mobile and called the burner phone that Sakharov set up before the trip. She didn't relish the impending conversation.

"Katarina, it's Leine. Did I wake you?"

"How can I sleep? Have you seen the news? Someone released sarin gas at a casino in Las Vegas."

"Yes, I know. That's partly why I called."

There was a pause. "How did the meeting go?" she asked. Trepidation had crept into her voice.

"Not as planned." *That was an understatement*, Leine thought.

"Is Anatoly with you? I tried his mobile but he didn't answer."

"I'm afraid Anatoly has been detained."

"He—what? What are you talking about?"

"Henderson had him arrested."

"On what grounds?"

"They think he's responsible for the Vegas attack, among other things."

Katarina didn't reply for a moment as the realization sunk in. "Oh, my God. But he had nothing to do with it!"

"I realize that. I need something—anything—that can prove your husband's innocence. Do you have access to his contact list?"

"Wait," she said, hope lacing her voice. "Anatoly asked me to send a file to you in case something went wrong." There was the sound of tapping on a keyboard. "I just sent it to you. The file has several pictures of a park in Moscow, so I'm not sure why they'll help, but he wouldn't have asked me to send them to you if they weren't important in some way."

"Do you know if the file was encrypted?"

"It is. He said you'd have the key."

"Good. Hold on while I take a look." Leine checked the throwaway email account she'd set up for communication between her and the Russian arms dealer and found the file.

"Got it." Leine entered the encryption key they'd agreed upon during Olga's rescue operation and clicked on the file. Inside were three jpegs—all seemingly innocuous scenes of Gorky Park.

"Looks like I need to run these through some software. Let me call you back."

Leine ended the call and loaded the photographs into the steganography software that she'd used for the pictures on Mikhail's flash drive. She stared at the results.

Bingo.

The quality of the three photos suggested surveillance images taken with a long lens. The first photograph showed General Tsarev on a tarmac next to a cargo plane, being greeted by a man Leine didn't recognize. The mystery man was several inches taller than the general. He had black, curly hair, and wore a pair of dark sunglasses, making identification difficult. Behind him, the plane's open cargo hold revealed several stacked containers with what appeared to be Cyrillic writing on them. The depth of field was such that it blurred the background, making it hard to read, and Leine enlarged the picture. She squinted, trying to bring the Russian letters into focus.

Explosives. Handle with Care.

In the second picture, the two men were smiling and shaking hands over a briefcase filled with euros. The mystery man had taken off his sunglasses, revealing a small scar above his left eye. The third photograph showed the general walking toward a black Mercedes Benz sedan, the briefcase in his hand.

She quickly downloaded all three onto her phone and sent the picture of the mystery man to Lou with a note to run it through facial recognition files. Checking the time, she picked up her bag from the bed and hit redial on her phone.

"Leine—all of Anatoly's American assets have been frozen. I can't access anything." Katarina sounded as though she was on the verge of panicking.

"Don't worry. We'll figure this out. I promise."

"Were the files helpful?"

"Very. I'm on my way to find Henderson. I'll explain everything later. Don't worry." *And don't do anything rash,* Leine thought.

Leine took the elevator down to the lobby and walked out the front doors. At two separate points, two unremarkable looking men wearing dark suits glanced at her as she passed by, but looked away, as if disinterested.

If she were a betting woman, she'd bet the general had taken the bait.

"Pull over here," Leine urged the taxi driver. She checked her watch. She hoped she wasn't too late. It had taken a fair bit of maneuvering, but she was confident she'd shaken whatever surveillance the general may have put on her. The driver pulled to the curb near the entrance of the underground parking garage of the mirrored building where she and Sakharov had met with Henderson. She paid in cash, exited the vehicle, and sprinted down the ramp. Ten yards from the entrance to the stairwell, the door opened and three people emerged, heading toward a waiting SUV.

Henderson and his security team. Relief swept through her. She'd made it in time.

"Scott," Leine called. Henderson turned to see who had said his name. The agents both reached for their guns and she slowed her pace, trying not to spook them. One was Danny. She didn't recognize the other agent.

The director frowned and murmured something to Danny before continuing to the SUV. The driver got out and opened the back door.

"Wait. Scott. Hear me out."

Ignoring her, Henderson placed his briefcase on the back seat and climbed in beside it. The three agents formed an impenetrable wall around him.

"You said you wanted proof."

Henderson hesitated, his hand on the door. He waved the agents away, creating an opening.

Leine held her phone so he could see the photograph of the general and the mystery man shaking hands. "Who is the man with General Tsarev?"

Henderson squinted at the image. After a moment he held out his hand for the phone.

Leine gave it to him. "There's more."

Pausing at each, he flipped through the next two photographs. Then he handed the phone back.

"Get in."

CHAPTER 39

Leine glanced at the news on their way to Henderson's meeting with the vice president. Reports were ominous. Reacting to the attack in Las Vegas, the US had deployed two of its nuclear submarines to the Bering Strait. The Russians responded with two of their own and tensions were running high. International headlines screamed, *United States in Nuclear Showdown with Russia!*

Tsarev's end game had become all too clear. Dmitry's cryptic reference to the war made sense now. Did Russia's leaders believe the US to be so weakened from committing its forces abroad that she wouldn't have the strength to win against Russia?

A dangerous game had been set in motion and the outcome wasn't assured. A nuclear exchange was a distinct possibility.

Henderson's SUV turned into the side entrance of the Eisenhower Executive Building and cleared security, then passed through the black metal gate to the inner parking lot. Henderson, Leine, and the two agents exited the vehicle and headed to the office of the vice president.

The Victorian-era sage-green and buff walls harkened back to another time in the political history of the United States, as did the delicate mahogany, maple, and cherry floor. Two black marble fireplaces stood at each end of the room, and several ornate chandeliers hung from the painted ceiling. In the center of the room stood an oval table that could easily seat a dozen.

Leine and Henderson entered through an arched doorway. Vice President Lawrence looked up from his desk at their arrival, a sheaf of papers in his hand. Secretary of State Eileen Miller stood next to him, her hand resting on the back of Lawrence's chair.

"Have a seat," Lawrence said, indicating an overstuffed settee across from two black leather armchairs. He rose from his desk and joined them, choosing one of the chairs. Secretary Miller took the other.

Vice President Lawrence looked as though he'd been through hell and back: with his sleeves rolled up to his elbows, his white button-down shirt was open at the neck, and his tie and suitcoat were nowhere to be seen. The dark bags under his eyes were a testament to the stress he was under. Secretary Miller was all business, dressed in a crisp burgundy suit and tasteful gold earrings. Her expression was grim.

"I understand you have information pertaining to recent actions taken by our Russian counterparts," Lawrence said to Leine.

"I do," she replied. "Information, that when taken as a whole will implicate General Tsarev and exonerate Anatoly Sakharov."

Miller raised an eyebrow. "I'm sure you can understand our skepticism."

"I can. But hear me out." It was make or break time. Leine pushed aside her reservations about Sakharov's true motives and continued. "Both Sakharov and Tsarev have the ear of the Russian prime minister, and both have much to gain from instigating a war with the US. As an arms dealer, a war would be quite lucrative for Sakharov. But I'd like to put forth another theory."

"And that is?"

"That Tsarev is interested in changing the course of Russian-US relations. That he objects to the cooperation between our two countries and that he wishes to restore his homeland to its former glory."

"Go on," Lawrence said.

"I have files that when taken in context can be seen as strengthening that theory." She pulled out her phone and brought up the files containing the photographs from Mikhail's flash drive. "The source who gave me the first set of files came by them through Anatoly Sakharov's son."

While Secretary ·Miller looked on, Vice President Lawrence clicked through the files, pausing occasionally to ask pertinent questions about what he was seeing. When he'd reviewed everything including the videos, he leaned back, a pensive look on his face.

"Blackwell won't believe this is a play by the general," Lawrence said. "The evidence you've shown me still points to Anatoly Sakharov."

She leaned forward and locked gazes with the vice president. "Of course it does. Which is exactly what Tsarev wants. I have one more set of photographs to show you."

Leine opened the file containing the photos of the general and the mystery man. Henderson had identified him as Omar Tafiq—a commander for Izz Al-Din. Just then, her phone vibrated and an alert displayed on her screen telling her she had a reply from Lou.

She scanned the message before clicking back to the picture. She handed Lawrence her phone and said, "As you can see, the man on the left is Tsarev. The identity of the other man in the photograph has been confirmed by two separate sources as Omar Tafiq, a high-ranking leader for Izz Al-Din."

Lawrence frowned at the photograph. "The CIA tells me they picked up chatter implicating the Kremlin in the Vegas attack. The way it looks, both the Russian president and the prime minister are in league with Sakharov."

"I'm not so sure," Leine said.

Henderson shot her a warning glance.

"Right now," she continued, "the only thing I am sure of is that General Tsarev supplied arms to Tafiq. If Tsarev was looking for someone to take the fall for arming the terrorists, why not use Sakharov? The general already tried to blackmail him into delivering more shipments by abducting his daughter."

"And you have proof of this?" Secretary Miller asked.

"I was part of the rescue operation."

"Misdirection," Henderson interjected. "One of the general's favorite tactics."

Leine nodded. "Exactly. If the general didn't agree with the new Russian leadership on how they were running the country and wanted to start a war with the US to change course, it wouldn't take much for him to push a rumor indicating Russia's involvement in the sarin attack."

"Scott?" Lawrence looked at Henderson. "What's your take on this?"

"She has a point. We need to vet the source of the rumors. Have you been able to talk to Prime Minister Fedorov?"

Lawrence shook his head in frustration. "The Kremlin cut off diplomatic relations two hours ago. Our direct line has been disconnected, and they recalled their ambassador. Blackwell is convinced that President Ivanov has been lying all along, and refuses to listen to reason."

"Give me twenty-four hours," Leine urged. "I recently floated the idea to an associate of the general's that I've got information vital to his current operation and am willing to part with it—for a price. If what Sakharov told me about the general is true, he'll do anything to get that information. I'm convinced one of his operatives will make an approach soon. I believe he already has my hotel under surveillance. If I can get confirmation that Tsarev's the driving force in this massive deception, that he's been playing the president and the prime minister as well as Sakharov, will you take the information to President Blackwell?"

Miller narrowed her gaze and asked, "You'll wear a wire?"

She shook her head. "That's the first thing they'll look for. Put me under surveillance. Then, once Tsarev's people make contact, you can eavesdrop using whatever method you guys have perfected since the last time I worked for you."

"What's in it for you?"

Leine looked at him in disbelief. "You have to ask? How about avoiding a nuclear exchange, for starters?"

The Vice President nodded. "Just checking. Apparently you're still a patriot." He rose from his chair, his expression grave. "You've got twenty-four hours."

CHAPTER 40

Leine sat at the hotel lobby bar, nursing a drink. Several tables were occupied, some of which no doubt hosted Henderson's surveillance teams. The couple over by the fireplace, perhaps. Maybe the three guys dressed in business suits four stools down, bitching about work. There were enough patrons for more than a few agents to hide in plain sight.

She didn't allow their presence to lull her into a false sense of security. So much could go wrong. Tsarev may have decided not to make an approach, believing the risk of what she knew was more acceptable than the risk of making contact. Or perhaps he was waiting to see what she'd do, whether she'd tip her hand by acknowledging someone in the bar, giving him the heads-up that a surveillance team had been put in place.

Another possibility was that he'd decided she didn't have additional information—that she'd used the bluff to buy herself more time. Dmitry had intended to torture her. Most people would try anything to avoid being tortured. The general wouldn't risk getting caught if that were the case.

Worst case scenario: he realized she was luring him into a trap. She'd need to counter his moves if he tried to eliminate Henderson's operatives. She adjusted the silver comb she'd used to put her hair up. It was the one she'd purchased at the leather shop in Athens when she picked up the semiauto before the gala. At least she had access to a weapon, although the blade's effectiveness against someone with a semiautomatic was questionable. The comb was more of an "up close and personal" remedy. She doubted she'd get close enough to Tsarev to slice through his jugular.

If he'd even taken the bait.

She checked her watch. 10:47. She'd been there since nine thirty, passing the time in conversation with one of the three men who had hit on her. He was cute in a lost puppy sort of way and at first was interesting to talk to, but the guy turned out to be married. Leine called bullshit on the sob story he used to try to play her and told him to go home to his wife. She felt sorry for the woman who had to put up with him, and was even more grateful than usual for not having to play the dating game.

Henderson wanted her to remain at the bar until eleven, and then take the elevator to her room. He'd wired her phone and had tapped into hotel surveillance cameras in case Tsarev made his move outside the bar. Henderson had incorporated a small recording device with an on/off button in the belt buckle she now wore, allowing her to control the transmitter when the general's men did a sweep. There was also a built-in homing beacon she was to activate as soon as she had confirmation of the general's involvement. Leine didn't plan on using either unless she was absolutely sure it was safe to do so. If the general had his people continually monitor for tracking devices and bugs and she turned it on they'd know she was wired.

She swallowed the rest of her drink, left a tip for the bartender, and picked up her purse. When she turned to leave, the married guy appeared at her elbow.

"What part of 'go home to your wife' do you not understand?" she asked, mildly annoyed. The man smiled and tightened his grip on her arm.

Keeping his voice low, he said, "Come with me. The general would like to see you."

She let him lead her through the lobby and out the front doors into a waiting sedan. He dumped her purse on the seat between them and looked through the items. Picking up her phone, he opened the back and removed the SIM card and the battery. Then he reached under the seat in front of him and dragged out a black metal case, which he opened to reveal a bug detector.

"Shoes."

Leine took off her pumps and handed both to him. He turned on the unit and waved the attached wand over them before handing them back.

"Watch."

Leine gave him her watch. He waved the wand over it, then took out a small screwdriver, which he used to open the back. Not finding anything suspect inside, he returned it to her.

"Belt."

Leine unbuckled her belt, slid it off, and handed it to him.

Frowning at the monitor, he ran the wand over and around the buckle several times. Had he detected something? Henderson had assured her that the device transmitted no signal when it was turned off. He held the belt up to look more closely at the buckle, then set it down beside him as he fiddled with the controls on the detector. Apparently the unit began to respond properly, because he waved the wand over the buckle again. This time, he gave the accessory back to her. Leine exhaled quietly and slid the belt back on.

He then tested the other items from her purse that were on the seat, and ran the wand over her. Satisfied she wasn't wired, he turned off the equipment and stowed it under the seat. Then he shoved the contents of her purse back inside, and handed it over the seatback to the man in front.

The driver executed several moves designed to lose anyone tailing the sedan. Leine wasn't worried. Henderson's agents wouldn't have any trouble following her. In addition to the teams on the ground, Henderson was using a surveillance drone. Even if his people lost her, they'd still be able to track the sedan. She decided to take a chance on the wire and get things rolling. When her captor's attention was diverted by something the driver said, she pressed the tiny concealed button, turning the recorder on.

"Where are you taking me?" she asked.

"I already told you—to the general."

"Yes, but where? I would have preferred somewhere out in the open."

He shook his head. "The general is not here for your convenience. You told Dmitry you wanted to trade information for money. We have been sent to find out if that information is credible."

Leine acted alarmed. "I told Dmitry that I would only speak to the general. If I don't check in with my contact every hour, they will release the information and compromise the general's operation." She emphasized the last point. "It's in his best interests to meet with me. I'm willing to give him this information for a price. If he wants his grand plan to work, then he needs to deal."

The man scowled as he pulled out his phone and tapped in a number. "*Da*," he said into the mobile. "She will only speak with you," he continued in Russian. "She says if she is not allowed to check in with her contact every hour the information will be released." He waited, listening. "Understood." He ended the call and slipped the phone into his pocket. He took a deep breath in through his nose and exhaled forcefully.

"He will meet with you."

CHAPTER 41

Rural Virginia, United States

They drove out of DC and into the quiet Virginia countryside. Few lights dotted the landscape. The tranquil surroundings of the large horse farms and estates were in extreme contrast to the glare and manic pace of Washington. The bucolic region allowed people of means a stress-free environment in which to escape the daily grind.

Miles from the nearest residence, the sedan pulled into a manicured driveway and stopped at a massive, gold-plated gate. The driver rolled his window down and turned toward the camera. There was a few-second delay before the gate opened. They continued down the long, well-lit gravel drive, coming to a stop outside a traditional white, two-story colonial with black shutters. Massive columns stood sentry along the wide veranda, giving the well-preserved mansion a stately, old-world air.

The gold-plated gate seemed more in keeping with a Russian general's style, although that was just conjecture on Leine's part. The four of them exited the sedan, and they walked in through the front door. An elegant mahogany staircase swept up in two graceful curves from the main foyer to be joined at the second level by a carved handrail. Antique furniture and a large oval rug graced the foyer, while Civil War-era paintings of long-dead residents lined the walls.

Definitely not the preferred style of any Russian general she'd ever met. Perhaps she'd underestimated Tsarev.

"Ah. The elusive Leine Basso." General Tsarev appeared at the head of the stairs on Leine's left and started down to meet her. He wore a crisp, navy blue tailored suit and blood-red tie, the ensemble accentuated by a pair of gold cufflinks and a pinkie ring. His thinning brown hair had been combed back to reveal a high forehead, broad cheekbones, and thick lips undercut by a substantial set of jowls.

"General," Leine shook his outstretched hand. His grip was firm and dry, his gaze cold and calculating.

Tsarev stepped back and indicated a room to her left. "Shall we?"

"I need to check in with my associate first. One of your men has my phone and SIM card. May I have them back?"

"Of course." Tsarev turned to the man who had picked her up in the hotel bar. "Do you have Ms. Basso's phone?" He nodded and fished in his pocket before handing the phone, the battery, and the card back to Leine.

"Thank you." She replaced the battery and inserted the card before texting a short message to a burner phone Henderson had set up. Then she handed the phone back to him.

The general followed her through the open doorway into a formal study and closed the double doors behind him. More antiques filled the room, with a massive mahogany desk as the centerpiece. The hardwood floor had been polished to a high sheen and there wasn't a speck of dust visible.

He studied her with an appraising stare. "I will say your comments to Dmitry were somewhat alarming. That you have information you are willing to sell to me, possibly to the detriment of your country, tells me that you are a woman with few principles."

"That's where you are wrong, General." Leine sat in a nearby wingback chair and gave him a direct look. "I am highly principled. I disagree with my government and would like to see things change. Apparently, you and I share a kindred vision."

General Tsarev's face betrayed no emotion although it looked like his respiration had increased. His florid complexion grew subtly redder as he moved to the chair across from her.

"Then why require payment? Isn't the possibility of a new world order enough?"

Leine gave him a slow smile. "Really, General. You must know I'm nothing if not pragmatic. Money buys a lot of patriotism."

The general smiled back. "How do I know this isn't a trap?"

"You don't. But as I said, I'm pragmatic. Surely your sources uncovered that personality trait. I sold Sakharov information he'd find useful—photographs of his diverted shipments, for instance." She leaned back against the chair and smiled again. "The rest is only of interest to someone with your ambitions. Or the Central Intelligence Agency. It's really your call, General."

Tsarev studied her in silence, his expression revealing only bland interest. Leine kept her own expression neutral so she wouldn't betray the thoughts running through her mind. Did he believe her, or had he caught on to the ruse? The recording device in her belt was still on, but the general hadn't yet implicated himself in anything. She was wary of prompting him. Anyone who had risen as high in Russian intelligence as he had would know when he was being played.

"And what of this covert operation you mentioned to my associate?"

Leine smiled. "An added incentive. I want you to get your money's worth. Happy customers and all that."

Tsarev frowned at her joke. "If you are so interested in change, why did you help to rescue Anatoly Sakharov's daughter? Surely you must have understood whoever instigated the abduction did so in order to further his or her plans."

Leine shrugged. "The money was good. And, if you look at the bigger picture, which I'm sure you have, you'll realize I was merely playing my part. In the beginning Sakharov didn't trust me. Now he does. I have no doubt his trust will serve me well in the future."

He leaned back in his chair. "But now he does not trust me."

"Exactly."

Tsarev narrowed his eyes. "You mean this was your plan all along?"

"General Tsarev, if I may speak plainly?"

The general nodded. "Of course."

She continued. "I'm an analyst for the CIA. The money's laughable when you consider the information that comes across my desk every day. You are a very rich man, as is Sakharov. I decided that if I could get him to trust me that I might ultimately be able to work out a business relationship with you, too. I didn't plan to make the two of you enemies. It just happened that way." Leine crossed her legs. "I see the writing on the wall. Although still relatively strong, the United States military is stretched thin, while Russia is becoming a much more valuable player on the world stage. And, with current US leadership more interested in policing the world than securing her borders, my country is dealing with significant unrest from within."

General Tsarev's expression still gave nothing away.

She leaned forward in her chair for emphasis. "The world is at a pivotal point, General. With a little trust I believe that you and I can share what I would consider a very lucrative relationship, and at the same time shift the balance of the world's power to Russia, a country better positioned to lead."

"And you're willing to betray your country to help bring this about?"

"You can't betray something you don't believe in."

Tsarev rose from his chair. "I'll let you know my decision within two days."

"Sorry, General. Once I walk out of this room, the offer no longer stands." She stood so she could look him in the eye. "This is a once in a lifetime deal. I advise you to take it. There are several other entities that would be quite interested in what I have to offer."

General Tsarev considered her for a long moment. Had she overplayed her hand? She couldn't tell by his expression. Leine searched his eyes for an indication of which way he was going to swing.

He inhaled deeply and let it go, and sat back down in his chair. "I'm interested."

She did the same, using the movement to cover her relief. "Good. How would you like to do this?"

"First, I must know what information you have."

"I can tell you it involves the sarin gas attack in Las Vegas."

"Oh? But I thought you knew. It's been determined that Anatoly Sakharov is responsible."

It was make or break time. Again, she had to go with her gut regarding Sakharov. If he was in league with the general, then Leine's ruse would be obvious. That could only end with one result, and it didn't involve letting her live.

"You must think I'm a fool." Leine shook her head. "Really, General. Why must we dance around each other like this? If we're to be business partners, I prefer direct communication. Anatoly Sakharov was not in any way responsible for the attack. That, my friend, was all your doing. I must say the operation went off flawlessly. I'm quite impressed with how you were able to play our agents so well. Obviously, your reputation is no myth."

Tsarev studied her for a long moment. Then something shifted in his eyes. "Forgive the ruse. I had to be certain of your veracity. The false intelligence was the easy part."

Leine's heart beat faster. He'd just implicated himself in creating misinformation about the attack. She'd been correct in her assumption—flattery tended to be a fatal flaw in many a powerful man's armor. But the implication wouldn't be enough. The man was Russian intelligence. He created lies in his sleep. She had to get something more, something that would convince President Blackwell that he was behind everything.

"How did you convince the prime minister and the president to sever communication with Washington? The two countries had been working well together."

Tsarev shrugged. "It took very little on my part. Do you really think decades of mistrust and betrayal is easy to forget? A whisper in the right ear was all that was needed."

Almost there. She nodded, a smile forming on her lips. "Shall we talk money, then?"

"Of course. Tell me what else you know and I will determine its worth."

"Earlier today the CIA initiated a covert operation that will undermine your plans unless it's stopped."

"To which plan are you referring?"

Leine gave him a thin smile. "The one you've orchestrated to destroy the US, placing Russia as the world's only super power."

Tsarev narrowed his eyes. "Tell me about this covert operation."

"Not until we agree to terms."

The general sighed impatiently. "Fine. If what you say is true, then it is worth a considerable amount to me. At least several hundred thousand."

Bingo. Leine shook her head and shifted in her chair, at the same time surreptitiously activating the homing beacon in the buckle. Henderson's team would be there in minutes.

"More like several million," she answered.

Tsarev's face flushed dark red. "Several *million*? I don't think—" The general was interrupted by a knock at the door. "Yes?" he answered irritably.

The door opened and the man from the bar strode into the room and over to where Tsarev was sitting. He leaned down and whispered in his ear. Tsarev's gaze snapped to Leine's.

Shit. He knew. Leine's mind raced to understand what had just happened. There was no way Tsarev's security guards had detected Henderson's team so soon. Unless...

The homing beacon. The device emitted a strong signal, one that could be picked up not only by Henderson's crew, but by sensitive Russian surveillance equipment.

Leine pulled out the comb in her hair and leaped forward, aiming for the security guard's throat. The knife-like blades sliced deep into his carotid artery. Blood spurted everywhere as his heart pumped harder, trying to keep his body alive. The general shouted for his guards, his hand reaching underneath his suit jacket.

As if in slow motion, Leine sidestepped the dying guard and retrieved his gun as he collapsed to the floor, then dove behind the massive desk as rounds from the general's semiauto splintered the wood. The door to the study slammed open. Leine rolled to one end of the desk and fired at the general's incoming gunmen. There were three of them. She shot two and ducked back behind the desk.

Someone yelled for the general to come with him. Seconds later, automatic gunfire erupted as someone sprayed the desk with multiple rounds. Leine dropped low, making herself a smaller target, hoping the desk would be enough to stop the bullets. She checked the magazine in the bar man's gun. Four rounds left.

A click told Leine the gunman had run out of ammo and was about to change magazines. Leine rolled to the center of the desk, aimed at the man with the submachine gun through the opening, and fired. The bullet carved a hole in his forehead and his head snapped backward. Two other men had taken cover behind the wingback chairs. Leine fired twice, aiming for the center of each chair, then dropped back behind the desk. One round left.

She'd have to make it count.

Shouts erupted outside the window. Moments later, the front door thudded open followed by shouts and the sound of feet pounding the floorboards. Leine chanced a look around the desk. Guns drawn, dozens of Henderson's people swarmed the foyer and study.

Leine left the gun where it lay and raised her hands as she slowly rose to a standing position.

All agents in the room drew on her. It was quite an experience to be on the other end for once.

"Put your hands behind your head!" barked one of Henderson's people.

"I'm Leine Basso and I'm unarmed," she said and quickly complied.

Just then, another agent walked into the room. He was one of the three suits who had been at the hotel bar. "Stand down, Pennington. She's one of us."

Agent Pennington lowered her weapon and relaxed. Leine exhaled in relief and leaned against the desk. The adrenaline had begun to recede, leaving her shaky.

"Did you get Tsarev?" she asked.

The agent in the business suit shook his head. "Henderson said he was low priority. The general managed to get to his helicopter before we showed up." He surveyed the bullet holes in the desk and the dead gunmen. "Mind if I ask what happened? Looks like a war zone in here. I doubt Tsarev's people knew we were coming that much in advance."

"The homing beacon set off a warning somewhere in the house when I activated it."

"And it blew your cover," the agent said.

Leine nodded. "But I got what we needed."

CHAPTER 42

Moscow, Russia - One week later

General Tsarov sipped the after-dinner liqueur as Pearl prattled on about her shopping trip to Singapore. They'd just made love and were relaxing in the bedroom of the apartment. Tsarev leaned against the voluminous stack of pillows on the satin sheets Pearl insisted he buy.

It had taken quite a bit of cunning to sidestep the questions raised by President Ivanov regarding his part in events leading to the breakdown in relations between Russia and the United States. Having the prime minister in his back pocket had certainly worked in his favor. Fedorov had argued tirelessly in the general's favor, trying to convince the president that Tsarev should be considered a hero. That he had rooted out the misinformation leading the two nuclear countries to the brink of war.

Apparently, Ivanov bought his argument. In a meeting just that morning, the president had commended his actions and hinted at more accolades to come. Tsarev would have to be satisfied with the direction his country was headed. For now. Already, his mind raced with ideas, ideas that would steer Russia to greatness. It would just take time. And planning.

So much planning.

With a sigh, Tsarev polished off his drink, leaned his head back, and closed his eyes. The Basso woman had played him. He'd let his pride and her guile ruin his grand scheme. He wasn't angry. As his mother always told him, anger rarely helped a situation. Basso had only done what she deemed best for her country. A grudging admiration for her had taken hold of him. He'd like to turn her, have her work for him, but doubted that would ever come to pass. The only weakness he'd found to exploit was her daughter. Unfortunately, Dmitry had been unable to locate the girl.

Something told him that course of action would be unwise.

No, her daughter would live. It was Leine Basso herself who had to be eliminated. He checked the time on his phone—his meeting with Salome was in one hour. He'd debrief her and then offer her the assignment. He was quite certain she'd relish the thought of taking out a CIA operative. Especially the one who had rendered her work in the general's grand scheme ineffective.

Dmitry was still out of service because of his injury. If Tsarev was honest with himself, the man was a much less effective assassin than Salome, although he had tracked down the Libyan munitions clerk at the squalid apartment he and his gay lover were renting in Paris. Dmitry killed both at no additional charge, so there was that aspect to consider. Even so, Tsarev had played with the idea of taking him off his roster. There was still time to make that determination.

Someone knocked at the bedroom door. Annoyed at the interruption he called out, "What is it?"

The door opened and a dark, hooded figure slipped into the room. Tsarev struggled to a sitting position. His security guards should have stopped whoever it was at the door. The figure paused and slid off the hood. Tsarev's breath caught. He instantly recognized the woman's olive skin tone and dark, flashing eyes.

"Salome. What—why are you here?" Frowning, he grabbed his robe from the end of the bed and stood. Pearl had finally stopped talking and turned to look at their guest.

"Hello, Roman." The ghost of a smile graced Salome's full lips.

"Who is *she*?" Pearl's eyes flashed with anger.

"Nothing to worry about, my pet. Only a colleague." Tsarev approached the dark-haired assassin. "Did you forget? Our meeting is not for another hour." His mind raced. *How did she find the apartment?*

Salome arched an eyebrow. "Forget? No. I was in the neighborhood on assignment and thought I should stop by."

"Oh? Are you freelancing, now?" he asked, drawing closer. Where the hell was Georg and the rest of his security team? Close enough now to see behind her through the gap in the door, two of his bodyguards were visible. One sprawled on the floor next to the ornate glass and metal coffee table, a dark hole above his right eye. The other had fallen face first over the arm of the divan. Tsarev felt the blood drain from his face as his gaze darted to hers. His mind dulled, unable to process what was happening. Salome studied his face, her expression calm, and raised the suppressed pistol in her hand.

"Please," he whispered. "I'll pay more. Much more." When the assassin didn't respond, he croaked, "Who sent you?"

"An old friend," Salome replied, and fired two rounds point-blank into the general's forehead.

CHAPTER 43

Washington, DC

The day dawned crisp and clear, and the sun shone brightly in an azure blue sky. Tourists swarmed the Lincoln Memorial and the National Monument like ants to honey, two symbols of peace and American strength and values.

Leine zipped her jacket closed against the light breeze as she waited. Scott Henderson requested the meeting soon after she returned from the Tsarev incident. She wondered what he wanted—she'd already given her version of events to his people at the agency, as well as to Vice President Lawrence. Lawrence had brought Leine's recording of General Tsarev's admission implicating himself to President Blackwell, and had convinced him to lower the threat level and recall the nuclear subs. He then enlisted the help of the French ambassador to set up a meeting between President Ivanov and Blackwell, at which Lawrence played the Tsarev tape.

Scott Henderson appeared over a small rise and walked toward her, his tan overcoat buttoned against the chilly fall temperatures. The sun glinted off of his aviator sunglasses and spit-shined shoes. She walked over to meet him.

"Thanks for coming," he said, and removed his sunglasses. There were a few more lines around his eyes, and he looked tired.

"I have to admit, I wasn't going to come, but I figured I owed you."

Henderson nodded. "You'll be happy to know we released Sakharov's assets and he's been cleared of all charges."

"That took a while. Do a little digging, did you?"

Henderson gave her a look. "The wheels of government spin slowly. Especially when the assets of an international arms dealer are under scrutiny."

Leine resisted the urge to argue that Sakharov's assets should never have been under scrutiny in the first place—she preferred to stay off Henderson's shit list. "What's going to happen with Libya?"

"The US will have to be more involved. The American people believe Izz Al-Din was responsible for the attack in Vegas." Henderson stared into the distance. "Perception is everything. We need to show strength against our enemies."

"Then the general wins. That's exactly what he wanted—to spread the US so thin that she would be vulnerable to attack."

"We're aware of that."

"Well, at least Sakharov's been exonerated." She sighed. "And we've stepped back from the brink of war. But what's to stop the attack in Vegas from emboldening our enemies, no matter how we spin it?"

"It won't stop anything. We live in a new world, where our friends are our enemies are our friends. The wind shifts, constantly bringing another deception. That's like asking how will the world survive?"

"Maybe it won't. One can only hope cooler heads will prevail." The odds of that happening weren't looking too good.

"Do you have a lead on the person who launched the drone in Vegas?"

"A few. CCTV feeds showed a thirty-year-old male we've identified as a freelancer who walked out of the casino and left the doors wide open near the time that the drone entered the structure. But someone had to have been working the controls—it wasn't him. So far we've narrowed it down to three suspects that were in the area. Two men and a woman."

Leine nodded. "Let me know when you ID the person?"

Henderson studied her. "We'll see. That's actually a good segue into why I asked you here in the first place. I have a proposition to make."

Leine squinted at him and shook her head. "Don't even go there, Scott. You know what my answer will be."

"Hear me out. You'll have complete autonomy, answering only to me. You can choose your assignments, and will have the full support and backing of my office."

"Like I said, you know my answer." She started to walk away.

"Wait. Leine. If it's money you want, there's more than enough to go around. You'll be paid very, very well."

She stopped and turned. "See, right there shows that you haven't got a clue what drives me."

"I'm listening. I want you to work for me, Leine. I need you. America needs you."

She looked across the Mall at the National Monument piercing the sky. The values of democracy were still there, buried beneath the spin and the rhetoric from the Beltway, but it took too much effort to find these days. She could never work for her old agency again. There was too much history.

Leine shook her head. "Goodbye, Scott."

As the distance grew between them, a great weight lifted from her that she hadn't known was there. She could start over now, without the baggage of the past. It was a feeling she hadn't experienced in a long, long time.

She was free.

ABOUT THE AUTHOR:

 **DV Berkom** is the USA Today bestselling author of two action-packed thriller series featuring strong female leads **Leine Basso** and **Kate Jones**. Her love of creating resilient, kick-ass women characters stems from a lifelong addiction to reading spy novels, mysteries, and thrillers, and longing to find the female equivalent within those pages.

Raised in the Midwest, she earned a BA in political science from the University of Minnesota and promptly moved to Mexico to live on a sailboat. Several years and many adventures later, she wrote her first novel and was hooked. *Bad Spirits,* the first Kate Jones thriller, was published as an online serial in 2010 and was immediately popular with eBook fans. *Dead of Winter, Death Rites*, and *Touring for Death* soon followed before she began the far grittier Leine Basso series in early 2012 with *Serial Date*.

D.V. currently lives in the Pacific Northwest with her husband, Mark, and several imaginary characters who like to tell her what to do. Her most recent books include *Shadow of the Jaguar, Dakota Burn, Absolution, Dark Return, The Last Deception, A Killing Truth, Cargo,* and *Vigilante Dead.*

Note from D.V.

Thank you for reading *The Last Deception*. I hope you enjoyed it. If you would like to find out more about Leine Basso or my other thriller series, go to **dvberkom.com**.

***Sign up for my Readers' List to be the first to find out about new releases and exclusive, subscriber-only special offers: **http://bit.ly/DVB_RL**

Acknowledgements

This book wouldn't have been possible without the generous help I received from people: first and foremost to my initial reader, plotting partner, and sounding board, Mark Lindstrom; eagle-eyed editor, Laurie Boris; developmental story goddess Ruth Ross-Saucier; bodacious beta readers Michelle Yelland, Brian Yelland, Larry and Beverly Van Berkom, Bill McElwee, Jenni Conner, Ali Mosa, KC Curtis, and George; early reviewers Cathy Speight, Charlie Ray, and BigAl; also huge thanks to my advance reader team (ART). Additional thanks goes to Dawn Gill for all things British; Katie Nielsen for all the great information and inspiration for the character of Anatoly Sakharov; TSODA134 for vetting the operations in the novel, as well as making some great additions to the storyline; and last, but not least, Ed Kovacs for so many great ideas and for bringing my attention to several issues that needed to be addressed. This book is so much better because of the stellar help I received from everyone. As I mention at the end of every book—writing is never a solitary endeavor.

More books by D.V. Berkom:

Leine Basso Crime Thriller Series:
A Killing Truth
Serial Date
Bad Traffick
The Body Market
Cargo
Dark Return *(see excerpt)*
Absolution
Dakota Burn
Shadow of the Jaguar

Kate Jones Adventure Thriller Series:
Kate Jones Thriller Series Vol. 1 *(the first 4 novellas in the bestselling action/adventure thriller series: Bad Spirits, Dead of Winter, Death Rites, Touring for Death)*
Cruising for Death
Yucatán Dead
A One Way Ticket to Dead
Vigilante Dead

DV BERKOM

A LEINE BASSO THRILLER

DARK
RETURN

A LEINE BASSO THRILLER

CHAPTER 1

Tripoli, Libya

LEINE BASSO GAVE her clothes the once-over, making sure she was presentable before leaning down to wipe the six-inch blade on the dead man's trousers.

Good. No arterial spatter. If only there was a mirror around when a girl needed one. She made do with the hem of her shirt and wiped her face and neck. The only stain visible belonged to sweat from the intense afternoon heat, which radiated through a pair of partially open, paint-deprived shutters.

The recently deceased thirty-something piece of shit lay on the ground in a pool of his own blood, sightless eyes staring at the fifteen foot-tall plaster ceiling above them. Leine experienced no regret at the loss of his life—not when the person she'd just killed had been responsible for dozens of women and children being sold into the horrors of sex trafficking.

One down, so many more to go.

The trafficker's death was merely a drop in a very large pool of the never-ending sex trafficking trade—clubs and organizations run by criminals that managed to materialize wherever the need arose. And the need arose pretty much everywhere. This time, she'd been sent back to Tripoli to weed out the scumbags trafficking marriageable young women to the terrorist group Izz Al-Din as bonuses for their freedom fighters.

As an elite former government assassin, Leine Basso's specialized skill set was in heavy demand, and she was glad to provide it for the cause. If she could, she'd clone herself and wage an all-out war against the dirtbags who profited from the sale of human beings, especially when those transactions included children.

But she was only one person, as her handler, Lou Stokes, liked to remind her.

"Take a break, Leine," he'd argued the last time they spoke. "You've been working too hard. You need to rest. Go home to Santa. Remember him? You can't save everyone."

It was that last line that irritated her the most. Maybe she couldn't save everyone, but she sure as hell could try. And of course she remembered Santa. She lived with the guy, didn't she?

Leine straightened and slid the knife back into its sheath. The trafficker's pistol was still tucked in his waistband. He hadn't been expecting her, didn't know she would be in the apartment when he returned with the girl. Leine had sliced his throat from behind before he could cry out. It happened so quickly he didn't have time to draw his weapon, let alone fire.

It was hard to beat the element of surprise.

She took out her phone and photographed the body, capturing the bloody details. It would make a good addition to the wall. She'd created a secret, eyes-only file on her laptop, plastering a virtual wall with photographic trophies of her work as an operative for SHEN, the anti-trafficking organization. The wall was a reminder of why she did what she did. If she'd thought about it, the idea was pretty macabre.

But she didn't think about it.

One down, so many more to go.

Careful to avoid tracking through the blood, Leine crossed the room to the girl she'd been sent to find. Eyes wide with shock at the violence she'd just witnessed, the fifteen-year-old American stood in the corner, gaze riveted on the dead trafficker. Dressed in a traditional floor-length abaya that hung off her thin shoulders, she wore a hijab with a veil covering the lower half of her face.

"We need to get you out of here before his friends show up," Leine said with a nod toward the door.

The girl, whose name was Chessa, looked as though she was just now emerging from a trance. She blinked and shifted her attention to Leine. "Is he really dead?"

"Let's put it this way—he's no longer a problem." Gently, Leine took her by the arm and led her past the corpse.

The young woman balked. "Why should I trust you?"

"My name is Leine Basso. I work for SHEN, an organization that helps women like you get out of shitty situations. Your parents, Adrienne and Richard Carmody, sent me to find you."

The confusion in Chessa's eyes cleared and she nodded. Compared to the photograph her parents had provided, she'd lost several pounds in the weeks she'd been held by Izz Al-Din.

She'd most likely lost more than that.

The upper part of her face flamed red and she cut her gaze to the floor. "I feel so stupid. I should have known he didn't love me."

She was talking about the recruiter she'd met online, a Lothario who preyed on naïve young women and promised love, acceptance, and adventure. What they got was misery and pain and a life of sexual servitude.

Leine softened her voice. "We all make mistakes, Chessa. That's the thing about second chances—if we're lucky, we get a do-over."

"But I believed his lies. He promised we'd be together."

Leine didn't have the heart to tell her that the recruiter she fell for had been cultivating more than a dozen similar relationships at the same time. He received payment only when he'd successfully delivered the "brides" to the terrorist camp. Chessa's parents hadn't thought twice about her request to travel to London for a semester abroad with a group from her high school. Once there, it didn't take long for the recruiter to make contact and offer to get her into Libya so that they could be together. There was a catch, though. If they were to be married, she would have to convert to Islam, which included several weeks of rigorous "religious" training.

Once she agreed, the hook was set.

Leine led the way down the stairs to the apartment building's entrance. She slipped a scarf over her hair and slid on a pair of sunglasses before scanning the street for unwanted company. Leine stepped off the curb and began walking at a fast clip.

"Where are we going?" Chessa hurried to keep up.

"The car's just over there." She nodded toward a white sedan idling halfway down the block. The driver,

Rami, sat in the front seat, smoking a cigarette. "Right now we're going to a safe house on the other side of the city."

"And then I can go home?"

"As soon as it's safe for you to leave."

Chessa stopped in the middle of the street, her eyes wide. "What if they're waiting for me at the airport? They have people everywhere."

Leine gestured for her to hurry. "You need to keep moving, Chessa. We've got it handled."

The former assassin jumped into the front passenger seat, while Chessa climbed into the back. Rami pulled away from the curb and headed for the safe house.

"You said you had it handled. How?" Chessa asked, craning her neck to look out the back window.

"One of SHEN's partners has offered the use of their private jet," Leine explained. "You'll leave from a small airfield not far from the safe house." The partner was Fitzpatrick Personal Security, Inc., or FPS, a security firm out of Los Angeles that worked primarily in North Africa and the Middle East. Occasionally, their objectives aligned with SHEN's, allowing anti-trafficking personnel and the victims they rescued to hitch a ride on one of their transport planes.

As Rami drove, Leine kept her head on the swivel, laser-focused on identifying threats. She doubted that the dirtbag she'd just offed was alone. Usually she worked Libyan rescue operations with Hamid, another operative for SHEN, but he was still recuperating from a recent injury and personnel were stretched thin. The office had received an anonymous tip early that morning with the address where Chessa and her captor were allegedly holed up. Rami, a relatively new employee, was the only one available to accompany her.

"They told me he died," Chessa said in a quiet voice. Leine turned in her seat and studied her. The girl stared out the window at the sunbaked buildings flashing by. "They said I was to marry another man to honor my fiancé's memory." Bitterness laced her words and she shuddered. She gripped the door handle so hard that her knuckles turned white. "They said he was a major supporter of the cause and that I should be honored to be the wife of the leader of an important madrassa. But he was *old*. And fat. Not handsome like Tarik." Anger radiated off her in waves.

That'll take some therapy, Leine thought.

Just then, an SUV pulled onto the road behind them.

"We've got company," Rami said in a terse voice as he kept one eye on the rearview.

"Put on your seatbelt." Leine said to Chessa. The girl didn't hesitate and snapped on her belt.

The sedan they were in wasn't exactly a speed demon. The SUV was a newer model Mercedes—one that could eat the older model Taurus for lunch. The Mercedes closed the distance between them and Rami stepped on the gas. The other vehicle kept up easily, staying about a foot off their bumper. They screamed through a residential area, racing past apartment buildings and single family homes, neighborhood markets, and children playing in the street.

"Get us away from here, Rami. Somewhere without a lot of kids." Leine pulled the semiauto from her waistband. "Lou said you knew Tripoli inside and out. Lose these assholes."

Rami nodded and mashed the accelerator to the floor. The sedan shot ahead, gaining some distance from the SUV.

Leine looked back at Chessa. Her face pale and knuckles white, she gripped the door handle in stony silence.

"Hang on," Rami yelled and spun the car onto a gravel side street. The sedan fishtailed wildly until he brought it under control. Leine checked behind them. The Mercedes overshot the intersection, but quickly reversed and was soon eating up the distance they'd lost. Rami drove to the end of the street and hooked a sharp right, raced down the block, braked hard, and spun the wheel again, threading the sedan into a narrow alley. They sliced their way past closed doorways and garbage bins, kicking up a rooster tail of dust behind them.

Chessa twisted in her seat and looked out the back window. "Did we lose them?"

Rami glanced in the rearview mirror. "Maybe." At the end of the alley he shot out onto the main thoroughfare, spinning right, tires squealing.

Once again he stomped on the accelerator, weaving in and out of traffic with little regard for stoplights or signs. The Mercedes was nowhere to be seen. Two blocks later, Rami stopped abruptly behind a line of gridlocked traffic. It wasn't long before a dozen vehicles stacked up behind them, blocking them in.

Leine checked her side mirror. The Mercedes materialized several cars behind them and oozed into traffic.

"They're back."

Rami inched the car to the left and straddled the low divider, waiting for his chance. Without warning, he gunned the engine and pulled into the opposite lane, barely missing a head-on collision with a BMW. He veered left to avoid a Mitsubishi compact, and at the last second swerved back into traffic. Inching slowly forward once more, Rami drummed his fingers on the steering wheel before he muttered something that sounded like *fuck it* in Arabic. He spun the wheel and rocketed away from the line of cars, heading the wrong direction down the opposite side of the street. Then he hooked a sharp left and shot down an arterial street, barely avoiding being smashed flat by a delivery truck.

Three turns and a double-back later, he pulled into a vacant, single-car garage and turned off the engine. He exited the vehicle in a flash and rolled the garage door shut. Leine got out and moved to the closed door. Chessa stayed inside the car.

"We wait," Rami said, his tone matter-of-fact.

Leine's breath echoed off the bare walls of the small space. With the sedan parked inside, there wasn't much room to maneuver. A moment later, the sound of tires crunching on gravel could be heard outside as a vehicle slowly rolled past. Leine held her breath.

The sound receded in the distance and Leine relaxed. They waited several more minutes before Rami nodded at Leine.

She helped him raise the door and walked outside to make sure there was no one nearby. Leine gave him a nod and he backed out of the garage. She climbed in the passenger side and they took off, keeping to the back alleyways and less populated streets.

Leine turned in her seat and said, "You can remove your veil if you'd like."

"I'd prefer to leave it on," Chessa answered.

"That's fine. We'll be there soon."

Forty-five minutes and several evasive maneuvers later, Rami parked outside of a plain concrete building next to a private airfield. Leine led Chessa through the double front doors to the reception area, where a young woman wearing a hijab sat behind the reception desk. Leine introduced Chessa to Fatima, who was working intake that afternoon. The former assassin sighed with relief as the teenager appeared to relax in the presence of Fatima's warmth. A victim of trafficking herself, Fatima exuded confidence and compassion and was a staunch defender of the women put in her care.

Leine didn't envy what lay ahead for Chessa. It would be hard work finding her way through the feelings of anger and betrayal, not to mention the weeks of terrorist propaganda she'd had to endure once she'd arrived at the training camp.

Fatima ushered Chessa into the back and Leine wrote up an abbreviated report, leaving out the part about the trafficker's death. SHEN operated in Tripoli with the unofficial blessing of the Libyan government, which could be compromised if news of a murder found its way into an official report.

Besides, one less terrorist wouldn't be missed.

Chessa would be looked after by medical personnel while at the safe house. Soon, she'd be on her way back home to Los Angeles where she would try to pick up where she left off. Back to a home where life—especially American life—would never again be the same.

With a weary sigh, Leine signed the report and slid it into Fatima's "in" basket. Then she slipped on her scarf and sunglasses and stepped back onto the street into the relentless midday sun.

CHAPTER 2

THE MAN IN the white suit wiped the perspiration from his forehead with a handkerchief and scanned the crowded market. He didn't recognize anyone, but that didn't mean anything. The organization had a long reach with many supporters, and had watchers everywhere. Pulling the brim of his hat down, he made his way through the milling throng, attempting to blend into the chaos of Tripoli's oldest and most popular souk.

He'd made it to the edge of the crowd and was about to disappear into the rabbit warren of passages that made up the medina when he saw them. A quick glance to his left confirmed his fear—two intimidating looking men, both with telltale bulges beneath their jackets, were threading their way toward him at a rapid pace.

Cursing the visibility of his white suit, he dove into the crowd in the opposite direction, barreling past vendors and shoppers, stirring up a wake of angry people.

Before he could stop himself, he slammed into an older woman carrying a basket. The basket tipped, spilling its burnt-orange contents to the ground. The fragrant, dusty-sweet scent of turmeric enveloped them both as he blindly muscled his way past her, trampling the spice with his expensive shoes. The woman barely had time to react before he was gone. He didn't bother to apologize.

I've got to get the phone to Paul.

His singlemindedness drove him on as he raced past tables of brass and copper. He chanced a quick look behind him and his heart stuttered. The gunmen were closing in.

He had to do something.

He tucked his chin and poured it on, shoving people out of the way and knocking a young girl flat on her ass. He ignored her and rushed past, fervently praying for a miracle.

"Hey! Watch out," she yelled after him.

The passageway branched in three directions. He flew past the first and careened down the second.

And pulled up short.

The deserted passageway was a dead end. *Shit!* Nothing but closed doors and barred windows. He pivoted wildly, willing an escape route to materialize, knowing that retracing his steps would be suicide. Moments later, a pair of footsteps echoed around the corner behind him followed by the unmistakable click of the hammer being drawn back on a revolver. Slowly he turned. The two men stood not five yards away, guns aimed at center mass.

Out of the corner of his eye, he caught a glimpse of the young girl he'd smashed into. Eyes wide, she poked her head around the edge of the corridor. *Go away, kid.*

You don't want to see this. He groped for his jacket pocket, but his hand hit empty.

The phone wasn't there. His thoughts raced. Did he lose it back in the medina? No, the pocket was too deep for it to just fall out on its own. He thought back to his mad dash through the market and zeroed in on the old woman with the basket, then discarded the idea as soon as it emerged.

The kid.

He closed his eyes. There was nothing he could do. He was a dead man. They would never let him live after what he'd done. Sweat rolled down his neck and slid along his back. He lifted his hands, palms up, to show them he wasn't armed. Too late, he realized it didn't matter.

The loud *bang!* echoed off the plaster walls, followed by searing pain that split him in half. He doubled over, clutching his chest. His hand came away wet and warm with his blood. He fell to his knees as the two thugs moved in, reaching him as he sagged to the ground. He opened his mouth, trying to suck in a breath, any breath, but all he could manage was a pathetically shallow gasp. The bigger gunman searched his coat and pants. When he didn't find what he was looking for, the thug kicked him in the ribs, sending excruciating pain radiating through his body.

"Where is the phone?"

The man in the white suit sucked in one last, tiny breath. Blood bubbled between his lips as the light began to fade. The gunman said something else that he couldn't understand. His voice sounded like he was speaking in a long tunnel...

Then everything went black.

Jinn gasped and covered her mouth. The two men heard her and both looked up at once. Heart thudding in her ears, she tore away from the deadly scene and raced back toward the market. She'd be safe there. She'd memorized all its nooks and crannies, and a lot of the shopkeepers knew and liked her. Especially when she brought them valuable items they could sell.

Her hand closed around the cell phone she'd lifted from the man in the white suit after he'd slammed into her. It was a newer model of a popular brand and would bring a good price. But the pick had been easy, too easy. She was a master of distraction, but he'd already been distracted. Now she knew why.

Jinn was no stranger to violence—two years of living on the streets of Tripoli had taught her a lot about human nature, and it wasn't all good. But she'd never seen anyone shoot someone down in cold blood.

And now they knew she'd seen them.

A fresh dose of fear spurred her on, giving wings to her feet, as she dove into the public market and the anonymity of the crowd. She weaved in and out of the throng of shoppers, not daring to look behind her for fear of giving herself away. She wasn't very tall for her age and could disappear among the larger adults with little problem. Like a wisp of smoke, one of the shopkeepers had said when he described her, and she liked the comparison. It fit with her name, Jinn, the Arabic word for a group of magical beings.

Genies.

She made a beeline toward the rug dealer's shop. There'd be plenty of places to hide and his vision wasn't as sharp as it used to be, so he wouldn't notice her slip past. She slowed as she neared the entrance, using the time to catch her breath. She was lucky today—Ebrahim was regaling a customer with tales of a tapestry's origins and didn't see her glide through to the back, past mounds of Berber carpets and imports from Iran and Afghanistan and the silver tea service with brilliantly colored glasses, reserved for a celebratory drink after a sale.

She burrowed into a narrow channel in a mound of seconds that Ebrahim only sold to those customers uninitiated into the secrets of quality, stifling a sneeze from the dust motes underneath. Several minutes passed before the old carpet salesman's voice grew louder as he walked near her hiding place.

"I told you, I haven't seen anyone matching that description come through here, but you're welcome to look."

Jinn held her breath and squeezed her eyes shut, willing herself to disappear, half-believing her own mythology. Jinn of the Marketplace, the other kids called her. She'd constructed a reputation for being lucky and smart with the lightest of fingers, but also for being fair in her dealings. She never stole from the vendors in the market, preferring well-off visitors as her targets, and would assist the older shopkeepers by carrying product and stocking shelves or watching a storefront while the owner had to leave for a moment or two. The reputation she'd established set her apart from the other street kids, and shopkeepers tended to like having her around.

The sound of heavy footfalls grew near, hesitated a moment, and then circled the jumble of carpets where she hid.

"What are these?" asked a gruff voice.

"Those? Ah. You have outstanding taste, sir! Those are of the absolute highest quality. I have them on special through today only. I've had people tell me the price I quote them is almost criminal. Would you like to see one?"

The gruff voice said something Jinn didn't catch, and the footsteps receded. She let go of her breath, relief sweeping through her. She would wait a while more, just to be sure that he'd gone.

Her hand closed around the mobile in her pocket. Obviously, the device held something of great value to the two men. They'd killed for it, hadn't they? She wondered if her friend, Labid, would be able to unlock the screen so she could see what was so important. The tech-savvy computer repairman was known in the market for being able to hack into almost anything. She'd have to pay him a visit. Maybe its contents were more valuable than the phone itself. Carefully removing the phone from her pocket, she slid it between the folds of the carpets.

She'd come back later, when she was sure the two men were gone.

She waited a few more minutes before wriggling out of the dusty hiding place and making her way cautiously to the front of the store. She searched what she could see of the market for signs of the men with the guns but saw nothing out of the ordinary. Ebrahim was sitting in his chair at the front, smoking a cigarette and watching people go by. Jinn didn't want to put him in a compromising position in case the men came back, so she slipped past him without saying a word and went the other way.

She'd almost made it to the end of the market when the little hairs on the back of her neck stood up. Slowly, she turned.

Jinn had just run out of luck.

CHAPTER 3

THE SHADE FROM the awning of the outdoor café was a welcome relief from the relentless sun as Leine sipped a glass of sweet tea and watched people hurry past. Her cell phone rang and she checked caller ID. Right on time.

"Hey, Lou. What's up?"

"First off, congrats on taking the initiative and going after that lead we received this morning," answered Lou Stokes. Lou was the director of Stop Human Enslavement Now, better known as SHEN, the organization Leine worked with. "If you hadn't done that, we may never have found Chessa. Once she's gone through the psych eval, she'll be ready to go. Her mother and father are beside themselves and are on their way to Paris to meet her when she lands."

"That's great, Lou."

"Yeah. Hey, I know I said you should come home for a while, but if you're up for it, would you mind staying in Libya a little longer?" Lou's voice had an edge to it that wasn't normally there.

"That depends. What have you got?"

"There've been reports of missing children from a refugee camp near the Tunisian border. The cases are sporadic, but concerning."

"Izz Al-Din?"

"Nobody knows, but that's one theory. The children who've been reported missing are quite a bit younger than their usual fare."

"How young are we talking here?"

"Under ten."

"Jesus." Anger rose in her chest. She was glad that she still felt something after all the evil she'd seen. "Too young to be a bride, at least for the majority of fighters. Are they taking them young so they can raise them to terrorist standards?"

"That's a possibility."

"So what's my story?"

"You'll be traveling as Ava Yardley, a reporter for *Slam*. Rami will take you to the refugee camp."

Leine took a deep breath as the memories of the last time she'd visited a Libyan refugee camp flooded through her. She'd lost a good friend and become embroiled in a deception with ramifications that reverberated through the upper reaches of both the Kremlin and the White House. Not something she wanted to repeat. But this was business. Compartmentalizing personal feelings was second nature for the former assassin. She'd deal with any fallout when she got back stateside.

"And?"

"You're scheduled to interview the director of the NGO that finances the camp. The added bonus is that whatever notes you take will be given to an actual reporter for the newsmagazine to turn into a story."

"I assume Fatima has all the necessary docs at the office?" She'd need a new passport, as well as credit and business cards, press credentials, etc.

"As we speak."

"Anything else?"

He paused. "You should come home after this one, okay?"

Leine stopped herself from telling him to mind his own business, that she was just fine, thank you very much. She sighed. No need to get into it on an international call. "No worries there, Lou. I'm pretty sure Santa would like that too."

"You sure you're up for one more?"

"Yeah. Absolutely. Besides, this sounds more like a fact-finding mission. I can share whatever information I gather with Fatima and the crew at the office for follow-up."

"Be safe."

"I will."

She ended the call and set her phone down on the table in front of her. Lou was concerned about her, and he was probably right. All the warning signs of burnout were there. Her refusal to listen to other people when they expressed concern for her well-being. Her inability to sleep more than a few hours at a time, punctuated by nightmares that would only go away with ever increasing amounts of alcohol. How her personal feelings drove her actions, often resulting in a corpse. The main indicator, however, was the empty feeling she got when she took a life.

And she'd been taking a lot of lives.

She was having a hard time convincing herself that killing should be a last resort instead of her first response. She finished her tea and dug in her purse for money, which she left on the table. She was about to leave when a voice cried out.

"Wait! No—"

Leine tensed. Down the block, at the entrance to an alley, a young girl struggled against two big, burly men, each holding her by an arm. The endeavor was proving difficult for the men. The girl writhed and bucked and slipped an arm free before one of the men recaptured it.

In a flash, the three of them disappeared into the alley.

Leine sprang to her feet and sprinted across the busy boulevard. She slowed as she came to the corner of the alley and peered into the gloom. They were several yards away, partially hidden by shadow.

"Let. Me. Go!" The young girl fought the two men with a ferocity that would have made a cornered lion proud.

Leine walked toward them, her hand closing around the hilt of the knife concealed in her waistband. "What do you think you're doing?" she demanded in Arabic.

"This is none of your business," one of the men snarled before turning back to the girl.

Without breaking stride, Leine pivoted and swept her leg in a low arc, forcing the man off his feet and sending him toppling backward to the ground. She delivered a sharp kick to his head, knocking him unconscious, before turning to the second man. A flash of anger crossed his face as he wrapped his arm around the girl's neck and pulled her in front of him, while at the same time shoving a revolver under her chin. A third of his body was exposed and vulnerable to attack, including his head.

She drew the knife free as she shook her head in mock sympathy. A split-second of indecision lit his face.

"Nice try, asshole," Leine murmured and threw the knife. The blade buried itself in his right eye, cutting short the scream in his throat. His grip loosened and the girl slipped from his grasp. She took off running as he collapsed to the ground.

Leine extracted her knife from the second body of the day and raced after the girl.

END EXCERPT of DARK RETURN:
A Leine Basso Thriller